MINE TO POSSESS

GEORGIA LE CARRE

MINE TO POSSESS

Georgia Le Carre

1

AMELIA

https://www.youtube.com/watch?v=tj4OgWq5OmE
-White trash beautiful-

I can't keep my heart from sinking when I see the sign loom up ahead of me.

WELCOME
to
Sunny Vale.

I'm sure when it was put up in the late eighties, the painting of the sun was a bright, happy yellow. Now, it's faded to a dirty off-white. The 'L' from 'WELCOME' is missing and the whole board is filled with tiny holes where kids have used it for target practice with their BB guns.

Maybe, back then when the sign went up, Sunny Vale

was a welcoming place, the name sure suggests it was. Now it's the exact opposite of that. It's dreary, depressing and wholly unwelcoming.

I sigh as I pass beneath it and step into the trailer park. The trailers are all as old and dilapidated as the sign. The front windows of one of them is boarded up. Another is slowly, sadly sinking into the ground as if in shame. But my mom likes to pretend we are lucky we live here.

"Good afternoon, Amelia," a voice calls from the step of one of the trailers.

"Hi, Mrs. Mason," I call back, giving the woman a half-hearted wave.

She stands in the doorway to her trailer, a mostly smoked cigarette dangling precariously from her lips. She's at least sixty, and from what I can gather she's lived here since the park opened its doors. I kinda feel bad for her. What sort of mistakes does a person need to make to end up living here all their life?

Maybe she's like my mom...

Unlucky in love and life.

You'd think by husband number four my mother would have understood alcoholics don't make good husband mate-rial. But no. She chose Dan. Another mean spirited, aggres-sive, alcoholic tyrant on the wrong side of two hundred pounds.

Even thinking about him makes me slow my steps towards his trailer.

His trailer is his pride and joy, which I really think says everything a person needs to know about him. He's not trying to better himself and get out of this shit hole. To him, living in the Sunny Vale trailer park is living the dream life.

I still remember the day Mom announced we'd be moving here.

At the time we were living in a tiny, one-bedroom apartment and she was working two jobs just to keep us in that. By then I'd already met the cleaned-up, sober version of Dan once or twice. He seemed like an ok guy, so when she said we'd be moving into his place, which had three bedrooms, one of which, I was informed, would be mine, I was ecstatic.

My very own room!

God, the dreams I built up in my head. And then she brought me here and all my dreams faded away like the painted sun on that damned sign.

In one day, I went from being Amelia from the ghetto (the charming name the kids in my school came up with to differentiate me from the other kid called Amelia) to Amelia the trailer trash girl.

But they couldn't stop me from loving school, and I longed for a chance at college, but no college for me, of course. When I hit sixteen, Mom asked me to quit school and contribute towards the household expenses.

Which was fair enough. I understood, Mom needed me out working because Dan couldn't work due to his 'disability'. Plus, I hated seeing my mother's tired face when she walked through the door after a long shift. I was glad to be able to help her.

I managed to find a job in a small clothing store, but it irked me no end that we were both working hard to keep Dan tanked up every night. I kept my mouth shut, but once, when I was giving over almost all my wages to Mom while Dan was passed out on the couch, I couldn't help remarking that his only disability was the one he found every night in the bottom of a whisky bottle.

For my trouble, I got a sharp backhanded slap from my mother and a reminder we were living in *his* home. That kind of closed that discussion.

Life went on, but my job only lasted until two months ago when Dan came into the store in a drunken stupor and demanded the owner give me a pay rise. He caused such an embarrassing scene Mr. Jones told me not to bother coming back.

I'm job hunting right now, but it's hard when the only employer I've ever had is unwilling to give me a reference and I have no real educational qualifications. Dan sure has a lot to answer for.

I reach our trailer and stand at the bottom of the steps leading up to it. I just stare at the steps, wondering how the hell my life came to this. The trailer is one of the slightly better ones in the park, but it's still a shack. One of the steps is missing and the window has a crack in it. Stained curtains that are never open sit pulled taut against the windows, an inch or two too small to close properly.

The outside is nothing compared to the inside though.

Mom and I do try to keep the place in some sort of order, but Dan doesn't make it easy for us. Every day the place gets littered with take-out cartons, empty beer cans, whisky or rum bottles and, of course, over-flowing ashtrays. Thank God, I have my own little room. My sanctuary.

I skip over the missing step and go inside.

"Violet? Is that you?" Dan shouts.

His voice is slurred. I can tell he's not close to drunk enough to pass out, but he's nothing like sober either. He's in that horrible middle place where he thinks he's a charming comedian, but one wrong move on my part can send him into a blind rage.

"No. It's me, Amelia," I shout back, praying he doesn't bother coming out to talk to me.

I open the grubby fridge and put the milk into it. As I close the door my eyes dart around. The ashtray is already full, and six beer cans are scattered around the living room. I cleaned the place only two hours ago before I went out. I should do it again; save my mom the trouble when she returns from work. Then a rebellious thought crosses my mind.

Fuck it, she chose this life.

I sure as hell didn't. A second later, I'm filled with guilt. All I've ever had is her and no matter what she does or says, she's my mom and I love her.

I quickly clean the mess, then make my way down the narrow hall to my bedroom. I close the door as quietly as I can and lean against it. I don't hear him moving around. Maybe he's fallen asleep. I look around my bedroom. It's by far the cleanest room in the trailer. There are no scattered cans, half-eaten take-away remains, or plates with gravy crusted onto them. It even smells like perfume which is really something considering the dense fog of alcohol fumes and stale cigarette smoke that hangs in the air in the rest of the trailer.

I hear Dan approaching, his footsteps shambling. The trailer rocks slightly as he stumbles and bumps into the wall. Shit. He is coming towards my room. I move away from the door just as he crashes it open.

Bastard!

He's wearing grey sweatpants that are covered in stains, stains I can only hope are beer rather than piss. He's shirtless – not a good look for him. His beer belly hangs over; the skin tight and shiny, and so white it almost glows in the gloomy hallway. He's also in desperate need of a shower. The smell of alcohol and old sweat that clings to him reaches me immediately and I try hard not to react.

2

AMELIA

"Where's your mother?" he slurs.

"At work. It's Friday," I remind as politely as I can, even though it's freaking irritating that he can't even keep *her* schedule in his head.

"And yet you're here. Why aren't you at work?"

I resist the strong urge to roll my eyes. I don't want to set him off on another rant about how ungrateful I am.

"You got me fired, remember?"

He snorts and I'm not sure if it's laughter or disgust. "You're too good for that place anyway."

Place comes out as "plashe", which tells me he's a bit more gone than I originally thought. I shrug my shoulders. I'm not sure what he wants from me and I'm very wary of saying the wrong thing and sparking his temper.

"Pretty girl like you, you should be a dancer or something," he says, a speculative, admiring look in his eyes.

I'm sure somewhere in his drink-addled brain, he imagines it's a compliment, but it sure doesn't feel like one to me. I feel disgust swirling in my stomach. He doesn't have to come right out and say it. I know exactly what he means by dancer. Stripper.

He smiles at me, and it's not a normal smile. It's... oh God, lecherous!

And just like that the disgust in my stomach turns to unease. For the first time I have to deal with Dan as a predator and me as his prey while I'm trapped in this small space.

When my mother is around, Dan is either mean to me or pretty much just ignores me. These things I can live with, especially when he ignores me. In fact, that's my perfect scenario with him. But recently, more and more, whenever we're alone together, which I try to avoid whenever I can, this new side of him comes out, where he looks me up and down like I'm a piece of meat he'd like to devour. I've not failed to notice either the way he brushes against me whenever we pass each other, even out in the living room where there's absolutely no need for it.

I keep my face totally impassive.

"I said you're pretty," he repeats.

"Yeah. Thanks," I say tightly.

Just go away, I think to myself, but he doesn't go away. He stands propped against the frame of my door. I don't move because moving would bring me closer to my bed and I don't want him thinking for even a second that it's some sort of invitation.

He grins. "You know, Amelia, we've always had this chemistry between us, haven't we?"

My eyes widen. Is he mad? I can't stand him. As a matter of fact, I detest him. I'm dying to tell him exactly what I really think, but I have to keep this little gem to myself. Sleazy Dan is bad, but angry Dan is worse, far worse.

"I should call Mom and tell her to bring home some orange juice. I forgot to get it at the grocery store," I say, mentioning Mom in the hope he'll remember to be loyal to her. Unfortunately, it's too subtle a hint for him.

He grins at me. "Aww... look at you. All shy and shit. But I get it, really, I do. You don't want to hurt your mom. And neither do I. Violet is great. Fantastic woman. One in a million and she takes good care of me."

I feel a touch of desperation. "Yeah, she does," I say with emphasis, but at the same time I don't want to risk angering him, or encouraging whatever the hell he thinks this is.

He pushes himself up off the wall and I flinch slightly. Dan notices and laughs cruelly. "Don't pee yourself. I just thought someone should tell you how attractive you are."

I feel myself blush, the searing heat rushing up my neck.

His eyes note my embarrassment, and he laughs, the sound unfamiliar. There is something cruel and sexual about it. For a moment it seems as if he wants to say something else, then he checks himself, turns and stumbles away, heading for the living room. I hear his body crash onto the sofa.

I step forward and quickly close the door. My heart is beating like crazy. Jesus, what the hell was that all about?

I check the time. My mom is due home in an hour. I'll just lie low and hope Dan forgets I'm home. It wouldn't be the first time he's done it. One time, I came out of my room and Dan ran from the bedroom he shares with my mom with a baseball bat raised over his head. I managed to duck as he swung it at me.

Instead of apologizing he lost his temper with me, scolding me for sneaking around like a thief, and telling me that I should have the manners to greet him when I get home. I bit my tongue and didn't remind him I'd been home for almost three hours, and I'd spent the first fifteen minutes of it making him a bacon sandwich. I think that was the time I realized just how drunk Dan could get.

The hole he made in the wall with the baseball bat is still not fixed. It is a constant reminder to me that Dan can be unpredictable and downright dangerous.

I move to my tiny bed, sit down, and pull my laptop towards me. My heart is still fluttering as I start browsing the jobs' boards. I have to find something. Something that keeps me out of here for most of the day.

I freeze suddenly.

I can hear him moving around again. The fridge door opens, then slams closed. A beer bottle is opened, and the opener thrown on the counter. For some reason his not bothering to put the bottle opener back into the drawer irritates me. To think that Mom's out there working herself to the bone for this lazy jerk. I mean how hard can it be not to get shit faced through the afternoon, and put the damn thing back into the drawer for fuck's sake?

Like, everyone else manages it.

But my rage is pointless. I grit my teeth and return my attention to my laptop. I find a few promising openings. A waitress at a diner. A shelf stacker in a grocery store. Shitty, low wage jobs, but better than being stuck here with him. I fill out the applications to a couple of openings, hit send, and shut my laptop.

I pick up my cell phone, ready to text Lucy to see what she's up to tonight. I might see if I can go over to her place. She lives in a clean and tidy little house and her parents are normal. They work for a living and her dad only drinks a glass of wine or two with dinner and the occasional night-cap. Like a normal man.

I hear Dan stumbling back along the hallway towards my room again. I put my cell phone down. Great. What now?

"Do you need something, Dan?" I call, hoping he just wants a sandwich made.

I hate that I'm practically Dan's unpaid hired help, but if making him a sandwich gets him away from my bedroom, then right now, I'll happily do it.

My door has no lock, and he opens it without knocking just as I stand up from the bed. He grins at me and blinks twice, fast. I frown and he does it again. Oh God, he thinks he's winking at me. It should be tragic, but it's not.

It's disgusting.

3

———

AMELIA

https://www.youtube.com/watch?v=IGVZOLV9SP0

"I've been thinking," he says, then pauses.

I nod tightly for him to go on, feeling that's what he's waiting for.

"You want me to notice you."

My eyes widen and my mouth drops open. For heaven's sake. What on earth is going on with him today?

"Don't give me that *butter wouldn't melt in your mouth* look. You strut around here in your little, short shorts and your skimpy little tank tops, tempting me. What else can it be?"

Has he gone stark raving mad? The only thing I've ever worn that even vaguely matches what he's saying is a pair of baggy shorts that are about six inches away from my knees, and not once have I strutted in them.

I swallow the thousand different sarcastic things that fly

into my head and make the mature decision not to respond. If I try to reason with him, he'll just get mad and who knows what could happen. I'm trapped here for the moment, but Mom should be home soon. I just have to keep him at bay until she gets here.

"I'm going to make a sandwich. Shall I make one for you?"

Dan doesn't seem to notice or care I'm not responding to what he's saying. He just keeps right on looking at me like he's undressing me with his eyes.

"I've tried to resist your coy advances, but I mean I'm only human, Amelia. I have to give it to you; you played your cards well. You knew I wouldn't be able to resist you for long. And I mean your mom is great, one in a million and everything, but she's not what she used to be, is she?"

My mom hasn't changed one bit in the time he's known her. Dan takes a step into the room, and I take a step backwards, the backs of my legs meet my bed. He grins, but it doesn't reach his eyes. His eyes are suddenly hard and nasty, lecherously moving up and down my body.

"You win," he grins. "You've worn me down."

I feel sick. Ugh! This is my mom's man. I'd rather die than have sex with him.

He steps closer again.

I try to think what to do, but my mind has kinda gone blank.

He takes another step into my tiny room.

I have nowhere else to go. Dan reaches out and caresses my cheek. My stomach rolls with nausea. His fingers smell of stale cigarette smoke and beer, and his palms are rough, although I have no idea why – it's not like he's ever done a hard day's work in his life.

"I'll be honest with you, Amelia. I've wanted this for as long as you have, but it felt wrong, you know? Still... now you're eighteen, you're a woman now."

"I'm only seventeen," I say in a panic. "I'm not eighteen for another five weeks."

He smiles and does the blink thing again. "I won't tell if you won't."

My whole body goes cold with dread. I want to hit him, but I don't want to escalate the situation. There must be a way to extricate myself without resorting to violence. He's drunk, but there is no way I could win against him based on sheer brute force.

Dan reaches out and pulls me against him.

I have to resist the urge to retch as his hard beer belly digs into my body. He tries to kiss me, and I turn my head to the side. He slobbers on my cheek, leaving it wet. His breath stinks of stale beer and something dirtier than that. I can almost feel bile rising in my throat as Dan lunges his lips at me again. I try to wriggle out of his arms, but he's shockingly strong and his vice-like grip is impossible to escape.

"Dan, stop it," I say as firmly as I can. If I can just get the upper hand here, I might be able to talk my way out of this.

"Dan, stop it," he mimics. "You've pushed for this for months and now you're going to pretend like you don't want it to happen? Why? You think you're too good for me all of a sudden?"

I think literally every woman on the planet is too good for him. "You're very attractive and all that, but this is not right. You're married to my mom," I say, forcing my voice not to become shrill with panic and rage.

He releases me from his hold, and I breathe a sigh of relief. It's over. Except it isn't. Dan is only just getting started.

"Since when has that bothered you?" he snaps and shoves me so hard on my chest I fall backwards onto the bed.

"Fucking slut. You really think you're something, don't ya? Well, let me tell you something about girls like you. You're only good for one thing."

Frantically, I scoot backwards across my bed, but it's so small there's nowhere for me to go. My back is already pressed up against the wall. I can feel angry tears filling my eyes as I try to think of something to say to calm my mother's husband down. Nothing comes to mind. Since there's nothing I can grab to smack him with, I get ready to kick him in the nuts. So hard, he'll crumple into a heap and that will give me enough time to get the hell out of this trailer.

Then I'm never coming back.

He smiles down at me, and his eyes shine wickedly. I don't know if he really believes I've somehow been leading him on, or if it's just something he's telling himself to justify what he's about to do to me. Either way, he's coming for me. As if he knew what I planned to do, he grabs both my ankles and clambers onto my bed. He pulls my ankles wide, and roughly pulls me so I am flat on my back. Then he clambers on top of me, breathing his disgusting breath all over me.

I try to throw him off, but it's like he's made of wet sand. His weight holds me in place, and he grabs my flailing arms. He pushes my hands together over my head and holds them in place with one large fist.

I'm screaming now, shouting for help at the top of my lungs, but I don't know how much good it will do. Our neighbors tend to keep to themselves, not getting into each other's business. And no one around here will call the police. Not if they don't want their windows smashed in as a paint can comes crashing through.

Dan is slobbering over my neck. It's only a matter of time until he goes further. My screams are doing nothing to stop him.

"Dan. Get off her right now," my mom commands suddenly from the bedroom door.

My scream freezes in my throat and Dan jumps up like I'm a bed of hot coals.

"Oh, Mom," I whispered, pulling my legs together, relief flooding into me.

Tears run freely down my cheeks now. My mom is here. Everything is going to be okay. She can see what a creep Dan is. She'll get rid of him, and it'll go back to just being the two of us. We'll find another little apartment, but now that I can bring in money too, we'll make it work.

"You just couldn't see me happy, could you, Amelia?" my mom asks.

For a second it doesn't compute. I shake my head in confusion and shock. "What?" I blurt out.

"How could you?" she screams suddenly.

"Mom..."

"Don't you want me to be happy?" she whispers, her voice suddenly breaking.

Happy? Am I stuck in a nightmare? "Mom, he's a fucking useless alcoholic who just tried to rape your daughter."

"You seduced me," Dan mutters, all the slur gone from his voice.

"Shut up," Mom throws at him viciously before she turns on me again. "You walk around here in your little outfits, begging for Dan's attention," my mom accuses, mirroring Dan's untrue observation about my skimpy attire.

"But I let it go. I told myself you were just seeking attention. You wouldn't actually try to steal my man, but "

"Steal your man? Can you hear yourself, Mom? You're delusional." I look Dan up and down and shake my head. "You think I want to steal *him*? I wouldn't have him if he was the last man on earth."

Mom steps forward and slaps me hard across the face, leaving behind a stinging, burning patch.

"Show a little respect," she snaps, her face white with anger and hurt.

Dan grins, triumphant. I have no idea how this has happened. My mom came home and literally caught Dan trying to force himself onto me, and somehow, it's my fault?

"Mom, you heard me screaming," I plead. "Why would I have been screaming if I wanted this?"

My mom pauses for a second and then the hard look on her face softens.

"You're a pretty girl, Amelia, and you like to show yourself off. It would be a strange man that didn't find you attractive. Maybe you're just naïve and didn't know this would happen. This is my fault. I should have warned you what you were doing. You need to be more considerate of Dan's feelings."

"It's not your fault, Vi," Dan says quickly. "It's hers. She's been flirting with me ever since you two moved in here. I should have said something, but I didn't want to hurt you."

My mom shakes her head and sighs. "I know it's been hard for you."

"I love you, babe," he says pathetically.

Mom nods. "I love you too, hon. Let's just put this behind us, ok? Amelia, apologize to Dan, then you can go and start peeling the potatoes."

I just stare at her, my jaw hanging open. This betrayal is too much. I almost can't recognize my mom. Does she really want me to apologize to him knowing what he just tried to do to me? Well, maybe it's ok with her, but I know I'm sure as hell NOT going to apologize to Dan.

"Amelia?" Mom prompts.

I stare at her defiantly.

"It's ok, Vi," Dan says sweetly. He puts his meaty hand on her shoulder, and she looks at him. "Give her some time to think about this. She'll come around. Right, Amelia?"

I'm too shocked and distressed to say anything. I can't bring myself to even look at Mom, but I shrug my shoulders. I want them out of my room, and I think this might be the only way to do it.

"Fine," Mom says in a hard voice. "Stay in your room and take a moment to think about how you could have broken our little family up. And don't come out until you're ready to take responsibility for your actions and apologize to Dan."

"And to your mom," Dan adds. "You've caused her a lot of stress over these last few months, but you really outdid yourself this time."

Mom leaves the room, and Dan follows her. On his best behavior now. He closes my door quietly behind him. I stare at the old wooden door.

I want nothing more than to lay on my bed face down and sob my heart out. How could my mom take his side? Turning a blind eye to his drinking and his temper is one thing, but this? He was going to rape me. Does she really think so little of me that she believes I tried to steal Dan from her? Even if I did flirt with him, which I would never do. Not just because he disgusts me, but also out of principle, how could she accept him back after this? She obviously doesn't think much of Dan either. She obviously thinks he's too weak to say no to anyone who flashes him a come-on.

I take a deep breath. No, I won't give myself the luxury of wallowing in self-pity.

I have to get out of here. Right now. I don't know where I'll go or what I'll do, but nothing can be as bad as this. I stand up and go to my tiny closet. I pull out a duffle bag and throw in some clothes and my makeup bag. Then I slide in my laptop and my cell phone charger. I move to the bedroom door and stand listening. I can hear Mom and Dan talking in the living room. If I'm quiet, I can get to the bathroom and back without them noticing.

I sneak to the bathroom and grab my toothbrush, half a tube of toothpaste, my deodorant, a razor and a bottle of shampoo. It'll have to do. I sneak back to my bedroom and pull a brush through my hair. I toss it into the bag with some underwear and a couple sets of light clothing and zip it up.

Then I open the tiny secret drawer in my trinket box and fish out the small amount of money I've managed to save. I count it. I have a grand total of one hundred and twenty-two dollars and fifty-three cents. It's not going to do much for me, but I'm going to have to make this work. I put the money in my pocket and straighten up. I pick up the duffle bag, take a deep breath and leave my bedroom for the last time. I make my way down the hallway to the kitchen. My mom hears me and looks up. She nudges Dan and they both sit looking at me. Dan is now bleary eyed and holding a bottle of rum. He takes a swig as he looks at me.

"Well?" my mom prompts. "Are you ready to apologize?"

"Yes," I say. "Dan, I'm sorry you're a fucking rapist who blames everyone around him for his actions." Then I look at my mom and I can't stop the tears that flow quickly down my face. My heart is so full of sadness my chest feels tight. "Mom, I'm genuinely sorry you think this is the life you deserve because you're too good for this. Never forget, I love you and I always will."

Then I turn and leave the trailer, leaving Mom and Dan staring after me with open mouths. I've officially burnt my last bridge, but that's alright. I'd sooner die on the streets than apologize to Dan.

I dash away the tears and make a promise. "One day, when I have(I've) made my fortune, I'll come back for you, Mom. I swear it."

The dusty road in front of me is empty so there are no witnesses to my forlorn whisper, but it's a promise I won't break.

4

AMELIA

https://www.youtube.com/watch?v=VcjzHMhBtfo

-just a small time girl-

I've been desperately walking the streets since I left three hours ago and I'm no closer to finding a job than I was at Dan's hell hole.

I've literally walked into any business I've passed that looks even remotely like they might need staff and practically begged them for work, but it's the same old story everywhere. They're either not hiring, or they tell me to send in my resume. I feel like curling up in the gutter and crying my burning eyes out...

But I won't do that. Or go back to the trailer.

I'll make it or I'll die trying.

To start with I've discovered the tiny amount of money I have will pay for two nights in a cheap motel, but I have no intention of using it up like that. I try to think where I can go.

Lucy's place is out of the question. Her parents are super strict about having people staying over. I know if I tell her mom what happened, she will let me stay, but knowing her she'll also probably want to call the cops and social services and God knows who else. I don't want that.

I don't want anybody thinking ill of my mother. No matter what, she is *my* mother and I'll never betray her.

I don't really have any other close friends. Sure, I have a few acquaintances, girls I hang out with now and again, but I can't just turn up at their doorstep and ask them to house me until I sort my shit out.

I had colleagues at work and did get quite close to some of them. I guess Jason might put me up for the night, but the truth is I really don't know him well enough to lay my problems on him. He might even have a girlfriend by now and me staying at his will go down like a lead balloon with her. The more I think about it, the more I shake off the idea. I've been ghetto Amelia and trailer trash Amelia for too long. I'm not going to let myself become slutty Amelia or seductress Amelia.

No, I'm on my own with this one.

I'm pulled out of my thoughts as a door of The Pink Flamingo opens to the side of me and a drunken man stumbles out, almost falling on top of me. He gives me a lopsided grin and I shrink back, but he just stumbles along on his way. I have to stop thinking everyone is like Dan. Just before the door closes shut, I see the inside of it. Dimly lit with wooden floors.

I scrunch my forehead. It is the biggest dive around here.

Always full of people drinking too much too early. And fights like you wouldn't believe. But I can't help but look again at the sign taped to the door.

Help Wanted

THING IS, I've seen it already since I've been past this place twice and I'm just going in circles now, figuratively and literally, but this is the one place I haven't been inside.

Do I really want to work in a place like this?

The answer is a clear no. I most definitely don't, but it's starting to seem like it might be my only option. I stand at the doorway, debating the pros and cons of going in.

I can't help coming to the conclusion that it can't be much worse than what I just left. Maybe this bar and I are a good fit. Maybe we deserve each other. We're both at the bottom of the barrel. We're both the thing people come to when they're all out of other options.

Maybe working here won't be as bad as I think.

I lean against the steamed-up window for a moment and think about it. If I can get a job here, I might make enough money to rent a little studio apartment, but even better if I stick it out for a few months and get some experience and a good reference, I might be able to find a better job waiting in a decent place. I lean against the wall by the door and think for another few minutes, pretending to myself that I have other options, but I don't.

This is my last shot.

I push myself off the wall, take a deep breath, and push open the door. A cloud of humid heat hits me. The place is jamming, and everyone looks drunk. The tables and booths are all taken, and several people mill around in groups, standing in the open spaces around the place.

The bar is crowded too and even from here I can hear people screaming, they're next. The jukebox is playing in the background; a song I don't recognize. It's barely audible over the sound of drunken laughter, conversation, and shouts.

Well, they all sure look happy. Actually, very happy.

No one is fighting or arguing. No one looks like they don't want to be here. In fact, everyone seems to be having a great time except the harried looking waitress who pushes through the crowd holding a tray loaded down with drinks high above her head. She does it with ease.

I could do that, I tell myself.

I push deeper into the room, squeezing through the throng. My rucksack hits the back of a seated man's head as I push through towards the bar and I cringe, waiting for him to go off on me as I stutter out an apology, but he just laughs and waves away my apology. Whoa. Maybe this place isn't as bad as I thought it was.

"What you got in there, honey? Are you running away from home or something?"

"Something like that." I grin back at him.

"Cheers to that," he says cheerfully.

He picks up a shot glass filled with clear liquid and swallows it down to a round of cheers and whoops from his table. The grin on my face widens. This place is sure growing on me.

I make it to the crowded bar and wait until the couple waving money in front of me are served, before I push my way into the spot they've vacated.

"Hi," I chirp brightly, when the bartender gets to me.

"ID," he barks.

"I'm not here for a drink. I saw your help wanted sign in the window," I explain.

He turns away from me, leaving me standing there, unsure of what to say or do.

"Larry?" he yells. "Someone here for the job."

He comes back to the bar, and ignoring me, moves onto the next customer. A voice yells something indistinguishable through an open door from the back of the bar. The bartender looks back to me.

"Go on through," he says, jerking his head towards the open door behind the bar.

I have no idea how I would get to the door, and I stand staring at him dumbly for a moment. He rolls his eyes which makes my cheeks sting with embarrassment.

"Coming through," he shouts at two drunk looking men who are standing at the side of the bar.

They back up a little and the bartender lifts a section of the bar up and beckons to me. I push past the men and squeeze through the gap. It's so noisy I don't catch a word the bartender says, but he points at the door behind him, and I step through it.

It's cooler back here and a little quieter. I square my shoulders and start moving along a corridor with worn, red and green patterned carpet.

"Hello?" I call out timidly.

"For fucks sake, get in here," a voice shouts impatiently.

I follow the sound of the voice and find myself in an office. It's a small room, carpeted in the same cheap stuff as the corridor outside. The furniture is shabby. There's an overweight man with a pasty complexion sitting with his booted feet up on a desk. A lit cigarette smolders in an ashtray on the messy desk. He is wearing a suit, but even that looks cheap and ill-fitting.

He looks me up and down. "Looking for a job, huh?"

5

AMELIA

I'm kinda speechless by the situation I find myself in, so I just nod.

He gestures to the chair in front of his desk. I don't really want to sit on it. It looks grubby and sticky, but I park myself on it. I need a job. I can always wash my jeans.

"What's your name, kid?"

"Amelia Madison," I reply.

"I'm Larry Hall, the owner of this fine establishment."

I don't know if he's joking or not when he says that. He doesn't laugh and I'm glad I didn't.

"How old are you?" He gives me a look. It's the same look Dan used to give me when my mom wasn't home.

I don't think Larry is the sort of man who is worried about following the law, but this is my last hope and I'm not going to blow it with honesty. I swallow hard. "Eighteen," I lie.

Larry's smiling at me now, a smile that makes me want to shrink away from him. The look on his face takes away any guilt I might have felt about lying to him.

"Good. Good. Have you worked in a bar before, sweet cheeks?" he asks.

I can't lie about that. Two minutes behind that bar and he'll know I don't know the first thing about bar tending.

"No, but I'm a very fast learner," I say quickly.

"Can you put on a pretty smile and carry a tray?"

I give him my best smile. "That I absolutely can do."

He laughs and shakes his head. "Yup, you'll do. You keep that smile up. The regulars here like their waitresses smiling and happy as a pig in shit... and they're big on cleavage. The more the better... It'll show on your tips. You get me?"

I get him alright. I nod, forcing my smile to be wider, showing even more teeth.

"That's better. If you work here, you'll be working late most nights. Definitely weekend nights. You ok with that?"

I nod again. It's not like I have any sort of social life, anyway.

"And there'll be none of this bleeding-heart feminism bullshit. Our regulars like a joke and sometimes, those jokes could be seen as offensive. Your job is to laugh at them and not get your panties in a twist. Clear?"

It's clear. If I work here, I'll have to accept all of the pervy comments thrown my way and any groping without complaint and with a big smile plastered on my face. But at least here, I'll be able to leave when my shift is over.

I nod again. "Sure. It's all said in fun, right?"

"That's the spirit. No snowflakes in this establishment." Larry grins. "One more question. Can you start right now? One of my waitresses called in sick today and I think you can see we're kind of short-staffed tonight."

My eyes widen, trying to take his words in. Wow, I got a

job! I actually freaking did it. The smile on my face is genuine this time as I nod vigorously.

Larry laughs. "You'll be working around twenty hours a week, maybe more. The pay is rubbish, but smile like that honey, and you'll make a king's ransom in tips."

Crappy hours, bad pay, horrible customers, and a lecherous boss. It sounds like hell on earth, but it's a job. A life saver! I can do this for a few months. I'm certain it won't be half as bad as living with Dan.

"Wait here," Larry says, pushing his heavy body upright.

He leaves the office and I take a moment to compose myself a little bit. I can't let myself seem too thrilled about this. Larry will think something strange is up if I do.

"Greg. Greg. Get out here," I hear him yelling.

He comes back into the office a few minutes later with the bartender I spoke to when I first came in.

"Greg. Amelia. Amelia. Greg. Amelia's starting as a waitress tonight. Get her a uniform and show her where everything is. Ten minutes," Larry says.

I get to my feet as Greg rushes me out of the office.

"Don't I need to fill out any paperwork or sign anything?" I ask.

Larry shakes his head, then he and Greg laugh. It seems like lying about my age had really been totally unnecessary. Larry and employment laws seem to be living in different worlds. I shrug. I remind myself this is not a bad thing. *Just suck it up, Amelia. You need the money. Badly.*

I follow Greg down the grubby hallway into what I assume is the staff room. It's reasonably clean and there are lockers, which must be a good sign.

"Grab locker two," Greg says.

There are only five lockers. I go to locker two, open it,

shove my bag in, turn the lock, take the key out, and turn back to Greg. He's looking me up and down critically. Not again. My disgust must have shown on my face because Greg laughs.

"Don't flatter yourself," he says. "I'm working out what size uniform would fit you."

"You could just ask me," I point out.

He grins. "I could, but it wouldn't help much. The uniforms are pretty old. Most of the labels are washed clean."

"Ahhh."

Greg nods and disappears, leaving me standing there. I'm still in shock so I appreciate the little alone time to gather my thoughts, but he comes back quickly, holding up a black short skirt, a frilly little apron, and a black top that looks smaller than what I'm used to wearing.

He looks at my sneakers and winces. "They'll have to do tonight, but for your next shift, you'll need black stilettos. At least three-inch heels, but the higher the better," he says. He holds the clothes out to me. "I'll wait in the hallway while you put these on. Don't be long."

I change quickly, wanting to make sure I don't give Larry any reason to come looking for me while I'm undressed. The skirt is a decent enough fit, but the vest... wow, it feels as if my boobs are falling out of it. I stuff my clothes into the locker with my bag and push the key into the pocket of my skirt. Then I open the door to go out.

Greg looks at me. "Not a bad guess, huh?" He smiles. "Hell, Larry always knew how to pick 'em."

I frown and he quickly makes his face expressionless.

"So basically, the left-hand side of the bar is table service. You'll find some people on the right-hand side want it, too. You can serve them if you want to, but your priority is the tables on the left."

He pauses his explanation for a second and hands me a notepad and pen before going on.

"They go in the pocket of your apron. Write down the orders, bring the tickets to the bar, and take the drinks to the tables. Think you can manage that?"

"I think so," I reply sarcastically.

Greg ignores my sarcasm, and nods to my top.

"Open the top two buttons," he says.

It is already so tight and small. I frown.

He shrugs. "Totally up to you, but if you want to make decent tips, you'll do it."

I almost don't, but I need money fast and so reluctantly, I open the top two buttons and show off even more cleavage.

He grins. "Perfect. Let's go." He turns and heads back towards the bar. He points to a door on his left. "That's the staff toilet. Unless you have a weird fetish for bodily fluids, never ever use the customer toilets."

"Got it," I say, instantly deciding I would rather pee in my panties than go into the customer toilets.

Greg leads me out into the bar and opens the hatch for me to leave through.

Before I can even respond he turns away and starts serving customers.

I stand at that spot, unsure of what to do, but I don't have long to dilly around wondering. A man spots me and beckons me over to his table. It's on the left side of the room, so I quickly make my way over, a massive smile on my face.

6

AMELIA

"**G**ood evening gentlemen. What can I get for you?" I ask, my notebook and pen out and ready.

The men at the table laugh.

My smile goes so wide my face is in danger of cracking.

"You're new here, aren't you?" one of them asks.

"First night," I admit.

"I can tell. You haven't gotten the standard Flamingo exasperated greeting of 'what'd want next' down yet."

"Ok, what'd want next?"

Another laughs. "She'll do."

"Yeah, she'll do all right. Here's a nice simple order to get you started, cream pie. "Five pints of pale ale; three rum and cokes, no ice, and eight shots of tequila."

I write the order down quickly and flash them another big grin. "Coming right up."

I go back towards the bar and stand waiting for one of the bartenders to spot me. Greg spots me and rolls his eyes, pointing to the end of the bar. The opposite end to where the entrance hatch is.

"You work here, Amelia," Greg explains dryly. "You don't have to wait in the line. When you have an order, come straight up here, ok?"

I nod and hand him my ticket. He turns away and another table yells, "Hello, sweet cheeks."

"That'll be you," Greg calls over his shoulder.

"Right." I plaster another smile on my face and head towards them. When I come back with their order, there's a large tray waiting for me with all of the drinks for my last order.

"I have to take all of these at once?" I ask the female bartender who holds her hand out for my new ticket.

She nods. "Yeah. And if you drop them, Larry takes the money out of your fucking wages, so watch your step."

Wonderful. I pick the tray up cautiously. It weighs an absolute ton, and my hands are shaking with nerves. Beer starts to slop over the top of the pint glasses, and I feel tears starting to form in my eyes. This is not fair. I've not even been given a chance to practice. Just thrown into the deep end without a float. I put the tray back down on the counter and blink hard.

The woman behind the bar comes back, obviously taking pity on me. "Like this," she says.

Then she crouches slightly and pulls the tray to the edge of the bar. She holds her palm out and slides the tray onto it. "Do it with both hands to start with it if you need to."

I nod. That does look easier than my way.

She quickly tops up the spilled beers and nods for me to go.

I take a deep breath and do it the way she showed me.

The tray sits neatly on my palms. Yup, I can do this. I take my other palm off. My arm shakes from the weight, but the drinks hold steady, and nothing spills. I take a deep breath and with my spine straight I make it to the table before I realize I have no idea how to get the tray back off my hand.

I look around frantically and watch another waitress. She takes the drinks from the tray one at a time, announcing them and handing them to the people who claims them.

I copy her actions, and I soon have all of the drinks off the tray and on the table. Breathing a sigh of relief, I thank the man as he pushes a ten dollar tip into my hand. I put the money in the tight little pocket in the ass of my skirt and go back for the next tray of drinks.

The next few hours go reasonably smoothly. Granted I make a few mistakes (as I run left, right and center, but I don't drop any trays, and most important of all, I manage to resist the urge to tell any of the customers to fuck off, even when they make comments about my body that men their age really should know better than to say to a girl.

Larry keeps popping out of his door to see if everything is running smoothly. A couple of times he catches my eye and nods approvingly.

Finally, the place starts to quiet down as the night wears on. Eventually, I'm the only waitress still working. The other bartenders also have finished their shifts and Grey is the only one behind the bar.

I know it's too late to have any chance of finding somewhere to stay tonight now. With the money I've made from tips I could probably get a room in a half decent bed and breakfast place now, but I know I need to save the money for a down payment somewhere more permanent. I decide to hang around here as late as I can and then I'll either sleep in that small, locked room or I'll spend the rest of the night walking the streets. Tomorrow, I'll try to find somewhere to stay.

My thoughts are interrupted when the entrance door opens and a group of three men enter. They're all wearing black suits. Two of them hang back slightly from the middle one, letting him lead the way. He is short, but broad with black hair and eyes that are strangely vacant and dead. There is something dangerous and cold about him. One of my tables is waving at me, but I'm so transfixed by this trio I pretend not to notice. Even I can tell these men are not here for a drink.

They give off bad vibes and make me strangely nervous.

These men mean business.

At that moment Larry suddenly appears at the door behind the bar, his face is drained of color, and his eyes dart towards the three men making their way towards the bar. He must have seen them on the surveillance screens on his office wall and rushed out.

"Mr. Sorokin," I hear him say as he flashes the main guy a smile, but his smile looks sick, and I can see the beads of sweat that have formed on his upper lip. "I wasn't expecting to see you tonight."

"Why not? Your payment is late," Mr. Sorokin explains in a thickly accented, but polite voice.

Greg passes me my drinks tray and, although common sense tells me to move away from the bar area, I can't help being fascinated as to what's happening here.

Larry licks his lips. "Um... why don't you come around to the office? We can talk there."

"Or we can talk here," Mr. Sorokin says softly.

"Okay, sure," Larry says, his palms in a downward placating gesture. "We can talk here. I know the payment is late, and I'm really, really sorry, but you know, sales aren't what they used to be. Covid, you know? I've had to spend a lot to accomodate the new governmental regulations. I've even had to give up some of my tables to social distancing rules. But don't worry, it's just temporary. I'll get the money to you as soon as I can, I swear."

Mr. Sorokin doesn't say a word. Just looks at Larry with those cold, dead eyes.

Larry tugs desperately at his collar... like it's choking him. "It's just temporary," he gasps nervously.

Then Mr. Sorokin curls his forefinger towards Larry in a beckoning gesture. Larry's head is shaking as he reluctantly steps forward. It's like a particularly bad B movie has become real. Lightning fast, Mr. Sorokin grabs the front of Larry's shirt and pulls him towards him, dragging him halfway over the bar and pressing his deadly calm face close to poor Larry's sweating, white one.

Jesus! That sure escalated quickly.

I look around me and it seems as if everyone else is too drunk to care or even notice. I try to catch Greg's eye, but he studiously ignores me. I know I should take my tray of drinks and move on, but I simply can't drag my attention away from the scene playing out next to me.

7

AMELIA

"**D**id I just hear you say, as soon as I can?" Mr. Sorokin asks with exaggerated pseudo incredulity.

"No, no...I... I didn't mean it like that. You must know, I didn't. You'll have the money. I promise," Larry says, his voice low and pleading.

"Listen you fuckin worm. Stop talking. The more you writhe and squirm, the more you piss me off."

"Sorry, I didn't mean to—,"

"I said, stop talking."

Larry nods vigorously, the sweat is pouring into his eyes, making him blink owlishly.

"I want last week's and this week's packet by Sunday. And by Sunday, I mean this Sunday. Two fuckin' days from today. And if I don't have it all, plus the interest, then you know what'll happen, don't you?" He pauses, letting the moment drip with menace.

Larry's eyes bulge like a squeezed frog's as he nods.

"Say it," Mr. Sorokin murmurs, his voice silky with enjoyment in his ability to make Larry totally submit to him.

"You will break every bone in my worthless body."

"Very good." Mr. Sorokin smiles coldly before he releases Larry.

Then the three men turn as if one autonomous body to head back for the entrance.

Panic seizes me. Oh God, I can't have Larry know I've seen him in such a humiliating position. He will be forced to fire me out of sheer embarrassment. Hastily, I pull my tray of orders from the bar counter and turn away, but I'm so totally shocked by what I've just witnessed, my fingers slip, and my tray jumps out of my hand as if it has a life of its own.

In helpless horror I watch as it flies into the air. In seemingly slow motion, I see the drinks launch into the air. Gold, amber, and white liquids splash upwards and spray everywhere. In a way it is all rather beautiful. Well, at least until the flying glasses meet the hard wooden floor. The crashing sound of the breaking glass echoes across the whole room making my heart stop in my chest.

In my wildest dream I could not have imagined myself in this scenario. Mr. Sorokin's suit jacket is so absolutely drenched with beer it's dripping from the edges. He turns in slow motion and trains his dead eyes on me.

He is the impersonation of evil.

My insides go cold. "Oh my God. I... I'm so very sorry," I stutter. "Let me get some napkins for you."

I turn on my heel to start back towards the bar, but Mr. Sorokin reaches out, grabs my arm, and spins me to face him.

He doesn't shout or scream as I expect him to do.

Instead, his voice is flat and emotionless. "You think you're
so clever, so brave. Standing up for that fat, worthless
worm."

My eyes widen with shock.

Oh shit! He thinks I did it deliberately. "No, no... I didn't
spill the drinks on purpose. It was an accident. I swear it.
Honestly. You have to believe me. It's my first day here. I'll
pay for the dry-cleaning bill, of course."

He doesn't say anything, just stares at me intensely, with
his tar black eyes. It's impossible for me to know what he's
thinking, but he is so close I can smell him. He reeks of
smoked mackerel. Strange, but his skin looks shiny and oily
as a fish. It takes everything I've got not to step away.

"Oh, you'll pay all right, but not my dry-cleaning bill."
Something I've seen in Dan's eyes glitters in his eyes.

First my jaw drops, then I feel a flash of pure fury. The
shock of having Dan almost rape me, the pain of my mother's betrayal, and the fear of not having a place to crash for
the night rush into one boiling emotion that burns in the
pit of my stomach. I straighten my spine and stare back
at him.

"I've said it was an accident and I'm really sorry. I've also
offered to pay for the cost of cleaning your suit even though
it will probably mean I've worked all night for nothing. So...
you can take up my offer or not, that's totally up to you, but
don't imagine you can ask me to sleep with you just because
I spilled some alcohol on your clothes. I swear, I'll call the
police if you try to force me."

His mouth quirks with amusement, as if he is the devil
himself playing with a helpless human. "Who said anything
about sleep. After I'm done with you, little pigeon, you can
call anyone you want, but think carefully first, it would be a

such shame if I had to ruin skin like yours. It is so smooth
and... young."

Suddenly, I feel fear like I have never known before.
Even with drunk Dan, I was just waiting for the moment I
could knee him in the nuts and while he was reeling in pain
make my escape. Sure, I was shocked, disgusted, and
annoyed, and maybe even a little scared, but it was nothing,
nothing like what I feel now, looking into this man's cold
killer's eyes. Goosebumps rise all over my body. My mouth
opens, but I don't know what I can possibly to say to save
myself from a fate worse than death.

Then from the shadows a voice like whiplash, calls out,
"Ivan."

To my amazement the devil in front of me freezes. As I
watch in disbelief his eyes narrow before he slowly turns to
face an imposingly tall man who has stepped out of the
shadows.

8

VIKTOR

https://www.youtube.com/watch?v=RDcaYbeXeUI

-in the heat of the night-

"Let go of the girl," I command in Russian.

There is a flash of confusion in his eyes, then he recovers, and lets go of the girl as one would something hot. "It's nothing, boss. She's just a dumb broad in a dive bar."

I frown, unexpectedly furious with him. She's no broad. She's just a kid. Hell, she looks like she just turned sixteen. Not that it is any of my business, but what the hell are her parents thinking letting her work in a shithole like this? I keep my tone pleasant so anyone listening would think we were just having a polite conversation in Russian. "Fuck off."

Ivan's eyes show frustration and impotent rage, but wordlessly he nods, and moves towards the front door, the two goons who came with him follow closely behind. There is fear in their eyes, but their faces are deliberately impassive.

I walk up to the girl.

Something about her caught my eye as soon as I walked into the dive, but I couldn't see her properly before. Now that I'm closer I clearly see she is not only too young to be working in this place, with its stink of stale beer, where she's probably groped at every opportunity, but that she is also very, very, very beautiful. With a heart-shaped face and one of those swollen mouths that look like she has just given some lucky guy an unforgettable blowjob. Her hair runs down her back in a thick golden plait. It's so long, it goes all the way to her ass. And what an ass it is. Rounded and full. The perfect ass to grab onto while fucking.

I shake my head. Annoyed.

What the fuck is wrong with me? She's obviously way too young for me. As a rule I don't like them young. When they are this young, they are too clingy and desperate for ever-lasting love. I like girls who've been around the block and understand the nature of the game.

Her sparkling baby-blue eyes jerk towards mine.

She is completely horrified, but as soon as she locks onto my scrutiny, her eyes widen with confusion and some emotion I cannot pinpoint. For a few seconds she simply stares at me, her entire body frozen, as if the world around her has stopped revolving, and there is only me and her. Then, as if remembering herself, she suddenly tears her gaze away, dropping it down to the ground. Her long, luscious lashes make blue shadows on her silky cheeks. My gaze drifts lower.

Her top is open too low.

Showing off her pert, little breasts and I can't fucking

help myself. The image of me sucking those breasts slams into my head. I shake the stray thought away, disgusted with myself. I hate predators like Epstein.

She's just a kid. A fragile thing that needs protecting, not hitting on.

How in heaven's name did I get here?

This is not me. Part of me silently fumes that through no fault of my own I'm now the owner of a loan shark outfit. In an ideal world, I'd never ever set foot in a place like this, but my cousin, Alexei, unable to meet all his financial obligations, ran away and left me with his mess.

So… I now own his business and I'm not sure I like being the owner of thugs like Ivan bullying small-time business owners like Larry, or being in the position of saving under-aged damsels in distress that I am disgustingly attracted to. It all leaves a bad taste in my mouth.

"Are you ok?" I ask her.

She shakes her head slowly, not speaking, and the tears that were shining in her beautiful eyes spill over. I should push a few thousand dollars into her hand, apologize for Ivan's brutishness and leave, but something about her holds me in place. I don't know what it is, but every instinct in me is telling me I need to protect her. Stupidly, I reach out to her.

She flinches back from me.

I raise both my hands, to show her I'm not going to touch her if she doesn't want me to.

"It's ok," I say in a reassuring voice. "I'm just going to take you outside for five minutes to get you some fresh air and let you calm down, ok?"

"I'll get fired," she whispers.

Larry is standing behind the bar, watching the scene with an open mouth.

"Are you in the habit of firing your staff if I ask them to step outside with me for a moment and they do it?" I ask.

"N-no, of course not," he stutters. Then he forces a smile to his white face. "Take all the time you want, Amelia."

Amelia. That's her name. It suits her somehow. I turn and begin to walk away. She follows me silently.

"Wait in the car," I tell Jerome, my driver, as I reach the entrance.

He nods without question.

I go outside and turn around to wait for her. She opens the door but hangs back as if she is afraid of me.

"I'm sorry you got caught up in that," I say. "Ivan had no right to put his hand on you like that."

"I should have been more careful," she answers, her voice breaking. She presses her lips together immediately and her eyes begin to swim with tears again.

"It was a bit of alcohol. No big deal," I say.

She swallows hard, as if she is unsure of my motives. All the while tears are pouring down her face.

I smile at her, trying to think of a way to stop the rolling tears. "You probably shouldn't be quite so clumsy as a waitress though."

She gives a short laugh and sniffs. "I sure made a great impression on my first night, huh?"

I laugh, which is odd in itself. I hardly ever laugh out loud, but I can't help it. Through all of this, she has managed to keep a sense of humor. Which makes her quite the little heroine in my eyes.

"Can I ask you something without you thinking I'm coming on to you?" I ask.

She shrugs. "Sure."

"What's a girl like you doing working in a hole like this?"

Her bottom lip wobbles again and I find myself regretting the question. Another odd emotion for me.

"Hey, it's ok. I'm not judging you or anything, I'm just curious."

She exhales, a heartfelt sigh full of troubles. One a girl of her age shouldn't have to express.

"You want the truth?" she asks.

"Nothing else will do."

"Are you sure? It's not a pretty story..."

I nod. "I'm sure I can handle it."

"Okay, today, my stepdad tried to rape me, but that's not the big deal. The real kicker is my mom took his side. So, I walked out of his house with a duffle bag of clothes and hardly any money. I took this job because it's the only one I could find. It was a choice between doing this or ending up on the streets. Which technically, I still am, but hopefully, if I can keep this job, not for much longer."

"You don't have anywhere to stay tonight?" I ask calmly, even though I'm furious on her behalf. I want to punch her stepdad and shake her brainless mother.

"Nope," she whispers. "But since the bar is open pretty late, I'm hoping to hang around here until the very moment it closes. And then it won't be that long to wait until daylight comes. I can hopefully find somewhere then."

I know I should walk away. This is the right moment to stuff some cash in her and walk away forever.

Amelia isn't my problem. I have enough of those. But there's something about her that I can't walk away from. I don't know what it is, but I tell myself it's because her tough talking doesn't hide the vulnerability in her eyes, or

the fact that I can see she's actually terrified of her
situation.

"How old are you?"

"Eighteen," she lies.

I frown.

"Well, I'll be eighteen in a month."

I sigh. I'm probably going to regret this, but what the
hell. "How are you at cleaning?"

She frowns. "Cleaning?"

"You know. Vacuuming. Polishing."

"That kind of shit, I can do with my eyes closed," she
replies quickly, as if she has come into territory she recog-
nizes and is comfortable with.

"Good. How would you like to join my team of maids?
You'd be cleaning my private quarters and maybe one or two
of my offices. Fifteen dollars an hour plus accommodation."

"Why would you do that?" she asks, raising an eyebrow
suspiciously.

Why indeed? I shrug. "Because you look like you could
use a break." I glance at my watch. "I have to be elsewhere
soon, do you want the job, or do you want to go back in
there and keep working for Larry?"

"I want the job," she says quickly, flashing a big smile
at me.

"Right. Go back in and get your stuff. I'll be right here if
Larry gives you any trouble."

She nods then turns and walks back into the bar; her
head held high. I can't help but watch the way her ass sways
in the tight little skirt Larry has her wearing.

As the door closes, I turn away, frowning.

Deliberately, I put her out of my head and turn to the
very real problem I have to solve: Alexei's 'business' that I

have unwillingly inherited is basically a loan shark enterprise enforced by brute criminals. I came to this bar to observe first-hand the operation he ran, and I'm not impressed at all. At the very least, I should get rid of Ivan and his goons. And I will, when Marcus, my operations manager comes back from vacation.

Right now, I'm a man down, but I'm not going to put up with this psychopathic bullshit for another week. I'll have to get Larry to go up to my offices to work out something reasonable with one of my guys and put a very tight leash on Ivan until Marcus's return.

9

AMELIA

One month later

S o much has changed over the last month that I have to keep pinching myself to make sure all this is real. I've gone from living in hell in Dan's trailer, to being homeless, to having my very own place. Of course, my apartment is small, a one-bedroom affair, but it's clean with freshly painted walls and cozy with warm rugs on the wooden floor. I'm so happy here. In fact, right now, I'm happy with every aspect of my life, something I've never been able to say before and something I was beginning to fear I might never get to say.

Who would have known? Dan showing the full extent of his true colors turned out to be a good thing for me. If he hadn't pushed me over the edge that day, no doubt I'd still be living at the trailer park working in another dead-end job I hated, and totally stuck in a life I didn't want.

I think back to that first night I met Viktor Leshchenko.

My first thought was: *God, he is beautiful!* Wild with wolfish silvery eyes and midnight-black hair. Dressed from head to toe in black, he also radiated danger. When he spoke to the two goons quietly in a language I did not understand, I could only stare at him in open-mouthed shock.

Then he turned those silvery eyes to me, and it was like a punch to the gut.

At first, I was wary of accepting help from a man like him. I mean, he was just so out of my league, in every way possible. I could tell by the cut of his suit and the supreme confidence with which he addressed Larry that he was probably on Forbes richest list or something.

Okay, that night, in my naivety, I'll admit, I did think he'd be back to extract some form of payment in kind for his help, but as the days turn into weeks, I realize he didn't help me because he fancied me or anything of the sort. In fact, I'm starting to think he was sent to me for a reason.

He's my knight in shining armor.

Until the day he walked into the Pink Flamingo, I knew next to nothing about Russians. My knowledge, gleaned mostly from Tik Tok videos, had led me to believe they were vodka chugging Communists who kept massive bears as pets, and were ruled by a dictator called Putin, who was also a dangerous madman with access to a nuclear button that could incinerate the whole world at a moment's notice.

Instinctively, I knew what I believed could not possibly be true. Especially, if Viktor is any indication. So, I began to stay up late into the night, reading everything I could lay my hands on about Russia, its culture, history, literature, art, and even its politics.

What I learned fascinates and intrigues me.

But since that day I haven't seen him again. Apparently, he is away in Russia on business. I heard Mrs. Brent, the housekeeper, telling one of the gardeners she is worried what will happen now that there is talk of war with Russia. Will Mr. Leshchenko be targeted with sanctions?

None of the other staff suspects that I'm waiting impatiently for Viktor to return. The wait is almost unbearable. Sometimes the other maids will talk about him, and I'll listen intently without appearing too interested. I believe Katya might have a crush on him, but they all speak very highly of him. It even seems they are in awe of him, as if he's not quite real. A sort of foreign fantasy hero.

Like me, each one has her own rescue story to tell.

There's Lacey who ended up working here because her ex-husband, who used to work for Viktor, was beating her up. Viktor once saw her with a black eye and offered her a way out. Then there's Justine, a friend of Lacey's. who had been working since she was sixteen as a prostitute to feed her two babies. She jumped at the chance to come and work here.

From what they've said, it appears he is hardly ever around. The staff are governed by a management team that treats us well.

It is unanimously agreed that the Christmas bonuses are huge.

Not that I'm worried about a bonus. My wages are more than generous and I'm living comfortably for the first time ever. Plus, I actually enjoy the work. It's the sort of honest work that leaves you aching at the end of the day, but feeling good because you didn't have to do anything that made you feel dirty inside.

For the first time I'm not accountable or beholden to anyone.

It's pitch dark when I arrive at the office building. I pass the mirrors at the entrance and smile at myself. Yeah, life is good at the moment. I walk up the stairs to the second floor. It's my job to clean this entire floor. Fifteen small offices in a large open plan space with cubicles in the middle. There are also two sets of bathrooms and a long corridor to do.

The place is never filthy, and even the bathrooms are left in a reasonable state, but I quite enjoy cleaning everything to the highest standard possible. I always get a sense of accomplishment when my floors are all sparkly. Two and a half hours later I'm finished to my satisfaction.

I fill the kettle in the kitchen and open my packet of pot noodles while I wait. When the water has boiled, I pour it into the plastic pot, cover it, and carry it to the table facing the window. The sun is just rising, and sky is red, purple, and yellow. It's as beautiful as a Monet painting. I cut a thick slice of ham, chop it up and sprinkle it on top of my noodles, Then I sit down.

Alone and in perfect silence, I eat my breakfast.

The instant noodles are hot and delicious. It feels like a meal fit for a Queen. I feel lucky, so damn lucky. My mind drifts slowly. I think of Viktor, where he might be, what he might be doing. I remember that night sitting in the back of his black Rolls Royce and staring out of the window. I was scared and excited. What if I had jumped from the frying pan straight into the fire? Was I on an adventure to rival all adventures, or was I going to be the victim of a sick serial killer?

All kinds of horrible thoughts ran through my mind as

the car glided smoothly through the deserted streets. Slowly, his aftershave drifted into my nostrils, and it was nothing I'd scented before. It was subtle and mysterious, and my mind childishly concluded no one who smelled that good could be bad.

When the car came to a stop outside the place where I was to be housed, his staff, as if they'd been briefed in advance, came out to open the door and greet me. In a daze, I got out and the car pulled away from the curb. I watched it until it turned a corner. I never saw him after that night.

When my little noodle pot is empty, I throw it away, give the table a quick wipe even though I've not messed it up. I like to leave it all extra shiny for Viktor's employees when they come in later in the morning.

The smell of apple air freshener is still in my nostrils when I lock up and leave.

I take the bus to Viktor's house where today I'm supposed to help Justine and Leanne finish up. It is only a short walk from the bus stop, and as I arrive at the house, well, it is more of a mansion than a house. I can't help but marvel all over again at the sheer size of it.

Even after a month, I'm still overwhelmed every single time I see it. Surrounded by old trees and acres of green lawns, the house itself is something else. I swear, it's like something out of a fairy tale, rising tall in its own vast walled grounds.

Tall Roman pillars soar at least thirty feet into the air. As I go through the staff entrance, I nod at old George. I can't help feeling what a shame it is that this house is always empty except for the staff.

I walk up the driveway, reach the door, and ring the bell. Justine answers the door and shakes her head at me.

"How many times do I need to tell you that you don't have to ring the doorbell. Use your key, why don't cha," she admonishes.

Every time I'm scheduled to come to this house, Justine and I have some variation of this conversation. Technically, Justine is my boss and if she says I don't need to ring the bell then I don't, but it feels disrespectful just walking into Viktor's house without announcing myself. I mean, what if he's home? He could think I'm overstepping the line. I remember his silvery eyes again, and a shiver runs through me. He has amazingly light irises that seem to look right through you.

"Sorry, it just feels weird walking into someone's house without ringing the doorbell."

Justine steps back and I go inside the house. Together we head towards the staff area, where I take my jacket off and hang it and my rucksack on one of the hooks.

"Do you want a shot before you start?"

"Nah, I'm good," I say turning around. I watch as she takes a swig from her little silver flask.

"Fine. More for me then," she says with a naughty grin.

I grin back. She's not an alcoholic. She just likes a shot every now and again while she's working.

"What do you want me to do?" I ask, as she screws shut the cap of her flask and slips it back into the pocket of her apron.

"You can come upstairs and help me with the bedrooms."

It strikes me as a little odd she wants me to finish up upstairs rather than helping Leanne downstairs. I don't comment though. She's the boss and what she says goes.

I nod and follow her up the grand sweeping staircase

over the large landing and into one of the main suites of bedrooms. I've never been here before. This, I suspect, is Viktor Leshchenko's bedroom. In shock, I look around me. Wow, what a masculine room. Shades of gray with black accents.

Justine points to the sheets on the cart. Wordlessly, I start to change the sheets on the massive black leather bed, but to be honest I'm kind of in shock.

Does this mean Viktor is coming back?

Is this why we're changing the sheets on his bed?

While she polishes the furniture, she tells me about her youngest son and his excitement over his role in his school play. She tells me he's going to be a tree which basically means he's part of the scenery with no lines and unable to move around. I smile and make approving noises, but my heart is galloping like a freaking horse.

My God! Viktor is coming back.

"He doesn't see it as a bit part in any way." Justine smiles proudly. "He's so excited about it, insisting he's going to be the best tree the school has ever seen."

"He sounds so sweet," I say with a smile, but my mind is going crazy imagining Viktor's tanned, strong limbs slipping between these cool sheets that I have touched. I feel warmth course through my body.

"He is," Justine agrees heartily. "He throws himself completely into whatever he does. Mind you, that's not always a good thing. Some of that stuff is things he shouldn't be doing, like clambering up my kitchen cabinets to get to the cookie jar."

We both laugh, but mine is a little off. I'm sure my face must be horribly flushed.

Justine finishes the polishing and moves onto the vacu-uming and for a moment, our conversation is paused. By the time she's finished, I'm done making the bed. I'm dying to ask her when Viktor is coming back, but I can't. My throat is closed.

"Right. Let's go down to the kitchen. There's a lot of cleaning to be done still," Justine says, wrinkling her nose.

I help her gather up the cleaning equipment, and we move to the end of the hallway and put everything away into a large closet.

She gives me a weird smile as we head down the stairs.

"What?" I ask.

"Nothing. Aren't I allowed to just be happy?" she asks.

"Well sure," I reply. "But that's one weird smile you have going on."

She doesn't reply. She just looks away mysteriously. We reach the bottom of the stairs and go down a hallway towards the kitchen. At that point she does something strange. She holds back and nods at me to go in first.

I push open the door. The blinds are down, and the room is a little dark. Strange. This is always the busiest place in the house. I flick the light on and almost jump out of my skin when all the staff leap up from behind the kitchen island.

"Happy birthday," they all yell together.

I cover my mouth with shock. Leanne walks out from behind a wall holding a cake with candles on it. I laugh and shake my head.

"Wow! Thank you," I say, amazed. "How did you know it was my birthday?"

"It's in your file. You had to fill out your paperwork

before you started working here, remember?" Mrs. Brent says.

"Oh. Oh yeah of course." I grin.

"Come and blow out the candles and make a wish," Leanne instructs bossily, as she places the cake on the island.

10

AMELIA

Everybody starts to belt out a slightly tuneless but very enthusiastic rendition of the happy birthday song.

I look at their faces. I've only known these people for a month and yet they are almost family to me. This day last year, Mom had to work two shifts so I could hardly blame her for being too distracted to celebrate birthdays. I certainly didn't hold it against her when she squeezed my hand, wished me happy birthday, and gave me a Starbucks gift card.

I don't really know whether I felt sorrier for her or me, but I cried after she rushed off to work. When I heard my stepfather awaken, I slipped out and went to the bakery down the road, where I bought myself a red velvet cupcake and a candle in the shape of seventeen. Then I went to the woods, lit the candle, made a wish, and ate the cake. On my own with no one. It was a good cupcake, and that was the extent of my birthday.

This year, I have everything I want and so it's going to be an easy wish. I wished for nothing to change.

I walk over and blow out the eighteen candles. Everybody claps. Leanne starts to remove the candles and cut slices from the cake.

"So, what did you wish for?" Justine asks.

How can I tell her I wished for nothing, but the continuation of what I already have. I grin. "I can't tell you or it won't come true."

She laughs and shakes her head.

"Eighteen and you still believe that?" she teases.

"You're never too old to believe in magic," I say, making my voice sound enigmatic.

Mrs. Brent hands us each a piece of chocolate cake and we sit around the island eating and chatting. After a while most of the staff leave, only Mrs. Brent, Justine, and Leanne remain around the island. I feel conscious of the fact it's getting late, and I can't help feeling like I'm slacking when I should be working.

"Is there much left to do?" I ask.

"Put these paper plates in the trash and we're done," Justine says.

"But I just got here..."

"I know. It's something we always do on birthdays. One of the maids who isn't scheduled to work comes in and gives us a hand so we can have cake and a chat with the birthday girl. It's voluntary that you come in on your day off when it's your turn by the way."

"Oh."

"That's right. I only took you upstairs to help with the bedroom, because you're new and weren't expecting the cake, so we wanted it to be a big surprise. Unfortunately, you got here before the cake did so I just took you up there to keep you out of the way for ten minutes."

I laugh with them, appreciating the gesture and feeling like these women truly are more than just colleagues. They're starting to become family.

I hear a noise out in the hallway and my eyes widen.

"Relax, Amelia. It's just Mr. Leshchenko."

"Viktor?" I squeak, my heart racing like crazy.

"This *is* his house, you know," Justine reminds with a little laugh.

"It's not funny," I say, jumping up agitatedly. "How is it going to look if the first time he sees me since offering me this job I'm sitting around chatting and eating cake instead of working?"

"Hey, calm down. You're not in any kind of trouble. Viktor knows about our little birthday routine," Justine explains, her voice kind.

I shake my head unhappily. She doesn't understand. I didn't want our first meeting again to be like this. To top it all I must look a complete mess.

"Did someone say birthday?" Viktor asks easily, strolling into the kitchen.

"It's Amelia's eighteenth," Mrs. Brent informs. "Would you like a piece of cake?"

"Sure," he says, sitting down opposite me.

His presence has completely changed the mood in the room. He looks at me, and I feel my knees turn to jelly. With butterflies in my stomach, I sit back on the seat I just jumped out of.

"Happy birthday, Amelia." His voice is a dreamy combination of deep and warm, but his eyes are distant and unknowable.

I swallow the frog in my throat. "Thank you, Mr. Leshchenko," I eventually manage awkwardly.

"Mr. Leshchenko? Where did that come from?" His voice is teasing. Nothing like I remembered it. "Call me Viktor," he commands.

I nod mutely. I know I should say something, but when I open my mouth, I realize I can't think of a single thing to say, so I close it again with a snap. God, help me, but I'm acting like a total and complete idiot.

Leanne cuts a slice of cake and puts it in front of him. "Mrs. Brent baked it," she says.

He picks it up in his perfectly manicured hand, takes a big, manly bite, and chews slowly.

"Very good," he comments, looking at Mrs. Brent and nodding appreciatively.

Mrs. Brent blushes with pleasure.

He is either ignoring my awkwardness, too polite to point it out (not a likely option considering the way he spoke to Ivan), or best-case scenario, he hasn't noticed it.

I watch him as he informs Justine about a new club he has acquired and asks whether she will need extra staff to cover its cleaning. He seems so different to the man I remember. He still has that aura of power and primal dominance around him, but he doesn't feel dangerous here. He's deliberately relaxed, and his easy-going manner and easy smile are designed to put us all at ease.

The words flow around me, but I only register them as a buzz.

I can't understand why I cannot(can't) even look at Viktor. I mean, he is the most handsome man I've ever met, but this sizzling attraction I feel for him is far too strong and undeniable for it to be simply an ordinary attraction. In fact,

I don't ever remember getting wet just looking at a man like I am now. I shift uncomfortably in my seat, trying to take the pressure off, but the action just arouses me even more.

As if he can sense my clit is hot and swollen, he suddenly swivels those translucent, wolf-like eyes in my direction. I freeze with shock as our gazes collide. Something flashes in the silvery depths of his eyes, and the air around us becomes thick, almost liquid. I don't understand what is going on, but my heart misses a beat, and my breath comes out shallow and fast. Without warning a shutter falls over his eyes and nothing of those strange and wild emotions in those crazy seconds remain.

"Eighteen, huh? A big one," he drawls, breaking into a grin.

Jesus, I never noticed before, but his teeth are simply amazing. So wonderfully straight and white.

"I hear it's only downhill from here," I croak.

Viktor's eyebrows rise with surprise. "Hey, easy there. I'm nearly ten years older than you. The way you say it, my life is nearly over."

"Oh, Mr. Leshchenko, you're still so young and in your prime. Try being almost forty," Justine pipes up loyally.

"Almost forty is a fine thing. I look forward to all the wisdom the years will bring to me," Viktor says, before turning to me. "Big plans for tonight, Amelia?"

I feel my face flame with embarrassment. "Of course. I have a hot date with the new JoJo Moyes book."

"That's what you're doing on your eighteenth birthday?" Leanne asks, aghast.

Justine scowls. "Screw reading. You cannot spend this important day like that, Amelia. I won't allow it."

"Justine is right. You only turn eighteen once. I'm at a

loose end tonight anyway. Let me treat you all to dinner. What do you say?"

I swallow hard. Can I handle a night with Viktor Leshchenko without him guessing how utterly besotted I am with him?

"I can't go, I've got pottery class tonight, but you should definitely go, Amelia," Mrs. Brent urges.

I would be wiser to say no, but I really want to get out and have some fun. And the others will be there. It's not like it's going to be awkward.

I feel myself smiling and nodding my head. "Yeah, ok, that sounds great."

Viktor smiles, "Good."

"Actually, I can't make it," Justine excuses herself, a sly smile on her face. "I have my kid's school play tonight. He'll never forgive me if I'm not there."

"And I have a PTA meeting, so I'll have to pass too, but you two have fun," Leanne adds with a little wink at Justine.

I know for sure Leanne doesn't have a PTA meeting. Why are they all pretending they have prior engagements? Have I made my obsession with Viktor that obvious? I turn to look at him. He will call it off now I think, trying to ignore the disappointment I feel.

But he doesn't.

"Pick you up at eight?" he asks, one eyebrow cocked.

I'm so bemused I can only nod.

There is a strange look in Viktor's eyes as he stands up and heads for the door. I'm still staring at his broad back when he disappears out of sight.

Did I just agree to a date with my boss?

No, I tell myself sternly. It's nothing like that. It was meant to be all of us, but the others couldn't make it.

Telling myself that does nothing to ease the excitement swirling around inside of me at the thought of spending time alone with Viktor, though. I know nothing will happen between us, but it could still be fun... and it won't hurt at all that Viktor is so, so, so freaking easy on the eye.

11

AMELIA

The night is actually going perfectly well.

Viktor picked me up right on time and though he made no reference to my appearance, I caught the micro-second unconscious widening of his eyes when he first saw me and the instant and instinctive reaction to veil his expression.

I'm wearing a blue dress, the one I bought with part of my first paycheck. At the time, a voice in my head scolded that I was being frivolous, that I would never go anywhere nice enough to wear it, but I told myself it was a treat I deserved, especially since it was on sale. Boy, am I glad I bought it. This restaurant is definitely not the sort of place you go in jeans and a sparkly top.

It's one of those terribly upmarket, exclusive places, with tall ceilings and a bar area that is made from one long smooth piece of copper. Liveried waiters glide around silently serving classy people seated around pristine white tables.

"Why are there no prices on the menu?" I whisper.

At first, he seems surprised by my question, then he smiles, and I can't decide if it's a mocking smile or a self-deprecating one.

"It's a pretentious affection. Here have mine," he says, handing his menu to me and taking mine off me.

It is only then I realize I'm in one those restaurants where the woman gets a menu without prices.

Ouch, looks like I have just proved how unsophisticated I am. I hide my flaming cheeks behind the cream menu and try to appear unfazed as I gaze at the menu. The prices are a shocker. I can hardly believe what I am seeing. A hundred and twenty dollars for a tuna steak! Even more outrageous is something called marbled steak apparently from black cattle raised in Japan. That delicacy is four hundred and fifty dollars.

Jesus!

I can't even begin to imagine a piece of meat costing that much under any circumstances, but here it is. Rich people doing rich things. My eyes skim further down the cursive writing. Wow! They have taken the humble apple pie, served it with gooseberry ice cream, and are charging forty-three dollars for it. Okay, it's apparently flame grilled with Cognac, but even so... The cheese platter with five different cheeses flown in from Europe is fifty-five freaking dollars.

I put the menu on the table and look at him.

"What?" he asks, his face utterly expressionless.

"It's really expensive here, isn't it?"

He shrugs. "Are you worried I can't afford it."

I don't want to make a fool of myself, so I bite my lip to stop myself from saying more unsophisticated shit. "No, of course not."

For a few seconds there is silence, then he breaks it. "It's your eighteenth birthday, Amelia. Once it's gone, it's gone. I want you to remember tonight as something special."

To my horror tears flood my eyes. In my whole life no one has ever done anything this nice for me. I blink hard to stop the tears from rolling down my cheeks. Every freaking time I see him I end up crying and I don't want him to think of me as some kind of big crybaby.

I want him to see me as a confident adult not some sniveling, fragile child. I take a deep breath and force a smile. "Yes, I know you can afford all this. It's just... um... no one has been this kind to me for as long as I can remember."

"It's just dinner, Amelia," he says softly.

I stare at him. He is so unlike anything I've known. "I guess I'm just not used to such extravagance."

He lifts a finger and almost instantly a waiter materializes. "Two shots of Beluga Gold Line," he tells the man.

Two shots of clear liquid in frosted glasses comes faster than I expected. I assume it's vodka. My research has indicated Russians drink a lot of vodka.

"Drink up," he orders, raising his glass to me.

For a split second I hesitate and think of myself alone in the woods eating a cupcake. This is so different than any birthday I've ever had. My life has changed beyond recognition and that is an amazing, beautiful thing. No more Dan. In this new life I get to seize the moment with both hands. I smile at him as I raise my glass to my lips. Together we throw our shots down our throats. The alcohol is like liquid fire running down my throat. I feel it like a warm lick inside my stomach.

"Better?" he asks.

I beam at him. He was right to order the shots. I don't feel the way I felt before the drink. "Yes," I admit.

"Now, may I suggest the lobster and crab ravioli to start? I'm told it's very good."

A thought in my head wonders who told him that. Another woman he brought here? My eyes move towards the menu on the table. Sixty dollars. Wow! But in this new life I seize it all with both hands. "Okay," I whisper.

"And for the main course, especially, if you have never had it, you must try the Kobe steak. There's nothing quite like it."

Ah, the Japanese black cow. I nod. "Okay."

Wordlessly, I watch him order champagne. He is so self-assured and confident it is a pleasure to see him in action. I cannot help staring at his mouth. His lips are sensuous. The champagne arrives almost instantly. I listen to its hiss and watch the mist that comes out of the bottle. My mind records everything. This is a new experience and I want to savor it.

The waiter pours the bubbles out with flourish and places the tall flutes in front of us.

"To you," Viktor says, lifting his glass.

"To me," I echo in a daze.

A million cold bubbles pop on the surface of my tongue. I've never had real champagne before. A long time ago down by the river, I had a mouthful of some cheap imitation with some other kids. It was pretty vile, but this... this is delicious.

"So, Amelia, tell me about you," Viktor invites.

It must have been the vodka on an empty stomach, because I open my mouth and words rush out. I never stop talking as I babble away my whole life. Thank God, the food arrives.

It's like a work of art and it is... divine.

Honestly, I've never tasted anything so delicate or delicious as the handmade ravioli filled with lobster and crab mousse sitting in its small pool of creamy saffron cream sauce. It's my first taste of saffron and I'm in love with its flavor.

The first course is cleared away, and a bottle of red wine wrapped in a white napkin is brought to the table. It's to be paired with our steaks.

"What's your favorite movie?" I hear myself asking.

"I hardly have time for movies these days, but I was impressed with that old original 'Alien' when I was a kid."

I stare at him surprised. "I love alien movies and I've seen them all, even the old black and white ones from the sixties and seventies. And 'Alien' I(omit) gave me nightmares. God, the way that alien burst out of his stomach and skirted across the floor. Ugh."

He grins. "That was my favorite part."

I shake my head. "You're a philistine, Mr. Leshchenko."

He looks at me over the rim of his glass, a strange look in his eyes. "Guilty as charged."

"I was joking, obviously."

"I know. What's your favorite movie?"

I beam at him. "ET."

He laughs. "I should have known."

I laugh too, but I must admit I was a little worried it would be awkward between Viktor and me. We hardly know each other, and I couldn't help thinking his offer of dinner had just been a polite gesture. Or a sort of charity. His original plan might have been to drop in, have a drink with his staff, then leave us to it.

I even thought he might have been secretly a bit pissed off with the idea of spending his Friday night with me, but so far it doesn't feel that way at all. If he doesn't want to be here with me, he's hiding it very well. I've been watching him like a hawk, and he hasn't surreptitiously checked his watch or his cell phone once.

In fact, he's been extraordinarily charming, and somehow, he's got me to a place where I'm so completely at ease I've barely stopped talking all night.

"Penny for your thoughts," Viktor says.

I smile mistily. "I was just thinking what a really great night I'm having."

"Me too," he admits.

I feel my eyes widen. "You're just saying that to be polite."

His smile is mysterious. "Why not? The food is great, and the company is..."

"Is?" I prompt.

His eyes are liquid silver. "Intriguing."

Just like that something in the air changes. Suddenly, there is a flutter in my chest, and I feel quite breathless. I need to change the subject. Get myself back in line. I should ask him about his business. I have a feeling it's not exactly legit, and while it's none of my business, I'm very curious about it.

"What exactly do you do for a living?" I ask, choosing my wording carefully.

A mocking look comes into his eyes. "You mean am I a professional thug?"

"Are you?"

He laughs. "I get why you would think that after the way we met. I suppose you could say I'm an entrepreneur, although I don't like that word. It must have been invented by the same type of person who decided women were too delicate to see the prices on restaurant menus."

"Sorry, but I'm not in your camp. I actually dream of chivalrous men who open doors for me and want to protect me from restaurant prices that are sure to give me nightmares."

He regards me expressionlessly. "That's not very Gen Z of you."

"Gen Z or not, I wasn't privileged enough to ever think like that. I was never given the opportunity to be offended because someone tried to treat me like a little Princess. I've seen too much loutish behavior to ever want more of it." I shrug. "In fact, the lack of a father figure in my life made me dream of a man who would protect and care for me."

Something flashes in his eyes, and I fear it's pity, so I square my shoulders and quickly add, "In a way it was a good thing because I learned the invaluable lesson of independence and how to take care of myself, but we digress..." I sweep my hand in a circle. "What is it you do to afford all this?"

He leans back and pins me with his silvery eyes. "I have many businesses. You've seen some of the office blocks. I also own several nightclubs and a casino in Paris."

I stare at him. "Paris? As in Europe?"

He nods. "Hmmm."

I lean forward. "A casino in Paris sounds so glamorous and so far away from the goons I saw at the Pink Flamingo."

He looks down at the table. "All of my businesses are legit now, but it wasn't always so. I started as a teenager selling weed, before quickly moving on up to cocaine. Before I knew it, I was importing the stuff. In with the big boys and living it up. Hell, I was making so much money I didn't know what to do with it. The danger and excitement in that kind of life is a power rush. It pushes you to be bigger, to control more and more. I lived on pure adrenaline, and I thrived on it. You could even say I was addicted to it, but even then, I understood it was only a matter of time before I made one little slip somewhere and ended up behind bars. The expiration date for the big time drug lord is surprisingly short. Then something happened that hastened my departure from my life of crime. I used the money I'd made illegally to buy up legit businesses. That was five years ago."

"Don't you miss that power rush?" I ask curiously.

He leans back. "Not one bit. I'm not the same man I was."

I try to imagine him as a drug lord and remember the quiet yet utterly chilling voice he had used on the two goons. Yes, I can. "Have you become a good man, then?"

He shrugs. "That's not for me to judge, but those around me."

I ponder his statement. Where would I be without the job he offered me? Where would Justine be? Or Lacey? And those are just the people whose stories I know. So, he made a few mistakes when he was younger. It's not like I've exactly had a sheltered upbringing. Heck, I've bought weed in the past. Who knows? Maybe from one of his shipments. But...

I take a deep breath. Better to be honest. Put all my cards on the table. "Yes you are, but I kinda got the impression from our encounter at Larry's place that you are in the protection business, which is surely not a legit enterprise."

He frowns. "That is not actually my business. I unfortunately inherited it from my cousin, Alexei. It's not the kind of thing I would ever willingly invest in. I detest dealing with sleaze balls like Larry or Ivan so my first instinct was to walk away from it, but Alexei has implicated me, and I have to be careful how I dispose of it as there are a few unsavory characters who will come back to cause me problems later."

"So, you're not going to have me kneecapped if I don't properly clean the windowsills in your house?"

"Uh no... unless you're into that kind of thing, of course," he drawls, with a grin.

I laugh, but the sudden turn in the conversation into sexual innuendo makes me feel like I'm on slippery ground. Already, I can barely keep my eyes off him. It must be the alcohol, but I really wish I could touch him, kiss him. Yes, he has a past, but somehow, hearing about how he used to be and how he's changed now only makes him more attractive to me.

"You said something happened that made you realize you had to get out of the drug business," I croak. "What was it?"

For a second, his face clouds with some intense emotion I can't quite decipher. It could have been unbearable grief, or even pure hatred. I haven't known him long enough to know for sure. He covers his blip quickly and smiles at me.

"This is not the occasion to talk about such things." He forces a grim smile. "But enough about me. Tell me more about you."

"There's really nothing more to tell. I had a Cinderella-ish childhood, but I was rescued by a Prince."

Viktor raises his glass, and his eyes glitter. "I'm no Prince, Amelia."

I lift my glass too. "You could have fooled me."

"In that case, Cinderella shall go to the ball," Viktor says as he signals to our waiter to bring the check.

12

VIKTOR

Amelia is even more beautiful than I remember. Out of that sleazy barmaid uniform and without that haunted, terrified look in her eyes, she's as radiant as a fucking angel. I've never fucked an angel before.

Whenever I look at her, I feel my cock stir. I just want to take her to my bed and make her cum in my mouth. Then I want to fuck her all night long, until she's too sore to think straight or walk... whichever comes first.

I remember her as she was at the bar. Fearless and yet fragile. Even then she intrigued me in a way no girl had before.

A girl who clearly didn't have the best start in life, but no way was she quitting. With her looks she could have become a lap dancer or a stripper and brought in the big bucks, but she's out there working hard, earning her own keep. That's real independence. I admire her fierce courage. It reminds me of myself when I was a free spirited thirteen-year-old boy. When the whole world was my oyster.

It's only sometimes that her tough façade slips, and she

shows how naïve and vulnerable she really is. Those times I get the unreasonable and totally crazy feeling I want to lock her away from the world and protect her from its casual brutality, but I know that's just insane. She's not mine and she never will be. What happened to Lisa is never happening to her or anyone else for that matter.

Lisa was gunned down in front of my eyes.

Five years and twenty-two days ago, I held her in my arms and watched the life bleed out of her. We'd gone to a private party in a club, and she had refused to drink. She said she was too happy to drink. I didn't know it but she was pregnant with our child. As we came down the steps a man appeared to my left to distract me. While my attention was on him another one appeared to my right. He had a gun. She had instinctively thrown herself in front of me and taken the bullets meant for me. The bullets ripped through her chest and stomach, killing the precious life inside her and then her. She clutched her bleeding stomach and stared at me in horror.

"Our baby," she whispered brokenly. "He's killed our baby."

Then her knees gave way, and she began to totter like a doll. I caught her as she crumpled to the ground. Unhurt I watched the life extinguish from her eyes.

The shock was incredible. I walked away from the scene like a zombie. Inside I felt cold and empty. It hardly seemed possible, but Lisa was gone... forever.

I went back to our apartment, and everything was as we had left it. I went into our bedroom. It still smelt of her perfume. I sat on the bed and the cool night breeze blew in through an open window.

How stupid and arrogant I had been. I should have seen

this coming. In my mind I could see her clutching her stomach, blood pumping through her fingers. Her face white with horror, her lips moving, "Our baby."

I slammed my fist into a wall and felt no pain. Why? Why did she sacrifice her life for mine? I had never once even told her I loved her or made any kind of commitment. Guilt seared through me. So many times I had seen the look of sadness in her eyes because she knew I did not love her the way she loved me.

Her unthinking, selfless sacrifice changed me forever. Until that night I was seriously in danger of becoming a total psychopath. Now, I knew I had to get out of the dangerous life I'd chosen.

The man who'd ordered the hit was the man I would end up becoming if I stayed in that business, and that thought horrified me beyond belief. Lisa and our child were dead. I would honor their memory and do the thing she had always wanted me to do.

I would leave this life of sin. But first, I hunted down the man who had taken her from me and ended him. It was a pleasure.

Then I stopped all my illegal activities.

Just like that I walked away from it all. It took some adapting to, but I got used to it, and I came to see that the thrill I felt when I was working, the feeling I'd always told myself I needed to do something dangerous to achieve, didn't go away. The thrill came from making money, pure and simple. In time I found the same thrill with my legit businesses. I just wish I had found that out sooner, before Lisa paid the ultimate price.

Talking to Amelia made me relive the moment that Lisa died in my arms, and for a second, I was overcome with the old guilt and pain. I managed to swallow it down and continue as normal with Amelia, but it convinced me that I can't go there with her. I've made my peace with Lisa's death in a way. I've grieved for her, and I've allowed myself to move on, but even now, even though I'm out of that life, I know one day, it might all catch up with me.

There is still unfinished business. I killed the father and left the son, Igor, alive. I know I should have taken him out. It was just Revenge 101. Never leave the son alive or you will always be looking over your shoulder. But he was my age. I'd met him once, had a drink with him. More importantly his wife was pregnant with their first child. I spared him.

And he became my enemy.

An enemy who doesn't care that I'm no longer in the game. An enemy who is biding his time. So, it doesn't matter how much I feel myself wanting Amelia, I won't let myself go there. I can't and won't put her in the line of fire.

Once I was stupid and careless. Not anymore.

I've learned to live with the idea of never getting close to another woman again. Obviously, I date and sometimes, I even let myself see her more than once, but I never let myself get attached in any meaningful way. When I wasn't playing the field my mostly solitary lifestyle suited me very well. After Lisa, I never met a woman who made me want more anyway.

Until now.

I don't know what it is about Amelia, but she makes my body crave hers. Not even with Lisa did I harbor such deep lust.

I know, I'm playing with fire.

But... instead of wrapping the dinner up, dropping her off at home, and calling it a night, I find myself inviting her to the launch party at my new club. I lie to myself that it's not strictly a date. It's just a birthday treat. Plus, she'll be safe there. More security in and around that club than there is at Fort Knox.

I ask her to come to the club and she readily agrees, beaming up at me. I see her excitement at the thought of going to a club and feel her desire to spend more time with me. Not an unusual scenario for me to have women biting their lower lip, flicking their hair, exposing the soft skin on the inside of their wrists, or watching me when they think I'm not looking at them, but knowing the attraction isn't one sided makes Amelia even more dangerous to my peace of mind.

It would be much easier to back off and not let myself get too intoxicated by her. But not tonight.

Pushing aside my conflict, I pay the check and smile at Amelia. Tonight is her eighteenth birthday. She should be celebrating, and I intend to give her a night to remember. After tonight, I'll make sure our paths don't cross much, but for tonight, I'll just envelop myself in the perfume of her innocence.

"Ready?" I ask.

She nods and gets up. I call my driver and by the time we step out of the restaurant, my Bentley is idling on curbside waiting for us. Antonio, my driver, rushes to open Amelia's door and she smiles as she gets into the car. I go around to the other side, slip in beside her, and tell Antonio where we're going.

"What clubs do you usually go to?" I ask.

"I don't. I'm only eighteen remember," she says primly.

I raise an eyebrow.

"Fine," she confesses sheepishly. "I have a fake ID. My friends and I used to go to Human or The Max."

"Then you're going to love The Planetarium. It makes those places look like knitting clubs for grannies," I say.

She laughs. "This place had better live up to that."

"It will," I assure.

13

VIKTOR

https://www.youtube.com/watch?v=01IlptXTyK4
-Make you dance like Poco Lee-

My driver pulls up outside of the club. The large planet earth in the club's name is lit up with neon lights and shining over the street, turning the pavement blue and green. The sound of the music spills out of the door. I'm pleased to see that the line to get in goes right down the block. The launch party seems to be a success. Amelia makes a face as we get out of the car.

"What is it?" I ask.

"Nothing really. Just the length of the line. It's going to take us hours to get in."

I grin and she frowns.

"What's so funny? This dress isn't exactly thermal you know."

"Amelia, it's my club. Do you really think we're going to wait in line to get in?"

"Oh! This is *your* club. Right. Of course, we're not."

"Come on," I stretch my hand out to hers.

The second our palms touch, fire floods up my arm and my cock jumps. That was a bit of a shock. Hearing the gasp Amelia makes as our skin touches tells me she feels the fire too. I let go of her hand and instead place it gently on the small of her back. It does nothing to help dial back my lust for her. I try to ignore the lust pounding through me and lead her to the entrance.

"Good evening, Mr. Leshchenko," one of the bouncers greets with a nod, as he unhooks the small red velvet rope that leads to the VIP section of the club.

James, the new manager, rushes up to us, his face flushed with nerves and stress. "Mr. Leshchenko, I wasn't expecting to see you here tonight."

"Relax, James. I'm not here to check up on anyone, just to have a few drinks."

He clasps his hands and breaks into a big smile. "Wonderful. In that case, this way, please, Mr. Leshchenko. I think you'll be pleased with the turnout," he says, gesturing for us to walk with him. "The place has been rocking like this since we opened."

He takes us up the red carpeted staircase into the VIP area, which comprises a wide balcony that wraps around the entire club. It allows us a good view of the main dance floor. There's a big bar at one end and a smaller one at the other, and of course, the obligatory dance floor. No one is dancing up here yet.

James was right. Looking over the balcony into the main area, I see the place is absolutely packed and the dance floor is alive with people moving to the music. The DJ shouts something over the mic, something I don't quite catch, that gets an excited whoop from the crowd.

"May I get you a bottle of Champagne, Mr. Leshchenko?" James asks.

I turn to Amelia. "Champagne ok with you?"

"Whatever you're having will be fine."

"Champagne is good," I say to James.

He nods respectfully and turns away. As he waves down a waitress, I lead Amelia away from the railing and we take our seats on a nest of black leather sofas.

A waitress carrying a bottle of fizz and an ice bucket arrives with impressive speed. She uncorks the bottle, fills the glasses and leaves.

Amelia lifts her glass. "Here's to you. May you always be the richest man in the club."

"May you always be the most beautiful woman in the club."

Her eyes widen and confused color rushes into her cheeks.

Quickly she turns her head and looks out over the railings to the people on the dance floor below. She sways slightly, bobbing her head in time with the beat.

"I always envied people who managed to find a spot in a club where they can dance without other people's elbows in their ribs."

"That's the worst and best thing about clubs. The crowds. Without them there's no atmosphere, with them you must put up with elbows in your ribs."

"Yes, exactly." She glances at the VIP dance floor. "But it's amazing being up here. You get all of the atmosphere and none of the elbows or the showers of sweat."

"So, you like dancing..."

She swivels her head around. "Of course. Don't you?"

I shake my head. "I'm not much of a dancer."

"That's a shame."

We sip our drinks and chat. She tells me about some of the crazy shit her friends have done on nights out and I find myself regarding her with real curiosity, wondering about her life before I found her.

Eventually, Amelia excuses herself to go to the bathroom, and I watch her walk away, her hips swaying, her ass perfect in her dress. I notice the curves of her hips and I imagine myself running my hands all over her body. I want to touch her everywhere, taste her. I look away as she disappears through the door. God, she's gotten so far into my head so quickly. It's not just about the way she looks either. I'm really enjoying spending time with her.

Amelia comes back from the bathroom, her face flushed with excitement.

"Holy shit," she exclaims as she sits back down. "You should see those bathrooms. They're completely done up in glossy black marble and shiny chrome."

"I have. I approved their designs."

"I appreciate having doors that actually lock, soft toilet paper in each stall and thick hand towels, but the best part is what it doesn't have: an inch of liquid on the floor that you just pray is only water as you wade through it." She grins infectiously. "Heck, there's even free hand cream and perfume... I could really get used to this."

"Welcome to the VIP life," I murmur, staring at her. The women I date inevitably try to impress me with their sophistication or attempt to project a blasé attitude towards wealth as if they have seen it all. Not her. She just blurts it all out.

She holds out her glass and I refill it.

"To how the other side lives," she announces, then takes a drink, which somehow goes the wrong way and causes her to choke and splutter. "I guess you can take the girl out of the trailer park, but apparently, you can't take the trailer park out of the girl," she mumbles, embarrassed.

The change in her is instant and remarkable. Suddenly, she looks like a scolded kid. Miserably, she dabs at her red face with a napkin.

"Relax. It's ok," I say gently.

She puts the balled-up napkin on the table and bends her head with shame. "Thanks for being so kind to me. I'm afraid I just keep making a terrible fool of myself."

Her sense of disgrace is so disproportionate to her 'crime' that it startles me. My instinctive reaction is to want to hold and protect her, but obviously I don't. "It's not the end of the world, Amelia. Look, what can I say to make it better?"

She lifts her head slowly. "There is something you can say."

"What is it?"

She grins suddenly. "Say you'll dance with me. Please. This is my favorite song and it's nearly half gone." She reaches forwards and grabs my hand. "I love this song," she urges. "Come on. Please. Dance with me, Viktor."

I'm too surprised by the trap she set to react properly. Dancing isn't really my scene, but I'm intrigued and more than a little seduced by her, and it's also a shock to realize how much I want to be with her, so I allow her to pull me to my feet and let her lead me out onto the empty dance floor.

"Loosen up, Viktor," she orders. "Dancing is meant to be fun. You look like you're being punished."

I move my hips a little and she nods approvingly. "Better."

She throws her head back and closes her eyes, her arms in the air. Her lips mouth the words as she sways and twirls. She looks amazing, and it takes everything I have not to pull her into my arms and kiss that swollen mouth.

Suddenly the song ends, and Amelia opens her eyes and looks at me. Her blue gaze hits me like a punch in the solar plexus.

"One more song," she begs and steps closer to me.

"You need to loosen up those hips, though," she teases with a grin.

Laughing, she puts her hands on my hips and moves them, pushing my hips from side to side. I try to appear unaffected and detached, but her touch is setting me on fire, sending shock waves of desire through me. The sensation is so intense it feels like I'm a horny teenager once more.

She looks up at me again and I see she's no longer laughing. She's staring up at me, her eyes darkening with desire. Her mouth parts as if in slow motion. As I watch tantalized, the little minx runs her tongue over her trembling lower lip.

That does it.

I wrap my arms around her, yank her closer and crush her lips to mine. She gasps with shock, but her hands snake up from my hips and wrap themselves tightly around my waist. I push my tongue into her mouth, tasting her sweet one.

She runs her hands up my back. I push one hand into her soft hair. The music beats around us, and it feels like Amelia and I are in a cocoon of lust and acute awareness. We are the only two people in the world at that moment.

My body responds to her touch, like fire in my veins

spreading out through me, making me want more and more. Amelia's kiss is passionate and as hungry as my own. She presses her body tightly against me and I can feel the heat of her body through my shirt. Her hard nipples dig into my stomach. Amelia's clean scent of shampoo and soft perfume consumes me, taking over my thought processes, not letting me get any reprieve from my raging hard on.

And fuck me, I kiss that girl like I've never kissed anyone before.

My heart pounds in my chest like a wild animal, urging me to throw her over my shoulder like some Neanderthal and carry her back to my cave. The thought of what I would do to her in my bed makes me lose my head... until I hear her moan into my mouth. With that small, almost innocent sound my outrageous fantasy comes crashing around me. Reality hits like a bucket of cold water over my head.

I can't do that to her.

I can't let myself get attached to her. And she's not the sort of girl I can fuck and forget. I know I should end the kiss, but instead, I deepen it.

I can't seem to stop, even though I know I should.

14

AMELIA

I was starting to think Viktor was never going to kiss me.

At first, I thought the attraction was one sided, just a crush I'd developed. The more I flirted with him, the more convinced I became he was uninterested in me in that way... until that time our skin touched. And then I knew.

He'd felt that spark too.

But I could tell that he was trying to keep his distance. Then finally he got the hint when I put my hands on his hips and started to loosen him up a little bit. I never would have been brave enough to do that without the champagne, but it worked like magic. It showed Viktor I was into him, and he didn't have to worry about kissing his employee. After all it's not like I work directly for him. Justine is my boss.

There's no need to think he's taking liberties, because I'm right there with him. I want him desperately, and if I'm honest more, much more than he wants me. And not just because I'm tipsy, but because I'm a little bit obsessed with him. Have been since the first night we met.

Whatever it was that made him kiss me, I'm so glad it finally happened. I was about to burst, waiting to see if something would happen between us. Well, it's worth the wait. He's the kind of kisser a girl can only dream about. The way he possessively crushes me against his body makes my knees go weak., but his kiss is deep and passionate. I've never been kissed like this before. I'm used to inexperienced slobbery kisses, not this sensual, passionate, deep invasion of my mouth. It lights up my whole body and makes me crave more.

One of his hands is twisted in my hair, the other is pressing on the small of my back. My own hands are moving wildly up and down his broad back, feeling the taut muscles that lie beneath the silky material. God help me, but I really want to rip his shirt off and run my hands all over his skin.

For those few moments I forget we're in the middle of a club. We're not alone. There are people around us, probably watching us.

My pussy feels hot and swollen. I can feel how slippery it is as I move. The dampness soaks into my panties. My nipples are hard and sensitive as they press against Viktor's chest and my clit is tingling in a delicious way, begging for Viktor's touch.

I rub myself against his body, needing to feel the closeness of him, needing him to take me, own me. I can feel that he's turned on too. His cock is massive and rock hard. It presses and throbs against me, like it's calling out to me, tempting me. I shift slightly in Viktor's arms so that my body pushes and rubs against his cock. Up and down that hard shaft. A moan starts up in my mouth and for a split second he holds me more tightly, then suddenly he steps back, pulling his mouth away from mine, surprising me and leaving me feeling strangely cold and bereft.

We stare at each other. My chest is heaving as I gasp for breath, but his eyes and expression are completely veiled. I smile shyly at Viktor as I wait for him to take me by the hand, to march me back out of the club and continue this moment somewhere a little more private.

He shakes his head slightly and rubs his hand over his cheeks and chin. "Fuck! I'm sorry, Amelia. I shouldn't have done that."

Disappointment floods through my body and I feel my shoulders slump. Suddenly, the club is too hot, the music too loud, and the alcohol in my stomach feels like it's sloshing about, making me feel almost nauseous.

"Amelia? Are you alright?" Viktor asks, frowning at me.

No, I think to myself. He doesn't get to kiss me like that, tell me it was a mistake, and then act like he gives a shit.

"I'm fine," I say. "I'd like to go home now."

"Of course. I'll take you home," he says immediately.

My paranoid mind thinks he sounds relieved. "No, I can get a cab."

He shakes his head. "No way. I'll make sure you get home safely."

I nod, turn, and walk away, heading blindly for the exit. I feel so humiliated hot tears gather in my eyes. I blink them away furiously. I won't give him the satisfaction. That would be icing on the cake of my disgrace.

I can hear Viktor's footsteps behind me. He's no longer trying to make conversation. I step outside, and the chilly night air wraps around me. I rub my hands on my arms as

Viktor signals to his driver. The car appears quickly, and we get in.

I sit pressed up against the door, looking out into the darkened night. I'm upset that our kiss ended that way, and I'm embarrassed about the way I handled it. I should have shrugged it off, made out as though it was no big deal. Instead, I acted like Viktor had done something terrible to me.

We got caught up in a stupid moment; Viktor kissed me and then he remembered that I'm trailer trash and changed his mind. It shouldn't be bothering me this much. I mean I barely know him. Logic isn't helping though. I feel like I've lost something special, and I know it's stupid, but I can't help the way I feel.

I shoot a quick glance at Viktor. He's sitting against his door, his posture matching mine, his face turned to look out of the window. It's a very different scene to the way we were on the way here, chatting and completely at ease with each other.

I should have known this was too good to be true. I shouldn't have let Viktor's kiss affect me the way it did. But I know he wanted it as much as I did, and that somehow makes his rejection of me worse. If he didn't feel any attraction to me, then I could deal with that, but this is personal. This is someone who does feel attracted to me but sees that I'm below their station – the hired help – and catches himself before it can go any further.

When the car pulls up outside of my place, we still haven't spoken a word to each other. I don't particularly want to break the silence. I feel so stupid, and I just want to go inside and close the door and forget the kiss ever happened, but I also can't help but think that would be kind of rude after Viktor made the effort to take me to dinner and then out clubbing for my birthday. I take a deep breath and turn to him.

"Thank you for a lovely evening," I mutter.

He turns his head to look at me and smiles politely at me, but it's a sad smile, full of regret. It does nothing to shift the lump that's starting to form in my throat.

"I hope you enjoyed your birthday," he says.

I nod. I did up until the last ten minutes of it when Viktor broke my heart. I scramble out of the car and tell myself off for being so dramatic. He didn't break my heart, that's stupid. It was a kiss that shouldn't have happened, and that's all there is to it.

The car doesn't drive away until I open the entrance door to my building.

I run up the stairs, open my front door and rush straight up to my bedroom. I throw myself on my bed. I don't even try to stop the tears when they come, releasing the lump in my throat.

It seems silly crying over something I never had, but I can't help the way I feel. For a brief special moment there, I felt like maybe I could have Viktor. That maybe he felt the same way as I did. I know I didn't do anything to put him off me.

It has to be the trailer trash thing. It has to be that he came to his senses and realized that powerful men like him don't kiss girls like me.

The bitter truth is I'm just a glorified maid. And he's a billionaire.

15

AMELIA

Somewhere in amongst my tears and bout of self-pity, I must have fallen asleep. I wake up in the morning with a banging headache and drag myself into the shower. I don't have any major plans for today, but I'm not going to spend the day moping around thinking about Viktor. Now that I'm sober, it's much easier to put it into perspective. It was one stupid, ok, fine, amazing kiss, but that was all it was. There was no betrayal, no heartbreak. I just need to move on.

I can put it all down to the music, the surroundings, the alcohol, and my childish infatuation with a man that is clearly out of my league.

There is nothing more to it.

I sit at the kitchen table sipping at a cup of coffee wondering what to do today. Maybe I should go to the mall and treat myself to some new boots. A belated birthday present to myself. I smile, content with the idea. I might grab a couple of new paperbacks too and spend the rest of the weekend curled up reading. Ooh and maybe I'll even treat myself to a fancy box of chocolates to eat while I'm reading.

I'm sitting debating whether or not a whole box of chocolates is a good idea. I mean, is chocolate ever really a bad idea? I'll go for a run tomorrow morning or something to make up for them I tell myself when the doorbell starts ringing. I'm not expecting anyone, and I wonder who it can be. Maybe Leanne has taken me up on my offer to drop in for a coffee if she's ever in the area.

I open the door and freeze.

It's Viktor.

And no matter what I've told myself, the sight of him affects me in a way that cannot be denied. He's wearing black jeans and a navy-blue hoodie. He shouldn't look good dressed like that, but he does.

"Can I come in?" he asks.

"It's your house. I can hardly say no, can I?" I say rudely, stepping away from the door.

"If you don't want me to come in I won't. This is your home, Amelia, and I'm not going to force myself in if you don't want me here," he says, not making any move to come inside.

The truth is I don't want him here. Just seeing him again is making me feel that loss I felt last night all over again, but I have to admit that I'm curious as to what he is doing here.

"You can come in," I throw over my shoulder and start to walk along the short hallway back to the kitchen. I hear him close the door behind him. "Do you want some coffee? It's freshly brewed."

"No thank you. I won't keep you long. I just wanted to

talk to you quickly about something. About last night," he says.

I change course and open the door to the living room. I drop into the armchair and nod towards the couch. Viktor sits down and leans forward, his elbows resting on his knees, and his hands clasped in front of him.

"Look, Viktor, we were drunk, and things got a little out of hand. You really didn't have to come here to dump me all over again," I say. "Trust me I get it. Guys like you don't kiss girls from trailer parks."

He scowls, which, damn it to hell, makes him look even more attractive.

"That's what you think this is about? You think I stopped because of where your mom lives?" Viktor asks incredulously.

Put it like that does sound like I'm one of those self-righteous, hopelessly pompous inverted snobs. I blush slightly.

"Amelia, I grew up in a one room apartment that I shared with my mom and my two brothers. My mom did her best, but we were dirt poor. Why do you think I started selling weed?"

Now I'm really confused about what happened. If Viktor isn't the shallow prick I had decided he is, why did he reject me? Some of the ice in my soul thaws and starts running away in rivulets.

"So why don't you tell me what happened then since clearly I'm way off," I challenge.

"First of all, I want you to know I'm sorry. I handled the situation appallingly."

I shrug and keep my expression casual. "It's fine."

"You're a beautiful woman, Amelia," he says. "Please don't think I'm not attracted to you, because I am. I'm more attracted to you than I've been to anyone for a long time. But I shouldn't have kissed you. Not because I didn't want to, but because it doesn't matter how I feel about you. I can't be with you... or any other woman at this moment in my life. I'm sorry for stringing you along. I swear, I never meant for last night to turn into what it did."

I nod, not trusting myself to speak for a second. So, I was right. Viktor is into me. And I didn't do or say anything to change that.

"Have a good weekend, Amelia." Viktor smiles as he stands up. "I'll leave you in peace now, I just didn't want to leave things awkward between us."

I walk him to the door. "Thanks, Viktor. For explaining, I mean," I say as he steps out.

He glances back, nods, and gives me a strangely lost smile.

Then I run to the window and watch him get into his car and drive away. It's only then I realize I didn't ask him why he can't be with me with or any other woman. Maybe he doesn't want to commit because of work, or maybe he's still suffering from a broken heart. That can't be true because of the way he kissed me last night. Like a starving man.

Still, I don't suppose it matters.

He seemed like his mind was pretty well made up. I'm just going to have to forget the kiss ever happened.

It's not going to be easy, but I do feel a little better now that I know it wasn't personal. Viktor hasn't rejected me because I'm poor. And it gives me hope that whatever his reason for not being able to be with me is, that maybe he will find a way around it.

I<small>T's</small> <small>BEEN ALMOST</small> a week since Viktor told me he does find me attractive, but he can't be with me or anyone else. I wish I could say I've gotten used to the idea, but I haven't. I know it was only one kiss, but it was a kiss I can't forget. It haunts me day and night. I even dream of it. It was a kiss like nothing I'd ever felt before so as much as I try to put Viktor or that kiss out of my head, I just can't do it.

My whole body is freaking calling for him. I *need* him to kiss me again.

And not just to kiss me either. I need more. I need him to make love to me, to make my whole body feel as good as my mouth felt when he plundered it. But I can't have him, and I think knowing that only serves to make me want him even more.

I haven't seen Viktor since he came over to my apartment and told me nothing can happen between us. It's most likely his plan never to be around me again. Or maybe it isn't. Maybe it's just a coincidence, because although he said he was attracted to me, I can't imagine a world where I have as much of an effect on him as he has on me. I really can't see Viktor planning his life around where I happen to be on any given day.

Yeah, it has to just be a coincidence.

With that thought in my mind, I'm not overly surprised to learn that Viktor is holding a client meeting at his house on the day I'm scheduled to clean there. Viktor and the client are having their meeting in the large breakfast room, and I've been given instructions not to disturb them, but to carry on with cleaning the rest of the house.

I'm almost finished cleaning when I look out of the

French windows and see Viktor out by the pool. He's lying on a sun lounger, wearing a pair of swimming shorts. I feel my heart start to beat faster as I look at him. To my horror my pussy gets wet from just watching that gorgeously toned body.

God, how I want him. I want that man like I've never wanted anyone before.

It's like a physical ache inside of me, one that I already know I won't be able to get rid of unless Viktor comes around and replaces that empty ache with his mouth. Even then, I think the ache will hang around until we go further, until Viktor is filling me up in every way a man can fill a woman up. My thoughts are doing nothing to stop the tingling between my legs.

Viktor looks up and catches me watching him. I freeze for a moment. Fuck. He wasn't meant to see me standing here spying on him like some kind of fucking creeper. What do I do now? How do I explain this in a way that doesn't make me sound like a desperate, lovesick idiot? I come up with a quick plan and push the door open.

"Hi," I call, giving Viktor a little wave. "I'm almost done in here and I just wondered if you wanted any refreshments brought out before I leave?"

"That would be great if you don't mind," Viktor shouts back. "I'd just about kill for a cold beer right now."

"Coming right up," I say with an exaggerated cheery smile.

I step away from the door, my heart still hammering hard in my chest. I'm relieved that he seemed to buy my reason for standing there ogling him. Talk about thinking on my feet. It would have been too humiliating if he thought

I was just perving on him. As I hurry towards the kitchen my crazy mind starts fantasizing about being out there with him, lying on top of Viktor, wrapped up in his arms.

Don't even go there Amelia, I tell myself. Just don't.

I rush through to the kitchen and go to the fridge and pull it open. I scan my eyes over the contents, grab a can of beer, and grab a tall glass. As I'm pouring the beer, Justine comes in.

"Right, that's me done." She pauses. "You drinking beer in the afternoon."

"It's not for me. It's for Viktor."

"Ok. I'm off. You'll be all right on your own, won't you? Everybody else has gone for the day."

"Of course. I'm finished too. I'll be going soon."

"Want me to wait for you and give you a ride?"

"Nah. I enjoy the walk to the bus station."

"Ok, see you next week then."

"Bye, Justine."

She gives a wave and exits through the door.

I drop the bottle into the recycling bin and check that I haven't left anything out of place. I haven't.

My hand is shaking because I'm so nervous. I tell myself to just get over it. It's not like I'm going out there to seduce Viktor. All I'm doing is taking him a glass of beer. I step outside into the warm sun and Viktor is no longer on the lounger. He's swimming lengths in the pool and right now he is at the far end. Has he done that just so that he doesn't have to bother talking to me?

I don't know and I'm not going to dwell on it. It's probably for the best anyway. I'd only end up saying something embarrassing if I had to talk to him. I go over to the lounger

Viktor was sitting on and put the glass down on the little table beside it.

I debate calling to him, letting him know it's there, but I decide against it.

If I wasn't into him, I wouldn't call to him while he was swimming just to tell him his drink was here. I'd leave it here and expect him to see it when he got out of the pool. That's it then. That's where this little situation ends, I think as I turn around to head back to the house. Maybe he will call out to me...

I slow my steps.

But he doesn't.

Then disaster strikes. My shoe slips on a wet tile and the ground flies away beneath me. My arms pinwheel and an involuntary scream escapes my lips. Even as I am falling, I don't think of the harm my body is in. Instead, my first crazy thought is: boy, am I glad Viktor is in the pool now. The thought of him seeing me falling clumsily on my ass isn't the look I'm aiming for.

Thank God, I manage to catch my footing before I land on my ass, but my humiliation isn't over. My foot slips again and I tumble forwards instead, heading straight for the pool. I try to stop myself, but there's nothing to catch onto, and my foot steps out into the air above the water.

I feel myself plummeting through the air and landing in the cold water with a loud splash and a strangled cry of help. Panic sets in as the water closes over my head and my feet don't hit the bottom of the pool. I can't swim and I'm in the deep end.

I kick desperately, managing to break the surface of the water long enough to snatch in a quick breath, but then I'm going down again, and when I kick my legs this time, I don't come back up high enough to break the surface.

I'm sinking lower into the water. My lungs are burning as I hold my breath and the chlorine stings my eyes. I want to scream, but I hold my breath instead. Bubbles float from my mouth as my body fights me, wanting more oxygen.

I'm going to die here.

16

VIKTOR

I swim with my head down, my face in the water, pushing myself; harder, faster.

I'm actually rather pleased with myself. The meeting I've just had has just resulted in me getting rid of my unwanted loan shark business and I managed to do it without incurring any loss. Not bad for a day's work.

I hear a loud splash and I stop and tread water for a moment. There's no sign of anyone around. My drink is on the table now though. Did she just deposit the drink and leave without saying goodbye? I fight off the disappointment.

But as I turn and start swimming towards the side to get out of the pool a blonde head breaks the surface of the water at the other end of the pool then disappears back under.

Fuck! She's in the water. All kinds of crazy thoughts start flooding into my brain. Each one is lustier than the previous one. All the staff are gone by now. Is she fucking naked? An image crashes into my brain. I've placed her nude body on the side of the pool, opened her legs wide and I'm greedily eating her out. The afternoon air is full of her moans of pleasure.

I watch the water around me, waiting to see her swimming over to me beneath the surface, but she doesn't appear. Bubbles float lazily to the surface of the water where she went under it. The bubbles get bigger and come faster and it hits me then. She didn't jump into the pool; she fell in.

Holy fuck, she's drowning.

Instantly, I lunge in her direction and start swimming towards her, pushing myself harder than I ever have before. How long has she been under? It can't have been more than thirty seconds, but that must feel like a lifetime to the drowning person. I see the black of Amelia's uniform through the water. She's almost at the bottom of the pool.

Quickly I dive beneath the surface of the water, grab her under the armpits, and kick back to the surface. I push her head up out of the water and turn onto my back, holding her with one arm and pulling myself along with the other. I swim to the nearest ladder and clamber up it with Amelia pinned to my side with one arm.

I lay her on the ground beside the pool. She's not breathing.

Memories of Lisa dying in my arms rush into my head. I kneel beside her and give her the basic CPR training I learned in school.

Amelia coughs suddenly, a violent spasm that wracks her whole body. Droplets of water fly from her mouth and I immediately turn her onto her side. She coughs again, though not as violently and retches out a flood of water.

She draws her knees up to her chest as she gasps and

coughs frantically. Tears stream down her face and her body trembles, whether from the cold or from panic I don't know.

"It's ok, Amelia. You're ok," I whisper.

I go get my towel and wrap her in it. She sits up and looks at me. Her hair is plastered to her face and she's still half crying with shock. Mascara trails leave black streaks down her face and her skin is pasty white.

"You don't have to go that far to get my attention," I say.

She looks at me blankly for a moment, then she laughs softly. It's music to my ears. She must be feeling better if she's laughing.

"Come on," I say. "Let's get you to my car. I'm taking you to the emergency room."

She shakes her head quickly.

"No," she says. "Honestly, I'm fine. I was just a little bit shaken up, but I'm fine now, I swear."

I consider insisting on taking her to the hospital whether she likes it or not, but we'll sit there waiting for hours for her to be seen and she'll be freezing in her wet clothes. She really does seem to be fine, and I can't see what the doctors at the emergency room could do for her. The water is out of her lungs and she's reacting normally, breathing normally.

"Just please don't fire me," she whispers.

I shake my head. "Fire you? For almost drowning? Jeez, Amelia what sort of a bastard do you think I am?"

She looks down into her lap and I realize that with the hand she has been dealt in life, she has no reason to think I would react to this, to her, with kindness. Well, I'm going to show her that the whole world isn't a bad place.

"Look, if you don't want to go to the emergency room then we won't. But you're going to have a nice hot bath and

I'm going to put those clothes in the dryer... if I can find where it is."

Her eyebrows rise. "You don't know where the dryer is?"

I shake my head. "Nope."

"It's in the laundry room next to the kitchen."

"Right. Let's get you out of your wet clothes then." I stand and offer her my hand.

As I pull her to her feet the towel slips, and I can't help but notice the way her wet clothes cling to her body. Fuck me, she certainly has curves in all the right places. Those hips. Those breasts. That voluptuous ass.

I force myself to look away from her body as I hold open the door for her to enter the house.

"Come on," I say briskly, and direct her towards the staircase. "I'll run a nice hot bath for you. It will relax and warm you through properly."

"Thank you," she says, her voice small and unsure.

I open my bedroom door and walk towards the ensuite bathroom. "Won't be long. Just make yourself comfortable," I throw over my shoulder.

I turn the water on. I look through the cupboard until I find some bath salts and add them to the water. I leave her a stack of clean towels and I put a bottle of shampoo on the end of the bath for her. Then I grab a fluffy white robe from the hook on the back of the door and go back to the bedroom.

Amelia is still standing where I left her.

"I didn't want to leave a wet patch on your bed," she explains.

She catches herself and blushes bright red at her choice of phrase. I pretend I haven't noticed the double meaning of her words and hold the robe out to her.

"If you want to go into the bathroom and put this on first and give me your clothes before you get in the bath, I'll get them into the dryer straight away."

She chews her lower lip. "Everyone's gone, haven't they?"

"Yup. No one will ever know you were in my tub."

"I just wanted to say, thank you for saving my life."

She goes into the bathroom. I don't have long to wait before her arm snakes around the door, holding her clothes out to me.

"Take as long as you want," I say. "Get warmed back up. Relax a little."

"Thank you, Viktor," she calls from behind the door.

I change into a clean pair of trousers and go down to the laundry room. I put Amelia's clothes in the dryer and notice she hasn't given me her underwear. Once the dryer is going, I go back upstairs to the bedroom. I pull out my laptop and look through some emails, but I can't concentrate.

My thoughts keep returning to the fact that Amelia is on the other side of the bathroom door, naked, her skin wet and slippery with soap.

My cock gets hard just thinking of her like that.

I remind myself again that nothing has changed, but that's not strictly true. Lisa died because my business was dangerous. Amelia almost died bringing me a glass of beer. Is it possible that she's not in any more danger even if she is with me? Is it possible that actually, anything can be danger-ous, and when your time is up, your time is up?

I think that has to be some sort of a sign. A sign telling me that resisting Amelia to keep her safe is futile. Maybe she's actually safer if she's with me. Yes, I have enemies, but I also pay a lot of people to keep me and those close to me safe. People who would risk their life to save my girl if it came to it.

By the time Amelia emerges from the bathroom, my mind is made up. I can't allow myself to live half a life because of something that happened in the past.

I want Amelia. And I want her like I've never wanted another woman.

She opens the door and steps out of the room followed by a whirl of steam. Her hair is damp but combed out and the mascara streaks are gone from her face. She isn't wearing a scrap of make-up and honestly, she has never looked more gorgeous. I stand up as she comes out of the bathroom.

She smiles at me shyly.

I close the gap between us, cupping her face with my hands and pressing my lips against hers. She responds to my kiss, kissing me back, and wrapping her arms around me. I push my hands into her damp hair, kissing her like I never want to let her go again. And I don't want to let her go ever again.

She's mine now, and nothing and no one can change that.

17

AMELIA

https://www.youtube.com/watch?v=9HDEHj2yzew

-come on let's get physical-

I don't understand Viktor one little bit.

First, he kisses me like a starving man on the dance floor, then he tells me we can't be together, and now he's kissing me like a starving man again. Any other girl with even an ounce of self-respect would push him away, but not me. I'm too crazy about him to resist in any way at all. My knees have turned to jelly, and I move closer to him and I let myself melt into his body. I wrap my arms around him and cling like a lost and found baby monkey.

I'm conscious I'm wearing nothing, but a robe and my dirty underwear is balled up in its pocket. Viktor is wearing dry shorts, meaning he's even closer to naked than I am. I feel a swirl of nerves in my stomach. I know this is it. We're going to have sex right here on Viktor's bed. Somewhere in my head there is a voice urging caution. Screaming I have to stop this from moving forward this fast, but I can't. My body is pulling me along in a giant wave of desire and I feel powerless to stop it.

Viktor starts to walk me backwards as he kisses me, moving us towards the bed. My stomach is whirling, excitement swimming through me, and my clit is pulsing with desire. I want him more than I've ever wanted anything or anyone in my whole life.

I know this could be a one-time-only thing. Once the heat is gone Viktor might revert back to his stance of not wanting to be in a relationship with me or anyone. I know I could regret this. But... even if it is just this once, I still don't want to miss this experience. I might never feel this way with another man ever again. Viktor's tongue pushes into my mouth and I stop trying to analyze my situation. I don't want to think anymore. In this moment, I just want to feel.

We reach the bed and Viktor turns around so that my back is to the bed and he's facing me. He takes his hands from out of my hair and moves his face back from mine slightly. I don't want the kiss to end. I start to reach for him again, but he shakes his head and pushes me backwards.

I fall onto the mattress behind me.

He looks down at me and I feel my heart racing at the look on his face. He stares at me possessively, like he wants to consume me completely. His desire is clear to see, and not just on his face. His cock is hard and straining against his shorts. I start to reach for him, but he reaches down and pulls the belt of my robe open, and it falls away from me, exposing my breasts and belly.

Viktor pulls it further open. "Jesus!" he whispers, as he hungrily feasts his eyes on my body. "I knew you'd be beautiful. But not this beautiful."

He runs his hands over my body. "Soft. So fucking soft and pale you are."

Then he leans forward and takes one pink nipple in his mouth. Gently, gently, almost reverently, he sucks it.

I'm practically crying at the delicious sensations coursing through my body. He lifts his head and I feel his finger swipe through the folds of my pussy.

"You're dripping wet, little Amelia." There is a wicked look in his eyes.

It's true. I'm so turned on my juices squish against his fingers. His beautiful silvery eyes never leave me as he brings his fingers up to his face. First, he smells them deeply then he licks them.

"Sweet, so sweet," he marvels.

He cups both my breasts with his large hands and runs his tongue luxuriously around my hardened nipples. My hips wriggle shamelessly with anticipation and need as he plants kisses down my stomach. Deliberately he grasps his hands around my knees. Still watching me intently, he roughly pushes my legs wide apart, exposing my throbbing pussy. His eyes leave mine and travel slowly down to witness my arousal. There is a look of greed and satisfaction on his face as he stares at my wide-open pussy.

He drops to his knees and lowers his head. I feel him run his tongue along my inner thigh sending goosebumps flooding up my legs and all over my body. He moves his lips higher up my inner thigh, casting more little feather sensations.

My stomach is afire with excitement and my clit is pulsing, desperate for his touch.

His tongue licks at my swirling flesh, moving closer to my clit. I suck in a breath. It feels amazing, warm and rough. It sends sparks of desire flooding through my body. Viktor licks me with a dedication of a cat grooming itself, sending shiver after shiver through me, and making my pussy clench tightly, and my legs tremble wildly.

"Please, please," I beg mindlessly.

Without warning he suddenly presses his tongue firmly against my clit, setting alight the nerve endings.

"Ahhh," I scream, and lifting my hips, absolutely grind my pussy onto his tongue.

He releases the pressure, teasing me, and goes back to his gentle licking. It feels so good, but I want more.

"More, more," I pant.

"So greedy," he teases.

I want that pressure on me again, bringing me to the edge. I start to move my hips, but Viktor reaches up and puts his hands on them, holding them flat to the bed while he continues his light, teasing touch.

Just when I think I can't take it anymore, he takes my whole pussy in his mouth, and pressing his tongue firmly below my clit, begins to suck, making me feel dizzy with sheer pleasure. I writhe uncontrollably as he sucks harder.

"Good God!"

Suddenly, he takes my clit between his teeth, and I make a little squeaking sound as pain and pleasure collide inside of me. I'm frozen in my clamped position.

"Please, Viktor. Let me come. I'm going insane here," I literally sob. I have never needed release this badly in my life.

Viktor releases my clit from his hold and hot blood rushes back into it, making me gasp with shock. It's the best pain I've ever had. He starts fucking me with his tongue, putting just enough pressure on to keep me on the edge of the abyss of pleasure, but never able to fall into it.

While his tongue finds all kinds of sweet spots around my clit, he slams two long fingers deep into my soaking pussy.

"Oh God, oh God. I'm yours. Please. Fill me up. Own me. Make me yours," I babble, almost incoherent with lust.

He starts to thrust it in and out while still sucking on my swollen clit. The combination makes me lose my mind.

My hips rock wildly and my jaws clench as the pleasure in me builds up. Until it happens. The bubble of tension inside me bursts. My legs quake, my whole body is bathed in heat, and my nerves all come to life at once as my orgasm plows through my body, making me writhe beneath Viktor and moan his name, again and again.

I feel my pussy clenching tightly and a rush of warm liquid runs out of me. Viktor keeps licking, holding me at the peak of my climax. I try to say something, but my words won't come out. I can't move, can't breathe, can't even think. The pleasure is like an assault, slamming through me and taking over my senses. It's a delicious assault, one I never want to end. I feel like I'm melting.

My hands ball into fists at my sides, tugging at the covers beneath me and I buck my hips. Viktor's hands stay on them, but he no longer pins me down. I press myself against his face, thrusting my hips up and down, wanting this moment to last forever.

"Come in my mouth," he snarls, as he eats me so fast and hard, I become almost delirious.

I float in a sea of ecstasy as wave after wave of pleasure crashes over me and wave after wave of my juices gush into his mouth.

Finally, Viktor lifts his face away from me and watches me from between my legs. His expression is deceptively lazy, but his eyes are waiting and intense. He waits while I come down from my orgasm slowly, enjoying the heavy warmth it leaves behind in my limbs. My body feels good, better than I ever knew it could, and I want more. I need more. My hungry pussy tries to hold on to his fingers as he tries to withdraw them.

He kisses my pussy lips lingeringly then stands between my legs and gestures for me to scoot up the bed. I do it, making room for him on the bed.

My heart is racing as I slowly regain my composure and get my breath back.

He pulls his pants down and I swallow hard, nervous suddenly when I look at his huge, hard cock. He smiles at me, and I smile back up at him. He kneels on the bed between my legs and looks down at me. I feel vulnerable, my legs spread like this, my body open to him, but it's a good sort of vulnerable. I feel safe with Viktor.

He reaches down and runs his fingers down my slit, spreading my juices around. His fingers linger over my now tender clit, and I arch my back and gasp a little as fiery pain flows through my pussy and up into my stomach.

Viktor grips the base of his cock with one hand and moves on top of me. His weight feels good, solid. I wrap my arms around his shoulders and look into his eyes as the tip of his cock presses against the opening to my pussy.

"Be gentle with me. I've never done this before," I whisper.

Viktor freezes and looks down at me, not moving.

"You're a virgin?" he asks incredulously.

"Yeah," I say.

He rubs his hands over his face. "Fuck," he curses, and nearly sprints off me.

18

VIKTOR

Amelia sits up and pulls the robe closed around her. "I can't believe you don't want me anymore just because I'm a virgin. What, because I didn't sleep around in high school, you don't want to know me? Is that it?" she demands, her voice all at once accusatory and hurt.

I sit next to her. "You think I don't want you? Look at that," I say, pointing to my dick. It is so fucking hard it hurts.

She looks down then back to me. "So, what happened back then? When I told you I'd never had sex before, you jumped off me like I burned you or something."

"I'm going to make love to you, Amelia," I say slowly. "You can bet your bottom dollar I'm going to do that. I'm going to show you what that tight little pussy of yours can really do, and I'm going to make you come so hard you won't know what to do with yourself. But not like this. Your first time should be special, not just a quickie like this because I have my staff arriving in less than an hour for a meeting."

"So, you still want me?" she asks with a little smile that

makes me want to change my mind and just fuck her brains out right now.

"Obviously," I say. "Let me take you out to dinner tonight, and afterwards, we can come back here, and I'll show you exactly how much I want you."

"Deal." Amelia grins.

I kiss Amelia on the mouth, a sensual, tender kiss. I really can't believe someone as beautiful as Amelia is still a virgin. I'll have to find the balance between gentle enough not to hurt her and still rough enough to make her feel really good.

She moves in my arms, positioning herself over my legs. I can feel how wet her pussy is and it's doing nothing to stop the urges inside of me. It takes all of my willpower not to grab her and throw her on her back and just start fucking her senseless. She pulls her mouth from mine and smiles at me. She has a wicked looking gleam in her eyes.

She puts her hands on my shoulders and pushes me backwards until I'm laid flat on my back. She runs her hands over my chest, her robe falling open again.

"Amelia..." I start, but she shushes me and scoots down my legs. She moves until she's on her knees between my ankles and then she leans forward and bends down, running her tongue along the length of my still hard cock.

"Amelia," I say again. "It's ok. We don't have to do this."

She looks up at me and gives a soft laugh.

"Just relax, ok. You're not pressuring me. I'm doing this because I want to. I'm not a total nun you know. I've done stuff, I've just never met anyone who I wanted to go all the way with before. Now shut up and let me return the favor."

She pushes my legs apart a little and crawls closer to me and then she lays down on her front and sucks my cock into her mouth. Her lips are satin soft, her tongue rough like velvet. Her mouth is warm and wet, and I have to bite down on my lip to stop myself from coming the second she sucks me into her mouth.

She starts to bob her head, moving her mouth up and down my cock, running her tongue over me. She pays special attention to my tip, licking it all over and drinking me in. She pushes her lips all the way down me, taking me right into her throat and I gasp as pleasure floods through me.

I'm not going to be able to hold myself back for much longer and I stop even trying to. I relax and let Amelia do her thing. She keeps sucking me, harder and faster, like she's trying to suck me dry. I moan her name as I feel my orgasm building at the base of my cock and spreading out through my whole body. I moan her name again as I feel my cock twitch and I spurt into her mouth.

She swallows, not letting me go. She keeps sucking as I spurt again. She swallows down every last drop and still she sucks my cock like there might be more. My body is on fire with pleasure, and every part of me feels my orgasm. It's so intense it's almost painful.

Finally, Amelia sits up. She wipes her mouth and smiles at me.

"Ok, that was my appetizer. The rest is for tonight. Now I need to get home and change for the dinner you promised me."

I laugh and sit up, pulling her into my arms and kissing her again. I don't know what it is about this girl, but she's damn special. And now she's mine, and I'm going to make sure nothing can ever change that.

AFTER AMELIA LEFT, I got in the shower again. All I could think about was how sweet her pussy tasted, how she sucked me like she was loving it. I couldn't get the visions of her out of my head, and my cock sprang back up to life. I found myself jerking off in the shower, images of Amelia filling my head. When I came, it was with her name on my lips.

I finished my meeting early because I couldn't concentrate. I then called my favorite restaurant and booked a table.

I drive to Amelia's place to pick her up. I feel my cock stirring again as she comes out of the house as I pull up at her gate. I get out of the car and for a second, I can't do anything but look at her, drinking her in. She's wearing a black bandage dress that shows enough to be sexy but leaves a lot to the imagination too. And boy is my imagination running wild as I look at her. She's wearing black high heels that make her legs look even more stunning than usual.

I catch myself staring, and Amelia's shy smile tells me she has noticed it too.

"Hey," she greets.

"Hey yourself," I say with a smile.

She reaches the car and I pull her into my arms and kiss her. I have to will my cock to behave as it strains against my jeans. God, how does this girl have such an effect on me that a simple kiss has me hard?

I open the door for her. She gets into the car, flashing a bit of her thigh as she does so. I close the door and move to the driver's side. I'm driving tonight because I want it to be just her and me.

"I think you'll like this place," I tell her as I start the car. "It's one of my restaurants and out of all my businesses, it's my personal favorite. It's Italian, and the head chef there trained in Naples."

Amelia's stomach growls as I talk, and we both laugh.

"Just in case you're a bit deaf and didn't get the message, it sounds very much like my sort of place," Amelia says with a laugh.

We arrive at the restaurant and the valet takes my car away. I offer Amelia my arm and she slips her hand through it. It sends sparks flying through me.

I smile down at her, and I can see by the flush of her cheeks that our contact is having a similar effect on her. Maybe we should have just gone straight back to my place and ordered in, but I really do think Amelia will like it here, and I want to show her that she's special to me, that this isn't about sex.

19

VIKTOR

We step inside and the hostess smiles at me.

"Your table is ready, Mr. Leshchenko. Right this way please," she says.

We follow her through a crowd of diners. The place is just right – busy enough to have an atmosphere, but not busy enough to make it feel less intimate. The hostess leads us to my favorite table. It's situated a little way away from the rest of the diners, right at the window which looks out onto an Italian garden full of the very herbs and spices the chef uses in the food.

A waiter pulls Amelia's chair out for her. She thanks him and sits down. I sit down opposite her, and the headwaiter appears.

He smiles expansively at us. "Welcome, Mr. Leshchenko." He nods politely at Amelia. "Signorina." He places a menu down before each of us. "Would you like any drinks now or do you need a minute?"

"A bottle of your finest champagne, please," I tell him.

He nods and moves away from us. Amelia picks her

menu up and I do the same. Even though I eat here nearly once a month, the menu changes weekly.

"Do you see anything you fancy?" I ask her.

"It all looks amazing," she smiles. "I'm thinking maybe the chicken alfredo."

"Great choice," I tell her. "I think I might have the same."

The waiter comes back with champagne, and I order the meals.

"I've told you everything about my past and you hardly told me anything about yours," she says.

"What do you want to know?"

"Tell me about your family. Are you close to them?"

"My father died before I was born and my mother decided many years ago, she wanted to return to Russia, so I arranged it all for her and visit her a few times a year."

"I never knew my father either," she says. "He left before I was born, and it's been an endless succession of stepfathers for me."

"That must have been tough."

She sighs. "It's no secret that I've always preferred it when it was just Mom and me. You know, that time in between stepfathers. Sure, we struggled for money and that, but we were happy. The men she chose were never really suited to family life and having them around just messed everything up. Of course, my mom couldn't see that. "At first, she thought there was something wrong with her, but I think my latest stepfather, Dan, has cunningly managed to persuade her that there's actually something wrong with me. She now thinks I'm a brazen seductress and Dan is the innocent victim, drawn in by my womanly charms."

She laughs suddenly at the irony of it all. It's a bitter laugh, and although her story makes me angry on her behalf, I keep my expression neutral. "Dan is a manipulative shit, I take it?"

Amelia's expression of disgust says it all. "That's the understatement of the year. Let's just say Dan thinks he's God's gift to women, but he's enough to turn any woman's stomach. And one day, Dan went too far so I left."

There is real sadness in her voice, and I can tell she is really hurt by her mother's betrayal. I feel something rise up inside my gut. A strong reaction. A feeling of anger at a woman who would be so stupid as to choose a useless man over her daughter and a feeling I haven't felt for a long time. A feeling of great affection for the girl sitting opposite me.

"It sounds like you're better off out of there for sure, and I definitely think you did the right thing to leave." I smile. "This is your fresh start."

"I think so too," Amelia smiles, and reaches out to grasp my wrist.

Her hand looks small and pale against my skin. I take it in my hand and open it. There are calluses on her palm. I trace them. There are a million thoughts running through my head. I want to protect her. I want to take care of her. I even want to save that stupid woman who she calls mother if it will make her happy.

The waiter comes back to the table with our meal, and she takes her hand away from mine. I miss the contact instantly. She smiles at me as she starts to eat, and I start to imagine my hands all over her later on tonight. I eat without tasting anything.

It doesn't help me to concentrate on something other than Amelia when she runs her toes up my leg, teasing me. She grins at me with a gleam in her eye and I shake my head, amused by her expression.

She giggles and takes her foot away. I take a moment to compose myself properly before I speak again.

"Have you spoken to your mom since you left?" I ask.

"Not since I left, no," she says. "While I was walking out of the trailer, I was so angry with her I kinda hated her. But as time passed, I began to miss her terribly." She pauses. "But I can never go back. Not while Dan is there anyway. For the moment it's probably for the best if we just don't see each other. Since Dan came into our lives, we haven't really had an easy relationship, and to be honest with you I'm sick and tired of always being second best to the latest guy in her life."

Amelia talks about her shitty mom in an even, almost detached way, but I don't think she truly has made her peace with the way their relationship is. I can see the flash of pain in her eyes when she says 'second best'. She looks so vulnerable I find myself desperate to protect her from the world around us.

"I can't imagine anyone thinking of you as second best, Amelia," I say.

"Yeah? That's because you haven't met my mom." Amelia laughs.

"Do you have any brothers or sisters?" I ask.

She shakes her head. "No, just me. I don't have any other family. It's been just me and Mom, and whatever loser she's shacked up with, since I was three. My mom's dad died when I was a couple of months old, and her mom died when I was five. I don't know if my father is alive or dead or if he had any family. They didn't stick around either so quite frankly I'm not interested in any of them."

I want to reach across the table and wrap Amelia in my

arms and tell her she'll never be alone again. Her childhood sounds heartbreaking.

Amelia looks up and sees my expression and smiles. "It wasn't always bad though. When she was between boyfriends, Mom would act like a regular mom. We'd go to the park or the mall and hang out like mothers and daughters do. Maybe one day she'll wake up to Dan and we can have some sort of relationship again."

"You'd consider that?" I ask, a little surprised to hear it after the way Amelia talked about her mom.

"Yes, of course," she says with a self-conscious shrug. "I mean, she is still my mom and I love her. And I guess I feel kind of sorry for her. She's looking for her fairytale ending, but she's just so bad at it. She always picks the frogs that don't turn into princes."

She flashes me a teasing smile that makes her eyes sparkle. "I hope I don't take after her in that department," she adds.

"Well, I have been known to sit around on lily pads in my spare time," I smile. "Just so you know."

Amelia throws her head back and laughs and I laugh with her. Her laugh is infectious. She winks at me. "Maybe I'll turn you into a prince tonight if you're on your best behavior."

"Are you sure you want me on my best behavior?" I ask with a grin.

"Well, when you put it that way, maybe it's best if you're a little bit naughty," Amelia smiles.

"Now you're talking," I say. "So, speaking of naughty, want dessert?"

We've both finished with our second course, but my craving is only for Amelia.

Amelia nods and smiles. "I feel like I couldn't eat another thing, but at the same time, I feel like dessert is essential, don't you?"

I grin at her as I raise my hand to flag down our waiter. "In that case."

Amelia purses up her mouth and nibbles on her bottom lip as she scans the menu. I can't help but laugh at the concentration on her face.

"What?" she says looking up and catching my eye. "Choosing the right dessert is a serious business you know."

"Fair point," I reply.

After much deliberation and back and forth, Amelia chooses the butterscotch cheesecake with vanilla gelato. I choose the cannoli purely to keep her company. I signal to our waiter again. As the waiter departs with our orders I stare at Amelia.

I still can't believe how quickly she's gotten underneath my skin like this. Even before Lisa, before I vowed off love forever, I was never one to get attached too easily, but I have to admit to myself that I don't just like Amelia. The feelings are getting intense, much more, by far more than I could have ever expected.

"So, Amelia. If every job in the world paid the same wages and you could be instantly qualified to do anything, what would you be and why?" I ask.

"Did you read that question on an ice breaker card at work?" Amelia grins.

"No, I'm just genuinely curious."

"Mmmm...." She does the pursed mouth thing again then she smiles and nods, her decision made. "I'd be a lawyer. I've always been into those courtroom dramas, and I've had plenty of practice negotiating with hostile parties.

Plus, I'm pretty good in an argument. What about you?" She pauses for a second. "And you're not allowed to say what you're doing now because that's just boring."

I smile. "In that case I'll go with psychiatry."

Her eyes shine. "So, you could learn everyone's dark secrets and blackmail them?"

"No." I laugh. "What sort of a monster do you think I am? I'd do it because what is more fascinating than the workings of other people's minds?"

"Now that you mention it, I'd love to get inside a serial killer's head or something like that, you know? Just see what makes them tick. I want to switch."

"No switching." I shake my head and look at Amelia solemnly. "You made your bed and now you have to lie on it. No deep diving into the psychopathic mind for you."

Her expression changes, becomes sultry and knowing. "You're right. I think I'll keep the bed I have already chosen to lie in tonight."

I stare at her, and she smiles slowly at me. Suddenly it feels as there is no one else in the world except us. Nothing else matters except her and me. The sensation is broken when our desserts come. I thank the waiter, barely looking away from Amelia.

I watch her take a mouthful of cake and the expression of satisfaction on her face as it melts in her mouth.

"Good?"

"Divine," she whispers. "Ok, my turn to ask a question. If you could be famous for one thing, what would you choose?"

"Hmm," I think for a moment. "Painting."

"You paint?" Amelia asks, looking surprised.

"No. But I'm a big fan of great art." I smile. "What about you?"

"I'd be a famous singer. I can't sing for shit, but I like the idea of touring the world, and that would be a good way to do it."

"What country do you most want to visit?" I ask.

"Italy. Rome specifically," Amelia says without hesitation. "The food, the culture, the architecture. Everything about the city screams come and visit me."

"I'll take you there one day." I say it on the spur of the moment, but as soon as the words leave my mouth, I know I mean it. I want to see her in Rome.

Amelia smiles at me, her eyes shining with excitement. "I'm going to hold you to that," she says. "Where would you go?"

"Australia. I don't even know why. I've just always wanted to go."

"Well maybe one day, when I'm a famous singer who moonlights as a lawyer, I'll take you there." She grins.

"Right, I'm holding you to that too then."

20

VIKTOR

Our coffees arrive and Amelia picks hers up and takes a sip. She winces as she swallows it.

"Oooo... hot," she says.

"Did you expect it wouldn't be?"

She makes evil eyes at me, and we both laugh.

She blows thoughtfully on the surface for a moment and takes another sip.

"Do you want children?" she asks.

That was so left wing I never expected it. Only Amelia would ask such a question before she has even had sex with someone. I think of the child that died in Lisa's body. The pain is still there, but I won't spoil tonight for her. "Why? Are you selling some?" I ask lightly.

"Viktor," she warns.

"To answer your question seriously. If God is kind enough to give them to me, I will take them when they come."

She smiles mistily. "That's beautiful. I've always wanted

identical twins, but seeing as there are none in my family, it's unlikely."

"How many do you want?" I ask.

"Four," she says, then winks cheekily. "And maybe even more than that so we'd better get started quickly."

After the words are out, she realizes what she has said, and I see her wait awkwardly for me to cringe or mentally withdraw from her.

"Makes sense," I say lightly. "We don't want to still be changing diapers when we're fifty."

Relief that I didn't make a big thing out of her teasing chatter and run away screaming floods into her face. Her smile is warm with gratitude. "Unless they are our grand-children," she jokes.

"I call dibs on not changing any diapers once my kids are old enough to do it themselves."

"Nice try," she says.

I shrug. "It was worth a shot."

Amelia laughs, a happy carefree sound. "Actually, I agree with you. Grandparents are not there for the hard thing, they're there to spoil their grandchildren rotten behind their children's backs."

"Here you will find no disagreement from me."

"I think…"

Amelia tails off mid-sentence when the sound of a large explosion rocks the restaurant. The swing doors of the kitchen fly open, and a ball of flames and smoke explode out into the dining area. She turns to look in the direction of the sound, her mouth hanging open in shock as the table-cloths on the tables nearest the kitchen catch fire.

The flames take hold so quickly, we're both still in our

seats, staring in shock at the sudden carnage. The smoke fills the air, and I can feel my throat and eyes stinging.

I jump to my feet.

"Come on. We have to get out of here," I say, taking Amelia's hand in mine and pulling her out of her seat.

All around us, people are screaming and shouting, jumping up from their seats and stampeding towards the doors. A fire alarm blares out, only seeming to add to the chaos.

21

VIKTOR

E ven as I try to head to the entrance, I can see we're trapped. There is a wall of fire between us and the nearest exit.

I scan around, trying to see a way through the wall of flames without being incinerated. Through the haze and smoke-filled air, I see people rushing for the exits. On the other side of the wall of flames a woman falls down, but no one stops to help her, and I have to look away too. She's probably going to end up trampled to death, but I can't get through to her. There is nothing I can do to help her.

The staff are pouring in from the kitchen where the fire originated.

Most of them are covered in burns and one of the chefs is actively on fire. I shout at her to drop and roll, but she doesn't hear me over the screaming and the roaring of the fire, and her own total panic. Everywhere I look is like a scene out of a horror movie. I force myself to look down at the ground for a moment so that I can think.

I position myself between the fire and Amelia, but I

know if we don't get out of here soon, I won't save her. It won't be the flames that get us – we'll be dead from inhaling the smoke long before that happens.

I wonder if we can make a run for it, dash through the flames and get to safety that way. I take a step forward, but that's as far as I can go before the intense heat drives me back. I can already smell the hairs on my arms singeing.

The smoke irritates my lungs and I resist the urge to cough, knowing it will only make it worse. Amelia has already succumbed to coughing behind me, and in my mind, I see it happening again. Lisa dying in my arms. Amelia dying because I brought her here. I refuse to acknowledge the thought.

I won't let it happen.

I turn back to our table and pick up the water jug. I pour the water over our napkins and pick one up. I press it over Amelia's nose and mouth and see the panic in her eyes and she lashes out instinctively, trying to push my hands away from her. I persist, pushing the wet napkin against her mouth.

"It will help you breathe," I shout.

My shout comes out as a hoarse sounding whisper and I'm not sure she can even hear me. I pick up the other napkin and press it over my own nose and mouth, showing her what I'm trying to do.

The relief from the smoke is instant when I put the cold cloth to my face. It's not total respite, but I feel like I can breathe again. I point to the napkin as another cough wracks Amelia's body and I don't know if she understands what I'm trying to do, or if she's just too weak to keep pushing my hand away, because I finally manage to get the napkin in place over her nose and mouth. Her coughing eases off a little and she reaches up and puts her own hand on the napkin, holding it in place.

I look around again and I know there's only one way out of here now. The whole place is a blazing inferno, and the fire is ravaging everything in its path. I turn to the window. The drapes on either side of it are burning, raging with fire. The heat coming off them almost drives me back, but I push closer. I reach down and take off my shoes.

"Amelia! I need you to listen to me," I yell.

She nods, her eyes wide and staring above the napkin. In some way panic has claimed her, but she seems to be trying to listen to me.

"I need you to crouch down, ok? I'm going to break the window and the air will rush in and make the blaze around us worse for a moment, but we have to go out through the window or we're not going to make it. Do you understand what I'm telling you?"

She nods mutely and drops down to a crouch.

I take my shoe and slam the heel against the glass. The glass cracks but it doesn't break. The smoke is getting to me now and I'm starting to feel dizzy as the fire uses up every trace of oxygen in the room. We don't have long at all to get out of here. I can feel my body weakening and I know if I don't get the window to break on my next swing, I might not have the energy for another one.

My head is spinning faster, but I swing my shoe with everything I have, and I feel a momentary relief as the glass shatters. I duck down, shielding Amelia with my body as shattered glass rains down on top of us. The flames jump and dance, swelling and burning more ferociously for a few moments, fed by the same air that rushes in through the now broken window.

I wait until the flames settle back down to their original intensity, then I push myself up and take huge gulps of the cool night air. I lean down and help Amelia back up to her feet. She steps closer to the window, throwing her napkin aside and takes great big sobbing gulps of air.

The window is lined with shards of wickedly sharp glass. I take my shoe again and smash them all out.

"We need to go out of the window," I shout as I put my shoes back on. "It's about a six-foot drop on the other side. I'm going to go out first so I can catch you when you jump. As soon as I shout up to you, jump. Ok?"

"Yes. Go," she shouts urgently.

The fresh air seems to have brought her back to her senses, blowing her panic away. I climb through the window frame and drop to the ground. The drop is a little more than I thought and the impact slams through my feet and up my legs. I suck in a breath, trying to ignore the pain in my legs. I turn back to the window and take a step back.

"I'm ready for you. Jump," I shout.

I see one of her legs poking out of the window and then her body starts to emerge. She's sitting straddling the window frame when another loud explosion sounds inside of the restaurant. Amelia screams and pushes herself off the windowsill. She comes tumbling through the air. I step beneath her, my arms raised to catch her.

I manage to grab her, but she came down a lot faster than I anticipated, and the impact of her body slamming into mine knocks me off my feet. I land hard on my back, with Amelia on top of me. Amelia looks down at me, concern etched into her face. There are black soot lines on her face, and she looks terrified.

"Viktor? Viktor? Are you ok?" she asks, her voice laced with panic.

I nod and suck in a painful breath. "I'm fine. Are you ok?"

I'm already sitting up as I say it, running my hands over Amelia's body, checking for any cuts or burns.

"I'm ok," she says. "I'm ok."

I wrap my arms around her and pull her against me tightly. She rests her head on my shoulder and she's half laughing and half crying when she speaks.

"We're both ok. I can't believe we got out of that alright."

I breathe in against her hair, smelling the smoky smell, and beneath it, Amelia's scent. She lifts her head from my shoulder and smiles at me, tears shining in her eyes.

"Thank you, Viktor. You're my hero, you know."

She leans in closer and kisses me. Her kiss is hard and desperate, like she needs to do this to convince herself we're really ok. Her mouth tastes of smoke and ashes, but I push my hands into her hair, kissing her back, equally desperate to reassure myself that this is real, and my Amelia is alright.

I break the kiss when I hear sirens in the distance. They're getting closer to us quickly.

"Come on," I urge. "We'd better get out of here and go and find the rest of the people who got out. We don't want a team of firefighters in there looking for us when we're safe."

22

VIKTOR

I wrap my arm around her shoulders, pulling her against my side as I lead her down the little winding path that cuts through the garden.

"Not everyone made it out of there, did they?" Amelia asks in a soft voice.

I want to tell her that of course they did, that everything is right in the world and bad things don't happen to people who have just gone to work or gone out to enjoy a meal, never imagining this would be their last night on earth. I want to protect her from the horrors of the world. I think of the woman who fell. Her shocked face locked in a scream of fear and panic. Amelia is not stupid. She knows how bad it was back there.

"No," I say, equally softly. "I don't think they did."

She moves a little closer to me as a shiver goes through her and I tighten my hold on her.

"What do you think caused the explosion?" she asks.

"I have no idea," I tell her. "But I intend to find out."

We reach the gate to the garden, and I open it and lead

Amelia through it. We come out at the side of the restaurant and make our way around to the front. A crowd has gathered there. Most of them are standing around watching the fire, expressions of shock on their faces. Some are lying on the ground with other people tending to them as best as they can.

The sirens are almost upon us now. Within moments the crowd is bathed in a flickering blue light as the first ambulance arrives. Another two are right behind it, followed by two fire engines and a police car.

I spot Marty, the restaurant manager, in the crowd. "Come on," I tell Amelia and make my way towards him.

"Any idea what caused the fire?" I ask.

"Yes. It was done on purpose, Viktor," Marty growls. He looks at me through slightly too wide eyes. Then he blinks and catches himself. "My apologies, Mr. Leshchenko, I don't know why I called you Viktor there. I..."

I shake my head impatiently. "Forget that" I say. "Why do you think it was arson?"

"Someone kicked the back door in and threw something into the kitchen. Before anyone could react, the thing exploded."

I scowl. Someone threw a Molotov cocktail into my restaurant! Instantly, I know who's responsible for this and I feel anger swirling inside of me. People are dead because fucking Igor has an issue with me. Why can't he just come to me, man to man, and have it out with me?

Amelia brushes against me and I glance down at her, wondering if she's gone into shock.

"Hey. Are you ok?" I ask, holding her tighter against me.

"Yeah. I'm just cold," she says through chattering teeth.

I wish I'd brought a jacket, but I haven't. Immediately Marty takes off his work jacket and hands it to her.

"Here, wear this," he offers.

"Oh no, I couldn't," Amelia says, shaking her head.

"Sure you can. It's all part of the service," Marty says with an attempt at a smile.

Amelia smiles back at him and thanks him. I help her into the jacket, then put my arm back around her shoulders.

"All right then. I'm going to have a word with the police," Marty says.

I nod and he goes off to find an officer. I should probably go and talk to them myself, but Marty knows more about this than I do, and I have no intention of telling the police my theory about Igor. I'll be dealing with him myself.

I look around the crowd again. Most of the people who were lying on the ground have been taken away in the first two ambulances, and the people left look for the most part like they only need basic first aid. The firefighters are fighting the blaze and a team of them are running in and out, pulling out bodies and covering them with white sheets that instantly turn black and red.

A firefighter stumbles out of the building with a woman slung over his shoulder. It's the woman who was on the ground. I recognize her bright pink dress, even though it's now streaked with black.

"Paramedic," the fire fighter shouts. "Paramedic."

Two paramedics rush in, passing by me and Amelia.

"We've got a live one," he says. "I suspect she has a broken leg. She was trampled as people ran from the fire, but I think that's what saved her life. She was so low down, she's inhaled a lot less smoke than the others who were trapped in there."

The firefighter puts the woman down on the wheeled stretcher the paramedics have brought over. She moans in pain as he puts her down as gently as he can. It's a sound that should make me cringe, but instead, it warms my heart. She's alive and conscious and that's way more than I expected of her. A broken leg seems like nothing in comparison to what could have happened to her.

Another paramedic wheels the woman away. Amelia coughs beside me and I look down at her with concern.

"We need to get you to the hospital."

She shakes her head and points. "Look," she says. "I'll just go over there."

Two paramedics have set up a first aid area where they're checking over people from the fire to assess if their smoke inhalation is bad enough to go to hospital or not and patching up minor burns. I nod and lead Amelia towards them. We join a short line, and within five minutes Amelia is in the hands of the paramedics.

"Are you ok here for a minute?" I ask her. "I have to make a call."

"Sir, wait," one of the paramedics says. "We really need to check you over. You could have inhaled more smoke than you think, and your hand is bleeding."

I hadn't even noticed the cut on my hand. I must have gotten it breaking and climbing out of the window.

"It's nothing,"

The paramedic looks ready to argue with me, but I'm already walking away. I move away from the crowd and pull my cell phone from my jeans' pocket and call Jerome, my main security guy. It's late, well after midnight, but he answers my call quickly.

"Jerome? It's Viktor," I say. "Any word on Igor's location?"

I know this could be a coincidence. It could be an act of mindless violence from some idiot, but I don't believe that. Since I killed his father, Igor has popped up on my radar several times, talking shit about me and causing trouble in one of my clubs. The bouncer there broke his jaw and I thought that would be the end of it, but that only made it worse.

I've tasked Jerome with finding Igor's location, but he seems to have gone underground, and Jerome's men have been having trouble finding where he's hiding.

"Not yet. I have men looking for him still, but honestly boss, it's like he's just vanished off the face of the earth," Jerome says.

"Except he hasn't. Because it looks like he's just gas bombed one of my fucking restaurants," I say.

"What?" Jerome exclaims.

"Yeah," I confirm. "He threw a Molotov cocktail into Papa's. And I'm going to make him pay. People have died in that fire. I was in that restaurant with my girl, and I swear he'll pay for that twice."

"Are you ok? Is she ok?" Jerome asks.

"We're both fine. Amelia's just getting checked over for smoke damage, but she's mostly ok. But she might not have been. Jerome, I want this search widened. Use any resources you need but find me that fucker. And fast," I say.

"Got it," Jerome says.

I end the call and go back to the first aid stand. The paramedic has just finished dealing with Amelia.

"Are her lungs clear?" I ask.

Amelia speaks up before he can though. "I'm sitting right here Viktor. You can ask me, you know," she smiles.

"So, you can pretend you're ok no matter what's been said," I ask with a raised eyebrow.

"Yes, exactly," she smiles.

"She has inhaled a little bit of smoke, but there shouldn't be any permanent damage. Are you able to stay with her tonight? If she has someone with her, we can let her go home, but otherwise, we'll admit her. Just as a precaution."

"I'll stay with her," I say quickly.

He grabs a leaflet and hands it to me. "This is what you need to look out for. Heavy coughing, any blood in her phlegm, dizziness or nausea. If she presents with any of these symptoms in the next four to six hours, you need to take her to the emergency room. If she presents with any symptoms in the next forty-eight hours after that, then a trip to her primary physician will be sufficient and they will advise on whether she needs to be taken to the hospital. Any other questions?"

I shake my head and the paramedic nods to me. I thank him for his help and turn to Amelia.

"Let's get you home."

23

VIKTOR

"Is everything ok?" Amelia asks.

I nod and lean in close to her, dropping my voice to a whisper. "Everything's fine. I just had a word with one of my men and told him to find the fucker that did this." I half expect her to pull away from me and demand I tell the police everything, but it's not my style, and if this thing with Amelia is going to work, she needs to know who she's dealing with. "He's going to pay for what he did."

Amelia surprises me when she pulls back from me slightly. Her face is set as she nods her head. "Good. People died in there tonight, and jail sometimes just isn't enough, is it? You take a life you should pay with yours," she says in a cold voice.

"Exactly," I say.

She smiles at me.

"You expected me to be horrified, didn't you?"

"Kind of," I admit with a shrug.

"Look, I don't agree with people going around kneecapping guys for a couple of dollars, but this is bigger than that, and our justice system isn't even close to doling out real justice. This guy murdered innocent people."

I realize the valet took my car keys. "I'll have to call my driver. Are you able to wait for about ten minutes."

"That's okay. I need to give your manager his jacket back too," Amelia says.

I call for my driver while Amelia scans the crowd. She spots Marty and heads off in his direction. I don't want to let her go, but I don't want her to think I'm too overprotective. She's only a couple of yards away from me, and the whole area is still crawling with police officers. Nothing is going to happen to her.

I can feel the old worries crowding back into my mind as I end the call with my driver and put my cell phone away. It's only the second time Amelia has been out with me, and she almost died. I'm dangerous to be around. I remind myself that this wasn't a personal attack on my life.

Igor or whoever he paid to do this didn't know I'd be in there tonight. Igor is targeting my businesses, not my life. I kind of hope that changes soon. At least then he'll have to get up close and personal with me and I'll be able to end this fucking thing once and for all.

Amelia comes back to me, looking a little chilly now that she's given Marty his jacket back. I open my arms and she steps into them, pressing herself against me. I wrap my arms around her tightly, trying to keep her warm. We don't have too long to wait before my driver shows up.

"Home," I say as we get in.

Amelia rests her head on my shoulder and by the time we arrive at my place, she's almost asleep. She groans when she has to get out of the car.

"Come on, sleepyhead," I tease.

She makes a face at me, and we walk up to my house. I open the door and Amelia steps inside. She's been here plenty of times as part of her job and she knows her way around. She heads for the stairs.

"I have to take a shower. The smell of the smoke clinging to me is turning my stomach," she says.

"Go ahead.' I start to follow her up the stairs. "I know what you mean about the smell. I'll grab you a robe."

I give Amelia a robe and open my mouth to tell her to use the master bathroom, but she's already gone past the door to my bedroom and heading for the guest bathroom. I go into the master bathroom myself and get into the shower. I watch the black soot and ashes run down the drain as I wash my hair.

It is only then it hits me what a close call Amelia and I have had.

Afterwards, I pull on a clean pair of boxer shorts, get into bed, and wait for Amelia. She comes back to the bedroom a couple of minutes later. I lift the covers up for her to join me.

"Do you want anything to eat or drink?" I ask as she moves towards the bed.

She shakes her head, slips her robe off, and gets into the bed beside me. She's totally naked and the little flash of her I got before she pulled the covers over her body makes my cock hard instantly.

I turn to Amelia and kiss her. She responds hungrily, but then pulls away.

"Viktor, I'm sorry, but do you mind if we don't... you know, have sex tonight? I really want to, but I just don't think I'm up to it after everything that's happened tonight."

"Amelia, sex is the furthest thing from my mind right

now," I reassure her. It's a lie, obviously. Sex is never far from my mind when I'm around her, but this is not exactly the special moment I'd planned.

She smiles and I see the relief behind her smile. "I will take a goodnight kiss though."

I lean in and kiss her, and the smile drops from her lips as they mold themselves to mine. I feel like my cock is going to explode as my desire for Amelia overwhelms me. I remind myself I don't want to put any pressure on Amelia, and besides, I don't want her exerting herself, at least not for the next four to six hours. I want to make sure she's ok before I even think about making her mine.

When I pull away, Amelia looks at me, her eyes shining with the same desire as I feel. Maybe it's a good thing to wait a little bit longer – the waiting is only going to make the sex even hotter when it finally happens.

I twist around slightly and prop my pillows up a little bit. I lay back against them and Amelia snuggles up to me. I put my arm out and she lays her head on my shoulder, and I wrap my arm around her. I pull her closer as she snuggles in.

I check my watch. It's two a.m. Roll on to eight o'clock, I think to myself. It's going to be a long night. The adrenaline rush has well and truly left me now and I can feel exhaustion setting in, but I need to stay awake and make sure Amelia is ok.

"Goodnight," Amelia mumbles, her voice thick and slurred with oncoming sleep.

"Goodnight," I say, kissing her forehead.

I think she's asleep before I say it. I look down at her and feel a glow of warmth spreading through my body. She's so peaceful looking. I tighten my hold on her, telling myself I'll never let her go. I so badly want to wake her up and make love to her, or even just hold her and talk to her, but she's been through so much and she needs to sleep.

I check my watch again. Barely ten minutes have passed since I last looked at it and I can feel my eyes starting to close already. I run my hand over my face, trying to wake myself up a bit. It's going to be harder than I thought to stay awake all night like this. Maybe I should just rest my eyes for a few minutes. Maybe even have a ten-minute nap. I don't want to be too tired to perform if Amelia is ready to have sex when she wakes up in the morning.

I'll close my eyes for just a second, I tell myself. I'm asleep within seconds.

I wake up to a loud groan. Amelia is thrashing inside the enclosure of my arms, her face twisted up as another groan is torn from her lips. She's having a nightmare. I gently shake her.

"Amelia. Wake up."

She groans as she comes awake suddenly, blinking up at me.

"You were having a bad dream."

She nods and sighs.

"The fire?"

She nods again and I notice she has tears in her eyes. I kiss her forehead and pull her closer to me.

"Nothing is going to hurt you, baby. You're safe. I've got you.".

I keep a tight hold on her, keeping my lips against her forehead as I whisper to her, promising her everything is ok, that I'm not going anywhere. I feel her starting to relax and after a couple of minutes, her body stops shaking.

"I'm sorry I woke you up," she whispers.

"You don't have anything to be sorry for," I tell her.

"I'm keeping you awake," she says.

"I'm not that tired," I insist.

"Liar," she says as I fight to keep my eyes open and prove my point. "Just go to sleep Viktor, I'm ok and if I'm not, I promise to wake you up. You've been through as much as I have tonight."

"Actually, I've been through more. I've had to deal with the fact that I could have lost you tonight."

"Don't kid yourself into thinking I wasn't feeling the exact same thing about you," Amelia says.

She closes her eyes then and I smile to myself. It feels so good to hear her say something like that. I don't suppose she would have said it if she wasn't half asleep, but I don't think that means she doesn't mean it all the same.

I wait until she's back asleep and then I close my eyes and let blackness take over.

24

AMELIA

I wake up in the same position I fell asleep in. Wrapped up in Viktor's arms, my head on his shoulder. Sunlight is streaming into the room. We didn't get around to closing the heavy drapes last night. We were both a mixture of too wired and too exhausted to think of much. Even the bedside lamps are still switched on.

Slowly, I turn my head and see that he's still asleep. I stare at him in wonder. He is so incredibly beautiful like this. I think back to last night. It wasn't the night I was expecting, that was for sure, but despite the way our night ended, I'm totally grateful we are both still alive.

Viktor was like an all-action hero when the fire broke out, my very own James Bond/Superman. He took control of the situation and gave me a wet napkin to help me breathe. He managed to snap me out of my panic, and I have no doubt in my mind that he saved my life.

I loved talking to Viktor last night, getting to know him a little better and laughing with him. And all through dinner my body kept me on my toes, keeping me on the edge of desire. Throughout the meal my clit kept tingling deliciously. I couldn't keep my eyes off him, and I could hardly wait to get Viktor home and have him take my virginity.

But after the fire, I just felt physically and emotionally drained, and while I still wanted Viktor badly, I knew it wasn't the right time. I want my first time with him to be memorable because it's good, not because it's tied up in my mind with the time we almost died in a fire.

I feel my pussy clench as I remember dropping from the window straight into Viktor's safe arms. The adrenaline was still flooding through my body and my skin was tingling. I kissed Viktor and I had never felt more alive in all my life. In that moment when I knew we were both safe, I knew then that I love him.

I know our relationship is moving too quickly, and some would say we hardly know each other, but I feel a connection to him that I have never found with any other human being.

I smile to myself as I very gently shift slightly, then push myself up onto my knees. Viktor starts to stir as I straddle him. He opens his eyes and I smile down at him. He yawns, stretches and smiles up at me.

"You can stay over more often if you're going to wake me up like this every morning."

"I had to do something to stop you snoring."

"I don't snore," Viktor denies.

"You so do," I say with a decisive nod.

"I so don't."

He sits up and wraps his arms around me. His kiss cuts off my silly insistence. I put my arms around his shoulders and kiss him back, feeling the tingling sensation move through my body as he brings my nerves to life. My spine tingles as his hands move over my back and I shift forward slightly, moving so I can feel Viktor's cock against my pussy through his boxer shorts. I move my hips a little and his cock rubs on my clit, sending shockwaves through my body.

He moans into my mouth as he kisses me. Bringing one hand around to the front of my body he caresses one of my breasts. My nipple springs to life beneath his touch, instantly hard, standing to attention eagerly. His palm presses against it, making it tingle and I feel my pussy clench.

Viktor moves his mouth from mine, kissing down my neck. I put my head back as goosebumps scurry across my skin, sending fire through me. Viktor moves his hand to my other breast, teasing my nipple between his fingers and making me moan out loud as intense shivers run down my body.

My clit is screaming for Viktor's touch, and I move my hips again, pressing myself against the tip of Viktor's cock, desperate for some relief from my insistent clit. He moans as he licks his way down my chest and sucks my breast into his mouth. He keeps working my other nipple in his hand as he nibbles gently on the one in his mouth. I gasp as more tingles pass through me, making me want Viktor more than ever.

My hips keep moving, speeding up almost of their own accord. Viktor pulls his mouth away from my breast and looks up at me, his eyes sparkling with longing.

"You have to stop doing that or I'm not going to be able to control myself any longer," Viktor says in a deep husky voice unlike his usual voice.

The lust in his voice and his words send a rush of liquid

between my legs. I don't stop moving my hips as I smile sultrily at Viktor. "Maybe I want you to lose control."

Viktor groans in frustration, putting his hands on my hips, he holds me still. "God, Amelia, you are driving me fucking crazy," he says in the same low, lust filled voice.

I bite my lip and smile at him. Then I lean forward and brush my lips across his before pulling back slightly.

"I want you to fuck me, Viktor. Right now," I say against his mouth. "I'm ready for this. More ready than I've ever been for anything."

"Let me get some protection."

I shake my head. "No, I just had my period. I just want to feel you inside me for this first time."

I brush my lips lightly across his again. He makes a growling sound at the back of his throat as his hands come off my hips and push into my hair, holding my head in place as he takes possession of my lips, pushing his tongue into my mouth. I kiss him back with equal fervor as my hands roam over his back and his sides. My hips are moving again, and Viktor starts to move with me.

I've waited so long for this moment, and I know I made the right decision waiting for the right man to take my V-card. I'm not even nervous. I'm excited, eager to know how it will feel to have Viktor moving inside of me, filling me up.

It's like he's reading my mind. He takes his hands out of my hair and grabs my hips again. He bucks his hips, moving me to one side, and before I know it, I'm flat on my back on the bed with Viktor on top of me. He kisses me again, and then he takes his lips from mine and kisses his way down my body until he reaches my pussy. He pushes his tongue between my lips, and this time, there's no teasing. He goes straight to my clit and licks it hard, pushing me straight towards the edge. He eats me out until I'm writhing beneath him, my orgasm almost upon me.

He comes up onto his knees and plunges his fingers into me, massaging my clit with them. The added pressure makes me gasp and my breath catches in my throat as pleasure explodes through my body. My clit is vibrating, pulsing with pleasure and my pussy clenches tightly as all of my muscles go rigid and my orgasm floods through my body in a warm wave of pleasure. I scream Viktor's name as I come hard, my body spasming as pleasure fills me.

I can't think for a second, I can only feel, as my body responds to Viktor's touch in a way I never imagined possible. As my orgasm starts to fade, another one washes over me as Viktor's fingers keep working me. My back arches, lifting me off the mattress. I want to scream Viktor's name, but I can't get any air inside of my lungs. I'm going dizzy but all that does is add to the floaty feeling of pleasure.

I flop back down onto the mattress, panting and gasping as the orgasm finally starts to fade, leaving me tingling all over. I open my eyes and smile up at Viktor. He returns my smile.

"Are you sure you're ready for this?" he asks. "Because I have to warn you, Amelia, there's going to be pain."

My pussy clenches at his words, spreading a delicious warmth up through my stomach.

"I'm ready," I whisper.

Viktor pulls his boxer shorts down and drags them off, throwing them to the ground. He kneels back between my legs. I spread my legs wider, opening myself up to him and he moans as he looks at my spread pussy.

"You're so wet," he says, his voice ragged with lust.

He runs his fingers over my clit, making electrical pleasure fizz through me and I gasp loudly. He smiles as he moves his fingers through me, spreading my juices around. He takes his cock in his fist and lowers himself onto me. He runs his huge cock through my lips, and I close my eyes as he pushes it against my opening.

I bite my bottom lip and take a deep breath as he pauses, but I nod at him. I close my eyes as he pushes into me. I feel my pussy stretching out, a stinging sensation of pain that makes me cry out and yet it is also a strange pleasure. It takes me a while to get used to the feeling of tight fullness I've never felt before.

Viktor runs his fingers softly over my cheek and then he pulls part way out of me and plunges in again. It stings again, but not as much, and by the third time he plunges into me, I start to relax into it.

It's beautiful.

He keeps moving, slowly at first, and I keep gasping as he fills me right up over and over again. Somewhere in his thrusts, the pain disappears, and the motion starts to feel good, really good. I move my hips tentatively, matching his thrusts. When I wrap my legs around his waist, he bends forward to kiss me deeply.

I push my hands into his hair and keep moving, and simply enjoy the delicious feeling between my legs. He pushes his tongue into my mouth, and I feel the fullness of it matching the fullness in my pussy.

Then he starts to thrust faster, and I match his thrusts with my own, feeling more confident now. The feeling of him moving inside me is starting to feel wonderful and my thrusts become wilder, my body taking over from my head. I move my hands over Viktor's back, feeling his taut,

muscular body and I moan as he moves in me, sending pleasure through my body now instead of pain.

He pulls his mouth from mine to ask if I'm ok. I nod,
eager for his kiss once more. He doesn't disappoint. He
kisses me with a deep passion that sets my soul on fire. I feel
my pussy clenching around his cock as my orgasm comes
on, taking me by surprise. I move my hips faster, needing
the release the orgasm will bring me.

When it hits, I dig my nails into Viktor's back, screaming
his name as my pussy clenches tighter and tighter, holding
Viktor's cock inside of me like I never want to let him go. I
feel fire spreading through my stomach and up into my
chest. My heart is slamming in time with my thrusting,
eager hips and I can barely breathe, but I'm in ecstasy,
loving every moment of the orgasm. My throat feels raw and
scratchy as I suck in noisy gasps of air.

Viktor pulls almost all the way out of me then slams
himself back in. I cry out as my orgasm blooms stronger
through me. My vision goes black for a moment as my head
spins dizzily. I feel my eyes rolling back in my head, and for
a moment, I can't breathe, but it's like nothing matters to my
body now except this feeling of intense pleasure. My body's
need for Viktor is greater than its need for oxygen.

Finally, when I feel like I'm about to pass out, my orgasm
fades slightly and my body responds to my commands
again. I finally gasp in great big gulps of air. Suddenly, a
scream of Viktor's name tears out of my mouth as pleasure
floods through me again. And I come again. Tiny whimpers
emit out of my mouth as the intensity of the feeling overwhelms me. I'm lost in a sea of pleasure, a giant nerve
ending being manipulated and kneaded constantly.

My whole body is alight; my skin tingling, my veins

running with fire. I call Viktor's name again and then my orgasm releases its grip on me, leaving me shaking and leaden and sated. Viktor is still moving inside of me, and my pussy clenches and unclenches, squeezing his cock, making me feel every inch of his length.

He's pumping into me faster and harder, and his breath is ragged. His face is twisted up like he's in pain, contorted with ecstasy as he fills me. He calls my name and then he leans forward and presses his face against my neck as he comes inside of me, a spurt of warmth that makes his cock twitch. He moans against my neck, his breath sending goosebumps scurrying over my skin. His cock twitches again and he says my name in a breathy voice.

I cling to him as his cock slips out of me and he lays on top of me, panting. I'm panting myself. I feel like I might never regain control of my body and my senses as I breathe in Viktor's scent, holding him against me. Finally, he rolls off me and we lay side by side, both of us gasping and panting.

"There's no way you haven't done that before," Viktor says beside me.

I roll onto my side and push myself up on one elbow. I run my fingernails over the skin on Viktor's chest and smile at him.

"I swear that was my first time," I say.

"Well shit. If you're that good now, what the fuck are you going to be like after a few more goes at it?" he says.

"Well, I'm planning on finding out," I grin.

"So?" he says, suddenly looking a little shy. "Was I worth waiting for?"

"Nah, you were terrible," I say. "I don't know what all of the fuss is about."

He looks at me, shocked for a moment, and I can't hold

my laughter in anymore. He grabs me and throws me onto my back again, laughing as he gets on top of me.

"Well let's see if you're still so cocky after this," he says.

He kisses me before I can answer him, running his tongue over my lips. He pulls back from me and smiles down at me.

"Seriously, Amelia," he says. "Did you enjoy it?"

"I can't believe you even have to ask. It was amazing," I smile honestly.

He kisses me again and then he smiles down at me.

"I'm just getting started," he says. "Ready to go again?"

Am I? I'm a little sore down there, but the answer is an obvious yes. I've waited eighteen whole years for this moment. I don't want to waste any more time waiting for round two. I nod and Viktor kisses me again.

He comes up for air, leaving me wanting more. He runs his hands down my sides making my skin pucker and tingle deliciously. He reaches my hips and grabs them, flipping me suddenly onto my front. I push myself up onto all fours and grin at him over my shoulder.

He returns my grin and then I turn back away as his fingers penetrate me, taking me by surprise. He pushes his fingers inside of me, finding my g-spot and pressing down on it. A strange sensation floods me. It feels like I want to bear down, and maybe pee a little all at the same time. The sensation passes quickly, and I feel a flood of pleasure instead. Viktor keeps working me and I hold myself in place, not wanting his fingers to slip away from my sweet spot. He keeps working me, and right when I'm on the verge of orgasm, he pulls his fingers out of me.

"No," I say. "Don't stop."

"Patience, Amelia," Viktor says in an amused voice.

He takes hold of my hips and pushes his cock into me. I gasp as he fills me once more. I'm a little tender as I suspected, but the slight sting is nothing like the first time. Instead of making me grit my teeth, it only heightens my pleasure as Viktor begins to thrust into me. He keeps his hands on my hips, pulling my body back to meet each thrust. His cock hits my g-spot with each thrust, and in seconds, his cock finishes what his fingers started.

I come hard, red spots floating in front of my face as I once more gasp for breath. My body comes to life once more, fire spreading through me and waking up my dormant nerves, nerves I didn't even know I had. My stomach contracts in time with my pussy and I scream Viktor's name as my pussy goes wild, clenching tightly around Viktor. He moans as my pussy holds him in place for a moment, and then my muscles turn to jelly as my orgasm fades and Viktor is moving again, filling me with desire for more even though my body feels as if it's slipping away.

He moves one hand from my hip and runs his fingernails down my spine. I arch my back into his touch as goosebumps rush over me, sending a shiver of excitement through my body. He runs his fingernails back up my back and grabs a fist full of my hair, tugging it. My scalp stings as my head is pulled back. The stinging sensation zings through my body, turning to pleasure as it cascades around me. Viktor releases my hair, and his hand moves over my back, across my side and over my stomach.

He pushes his fingers between my lips and finds my clit. He presses down on it, moving his fingers quickly from side to side as he continues to thrust into me. His fingers on my clit feel like electrical waves thrumming through me. The feeling is amazing, and it lights up my whole body.

I'm gasping and whimpering as another orgasm builds up inside of me, making my stomach muscles contract. I move with Viktor, pushing myself back as he thrusts forward, taking the full length of his cock into me with each thrust. I feel myself stretching to accommodate him and I feel my clit buzzing with Viktor's touch.

The sensations all come together to form one delicious ball of pleasure that bounces all the way around my body. As one wave crashes over me and begins to break, the next one comes, giving me no reprieve from the pleasure.

I struggle to get enough air as my body stops responding to me and starts responding only to Viktor. I don't know how much more of this I can take – each wave fills me with delicious pleasure, but it's so intense, and I don't get a second to catch my breath between waves. Viktor shows me no mercy though. He keeps the orgasm floating around my body, keeps me primed for the next explosion, and even as I scream his name at the peak of my climax, I know the next one is coming.

My body is putty in Viktor's hands, and he knows exactly how to knead me into shape. I feel another wave crashing over me and I scream over and over again as my stomach explodes with pleasure and my clit screams. I feel my elbows give way and I fall onto my face, but I still want more. I lay that way, turning my head so I can snatch in the few tiny breaths I can get, but still, I pump my hips in time with Viktor's thrusts.

His thrusts are getting faster and harder, short strokes that make me gasp with each one. He takes his fingers away from my clit and I don't know if I'm relieved or gutted. He puts his hands back on my hips and he holds me in place, stopping me from moving, frustrating me momentarily. His short strokes hit my g-spot full force and I see why he's holding me still as another orgasm crashes over me. As I scream his name, he loosens his hold on me, keeping his hands on my hips, but not holding me still now.

I try to thrust, but in the throes of my orgasm, I'm paralyzed by pleasure. Viktor tightens his hold again and pulls my body back onto his cock, moving me as he moves himself. He cries out my name as he holds me tightly in place as his own orgasm smashes through him. He keeps me pinned in place as his cock goes nuts inside of me, spurting and twitching. He calls out my name again in a voice that sounds pained, like the sound is being ripped out of him against his will.

Finally, he releases my hips and falls onto the bed face down beside me. He turns his head to face me as I push my legs out and lay flat. We're both a wreck, gasping and panting. I don't think I'll ever feel pleasure like that again. Judging by the way Viktor tries to speak and can't quite form any words yet, I think that was as good for him as it was for me.

We lay that way for so long that I start to shiver with the cold. I want to get back beneath the covers, but the thought of reaching down and pulling it over me is too much effort. Viktor must see that I'm shivering. He pushes himself up off his stomach and reaches down, covering us up. I smile gratefully at him and roll onto my side so that when he lays back down beside me, I can put my arm around his waist.

He wraps his arm around me and pulls me closer.

"Did the earth move for you?" he asks with a smirk.

"I felt like I was inside a washing machine." I grin.

He laughs and I start laughing with him.

"Seriously," I say when my laughter has passed. "That was so fucking intense. Is it always like that?"

"To be honest, I've been with my fair share of women, and I have never felt anything that even comes close to what we just had," he says. He pauses and then goes on. "But something tells me that with us, it will always be like that."

I smile as he leans closer to me and kisses me. My hold on him tightens as we kiss. This kiss is different from the other kisses we've shared this morning. The other kisses were full of passion and longing and a shared desperation for us to come together and I loved them. But this one is by far the best kiss.

It's soft and gentle, sensual in its nature. It's the sort of kiss shared by two people who are in love. The sort of kiss romance writers talk about, that no one really believes exists until they've had it. It's fair to say Viktor has just made a believer out of me.

We hold each other and look into each other's eyes for a long time. My body still feels too heavy to move and I can feel myself getting sleepy again. Viktor looks like he's about ready to fall asleep too. He moves his fingers in a lazy circle on my back and the sensation makes me feel sleepier and sleepier as he does it. I yawn and he smiles.

"I know that feeling," he says.

He closes his eyes and I do the same, but a second later I open mine.

"Viktor?"

"Mmm," he replies sleepily.

"When can we do that again?"

"Are you trying to finish me off?" he laughs.

"No," I say. "But there are way worse ways to go right?"

"Damned right," he says.

He opens his eyes long enough to kiss the tip of my nose and then closes them again.

"Soon. We can do that again soon," he mumbles.

His fingers stop moving as he falls asleep, and I feel his arm getting heavier on me. I lay awake for a while, just watching him sleep, marveling at how someone like me could ever get so lucky as to have a man as gorgeous as him want me. I don't want to go to sleep. I just want to lie here and enjoy this moment for as long as I can, but try as I might, I can't resist the pull of sleep for much longer, and eventually, I snuggle closer to Viktor, close my eyes and let sleep take me.

25

VIKTOR

Marcus, my right-hand man, calls to say his vacation is going to be a long one as he has been in an accident and broken his leg. I tell him to take as long as he needs to heal. I have bigger problems, much bigger problems to solve.

I spend the next few days focused on the fire. Or rather the aftermath of it. I speak to the police several times, although it feels pointless. I'm certainly not about to tell them anything about Igor – I'll be dealing with him personally – and they don't seem to have any leads at all.

A whole fucking building was blown up and people lost their lives, and the police don't have a fucking clue what happened or why. And then they wonder why people take justice into their own hands.

The officers investigating the fire claim that it's a priority, but it sure doesn't feel like it is. If it was, they would have something by now. Whether Igor set the fire personally, or had someone else do it for him, that person didn't just materialize in the kitchen out of thin air. A surveillance camera must have picked him up or someone had to have seen him coming or going from the restaurant.

None of the staff got a proper look at him. It's a busy kitchen and people are constantly moving around, so his movements wouldn't have attracted their attention. All anyone saw was his back after he threw the gas bomb and turned to run – a man dressed all in black.

Not only have the police failed to find any witnesses, they don't even seem to be trying to find out where the arsonist bought his supplies from either.

They aren't the real problem though. I accepted long ago that unless a crime goes viral for some reason, the police don't exactly rush themselves to solve crimes. The real problem is the damned journalists. I get calls from them all day long asking for a comment on this or that. At first, I refused to speak to them at all.

It was Amelia who convinced me I should do an interview with at least the local paper. She said my lack of comments made it look like I didn't care. I do care. I hate that people died in one of my restaurants and that people got hurt. I wanted to show that and so I did end up doing an interview. Unfortunately, someone brought Amelia up to the stage, and stood her by my side.

There was nothing I could do but carry on.

I talked about how angry and saddened I was about the loss of life, and about how someone must know something, and pleaded with them to come forward.

I made all of the right comments about the investigation, saying the police were doing their best and that they had a few lines of enquiry ongoing and so on – it was all bullshit of course, but it was what they had told me - and the interview made the front page of the local newspaper. The photo and a few direct quotes from the interview have made other papers too and at least now the journalists seem to have lost interest in me for the most part. I guess the scoop isn't much use when you're not the first one to get it.

I've filed a claim on my insurance for the building and its contents, and I already have a team in place starting to work on the rebuilding of the restaurant. And it's going to be a total reconstruction. The place pretty much burned to the ground and the empty shell the fire left behind was deemed unsafe. My developer knocked the shell to the ground, and he now has a team of contractors working around the clock to rebuild the building.

All of the staff from the restaurant who survived the fire have been given a generous compensation payment, and anyone who needed hospitalization has had their bill picked up by the company. They're all on retainers now, still getting paid their full salary on the understanding they come back to work when the new restaurant is built.

None of this is able to distract me from the fact that Jerome and his men still haven't been able to find Igor. Fucking Igor. He's the bane of my existence and it really pisses me off to know I gave that son of a bitch a chance and I am now living to regret it. It's like he's just vanished into thin air. But he hasn't. He's not his father. He's a spoiled, entitled little shit, and he'll fuck up somewhere along the line and reveal himself... and when he does, I'll be waiting. I'd feel better if that was sooner rather than later though. After the picture of Amelia and me appeared in the newspapers, it became clear I have someone I care about.

Someone who can be used against me.

I have barely let Amelia out of my sight since the fire. Of course, I have to go to work, but while I'm there, I'm confident she's safe. She works exclusively from my home estate now. I have convinced her to begin studying to be a lawyer. I have increased the security on my estate, and I know she's safe there. As soon as we finish work, we spend the evenings together.

She wants to go out tonight though.

I tried to talk her out of it, but she wouldn't be put off. She said she refuses to live like a recluse and if I don't want to go out, she'll go out on her own. That persuaded me. How can I keep her safe if I'm not even with her? We're going to one of my clubs. Although I'm a little nervous about Amelia's safety, I'm also kind of looking forward to it. It'll be nice to think about something other than Igor.

"You're still not ready," Amelia says, sticking her head around my office door.

She's wearing a dress I bought for her. A black dress that clings to her curves and shows off her amazing legs. Suddenly, I don't want to go out. She looks fucking amazing in that dress, but she'd look so much better out of it. I know she's got her heart set on going out though. I shut down the computer, stand up and smile at her.

"I only have to change my shirt."

"Yeah, I've heard that one before and then it takes you like two hours to get ready," she says, giving me a teasing smile that makes me want to rip that dress right off her.

I pause on the way past her to kiss her. She presses herself against me and kisses me back. She pulls away long before I'm ready for the kiss to end.

"Go," she orders with a laugh.

"See, this is why everything takes so long. You stand there all irresistible and shit," I laugh as I head for the bedroom.

"Of course, it's got nothing to do with you not being able to choose which shirt to wear," she calls after me.

"Look at you projecting." I'm still laughing to myself as I get to my bedroom. I don't take long to get ready at all. I pull out the first shirt I see. It's a plain black one. Yeah, it'll do. I change into it, spray some cologne, and go to the living room where Amelia is waiting for me.

"See. That wasn't bad, was it?" I say.

"No, but it was only because you were trying to make a point." She grins. "Now, let's go before you start thinking about getting changed into something different."

"Why would I get changed? Don't you like this shirt?" I ask.

"It's fine. You look great," Amelia says.

"Ah, you're just saying that aren't you. I should change it."

"No. Really. It's fine," Amelia says, the frustration showing on her face.

I start to laugh. "Got you."

She shoves me playfully. "Come on then."

"Yeah, let's go before you beat me up."

Amelia laughs and shakes her head. My driver is already waiting for us, and I grab my keys, wallet, and cell phone. Then we step out of the door and hurry to the car. We head out to the club with Amelia chattering away about how it's been so long since she's been out. I remind her it wasn't that long ago when I took her to the launch night of another of my clubs.

"That was ages ago," she says with an adorable little pout.

26

VIKTOR

The place is rocking, and Amelia looks happy as we step in. The wall of heat and thumping music hits us instantly. When Amelia tries to talk to me, I can't hear a word she's saying. I shrug and mime to her to see if she wants a drink. She nods her head and mouths 'yes please'.

I go to the bar and get us some drinks and when I come back to where I left Amelia, she points upstairs. I nod and lead her back across the packed club and up the stairs and along the short hallway to the VIP rooms.

"That's better," she says as we step into the VIP lounge. "At least we can hear each other up here."

It's still busy, but it's nowhere near as busy as it is in the main club. Amelia takes my hand and leads me over to the dance floor. I think she's really starting to enjoy the VIP lounges I bring her to, where she can move more freely. That has its disadvantages though. Like the fact I can't claim it's too packed to attempt to dance.

"No way," I laugh. "We haven't even had one drink yet."

"You don't have to have a drink to have a good time, do you?" she asks mischievously.

"No. But I do have to have a drink to dance in public," I reply dryly.

She shrugs and changes direction, leading me to an empty booth where we sit down. It's not long before a waitress comes over to see if we need more drinks. Amelia purses up her lips and nods her head.

"Yes please. We need some cocktails. And shots. Lots of shots," she grins. When the waitress has gone away, she looks at me with a gleam in her eye. "I'll have you out on that dance floor soon enough."

"At this rate, I'll be home in bed by midnight."

"Maybe you will if you play your cards right..."

The gleam in her eye tells me that she isn't joking. My cock responds to her words, and I shift in my seat. The waitress returns with a giant fishbowl of something bright red and a tray full of shots of various colors.

"Thanks," I say. "Just put it all on my tab."

The waitress nods and walks away. Amelia pushes a long, neon green straw towards me. I grimace slightly as I taste the sweet but potent drink.

"It's good, isn't it?" Amelia laughs.

She grabs a purple shot and holds it up. I take a blue one and we clink glasses and drink them. The shot is slightly less gross than the cocktail. Only slightly though. Why didn't I specify we wanted Tequila or a decent whiskey or something?

We sit drinking and chatting for a while. I can feel myself relaxing and Amelia is starting to get a little giggly. She's also getting a little more handsy. She keeps touching my arm when she talks to me, and every time she does it, I feel more and more turned on. It's taking a lot of willpower not to just demand we go home right now.

"Are you ready to dance yet?" she asks me.

"Not yet," I reply with a laugh.

"Well then you can just watch," she announces with a sultry look.

She slides out of the booth and begins to dance at the end of it, swaying her hips, her arms in the air. She throws her head back, twirling and moving. Watching her is like being slowly tortured. She looks so fucking good, and my cock is well and truly hard now. I just want to grab her and throw her onto the table and fuck the life out of her. She dances like she fucks; with no self-consciousness whatsoever, just enjoying the way her body feels.

She holds her hand out to me, and although I'm still far from ready to join the small crowd that is dancing up here, I can't resist her any longer. I take her hand and let her pull me to my feet. She doesn't waste any time. She presses herself against me and smiles at me. She turns so she's facing away from me and slowly drops to a crouch, pushing her ass against my body. She comes back up and I feel her whole body moving over mine. I know she can feel how hard I am. She sways her hips, purposely rubbing herself against my rock-hard cock.

She turns back to face me, and I wrap my arms around her, swaying with her. I lean down to kiss her, but she ducks away laughing. I can't be mad at her. She looks so good as she sways and twirls. I can't wait any longer. I have to have her. Now. Here.

I reach out and grab her hand. I don't speak, I just lead her back across the lounge and out of the room.

"Viktor, no, not yet. I'm not ready to leave. "We've only

been here an hour or so," she says as the door closes behind us and the sound of the music is mostly cut off, just a thumping beat remaining.

"I'm not ready to leave yet either," I say, looking at her over my shoulder with a grin.

She takes my meaning, and her pout becomes a smile as I lead her down the corridor and through a door marked staff only. I continue on to my office. I open the door and pull her inside. I don't bother to turn the lights on, I just grab Amelia and pull her into my arms. Her kiss is like electricity flooding my body and making my nerves hum. I kiss down her neck and she puts her head back, moaning as my hand slips beneath her dress. I push her panties to one side, slip my fingers between her wet lips and massage her clit.

She moans again as I rub her faster, harder, bringing her close to the edge. I kiss my way back up her neck and cover my mouth over hers as I bring her to orgasm. I feel hot liquid running over my fingers as I keep working her clit. She pulls her mouth from mine and whispers my name as a shudder goes through her body. I push her dress up over her hips and she reaches for my jeans.

She fumbles my jeans open. Reaching in she grabs my cock and moves her hand up and down it, sending flames running through my body. She pushes me closer to the edge. I grab her panties and push them down as she works my cock. She steps out of them without missing a beat. I have to be inside of her soon or I'll explode. I'm going crazy with need. I start to move, walking backwards in the darkened office, heading for my desk. Amelia comes with me, her hand still working me as we move, her mouth seeking out mine.

When I feel the desk against my ass, I wait for a

moment. I want to be inside of her now, but I also don't want to stop her hand on my cock. It feels so fucking good – she's using the perfect rhythm and just the right amount of pressure. I know if I don't stop her soon though, I'm going to come and I don't want to come until I'm inside of her, claiming her pussy with my seed.

I run my hands over her ass and the tops of her thighs and then I move them back to her ass, cupping it and lifting her off the ground, forcing her hand away from me. I instantly miss her touch and I almost put her back down and let her carry on, but instead, I turn around and sit her on the edge of my desk. I move between her legs, pushing them further open and I shove my jeans and boxer shorts down and I push my cock into her tight, wet pussy.

She moans as I enter her. Leaning backwards, she rests her weight on her palms as we begin to move. I pound into her, my cock moving through her slippery tunnel. She grips me like a glove, and I have to bite down on the inside of my cheek to stop myself from coming too soon.

I slow the pace, filling Amelia with long, slow strokes that make her throw her head back and gasp on each thrust as my cock glides over her g-spot. The tendons in her neck stand out, coated with a light glistening layer of sweat. I run my fingers over her stomach and up her breastbone finally reaching her neck and the bare skin there, watching the goosebumps chase each other up and down her body under my touch.

I feel her sweet pussy tightening around me, and I know she's almost there. I reach down and lay my palm over the hood of her clit and grind it slowly in time with my thrusting. She moans, a sound so full of pleasure and longing that it sets my soul on fire and almost pushes me over the edge.

She calls out my name as a great, racking shudder goes through her body. Her orgasm fades and she gives me a passion soaked smile as she comes up off her hands, and wraps her arms around my shoulders. I move my hands around to her back, caressing her skin and moving them lower. I cup her ass and lift her. She wraps her legs around my waist as I thrust into her, moving across the office and pressing her up against the wall.

I thrust fast and hard now, unable to hold myself back any longer. Amelia moves with me, making 'ahh' sounds with each thrust. Her nails dig into my shoulders as pleasure fills her. I keep moving, feeling the heat in the base of my stomach and cock.

Amelia tightens her pussy around me, clenching and unclenching. The feeling of tightness as I slam into her sends me over the edge. Pleasure floods my body as my orgasm roars into me. I pull Amelia up off the wall and we cling to each other as I spurt into her with a low growl.

As my orgasm fades, she unwraps her legs from around me and I set her down on her feet, but we still keep holding each other. Amelia leans against my chest panting for air. I breathe in the scent of her hair and kiss the top of her head. We stay like that for a few minutes, not talking, just breathing in the scent of each other. When we break away, she pulls her dress back down, retrieves her panties and pulls them on while I pull up my boxer shorts and jeans, zipping the fly and fastening the button.

"So now are you ready to dance?" Amelia asks me with a grin as she pulls her fingers through her hair, trying to tame it slightly.

"Do I have a choice?" I ask her with a soft laugh.

"Not really," she grins.

She moves to the door, pulls it open, then turns back to me with a slight frown.

"Do you know that door wasn't even locked?"

"No one ever comes in here but me," I reply with a shrug.

"You owe me two dances for that," she says with a laugh. "Because you can almost guarantee the night you don't want anyone to come in is the one time they do."

I follow her back along the hallway to the club's VIP lounge.

"How does that equate to two dances?"

"I'm not sure. It just does."

"Right. "Well as long as there's a good and logical reason for it," I say.

We step back into the VIP area. It's a lot busier now and the dance floor is pretty busy. Amelia takes my hand and leads me towards it and finds us an empty spot. She grins at me and purses her mouth up in that way I like and then she beckons to me. I lean in and she whispers in my ear.

"Dancing will put me right in the mood to do that again when we get home," she purrs as she sucks my earlobe into her mouth.

I groan already feeling my cock stirring again.

She moves back and winks at me. "How's that for a good reason to dance with me?"

I think the fact I start dancing pretty damned enthusiastically with her is all of the answer she needs to that question.

27

AMELIA

I hum to myself as I stand in front of the wardrobe looking at my clothes hanging in Viktor's bedroom. It gives me a little thrill each time I open the closet or one of the drawers in the chest of drawers and see my things in Viktor's bedroom. I think I've pretty much moved in with Viktor now. More of my stuff is here in his main house on the estate than back in my little apartment. He hasn't officially asked me to move in with him; it just kind of happened.

After the fire, we just seemed to get closer, and every time I so much as suggested going back to my place, he wouldn't hear of it. He would make some excuse why we should just stay here, and I went along with it, because I wanted to be with him and ultimately, I didn't care if it was here, at my place, or anywhere else in the world really.

We dropped into my place one afternoon after I put my foot down and told Viktor I had to go home because I was sick of wearing the same thing over and over again or hanging around the house in one of his shirts. He agreed to drive me and said we could stay long enough for me to collect some of my stuff, but for some strange reason I could tell Viktor was on edge. That's when I really knew there must be more to why I had to be at his place than he was letting on.

He hasn't come out and said it, but I think he's secretly worried that whoever started the fire will come after me next as a way to get to him. Maybe I should be a little more worried about that happening, but the truth is, I'm not. Of course, the idea of someone coming after me or someone coming after Viktor is truly frightening if I sit down and think about it, but I'm not doing that.

I'm floating around on the sweet cloud of love and romance, and I dig the idea that he cares enough about me to think that someone could use me against him. And I love to see the lengths he will go to keep me safe and stop that from happening. It tells me he feels for me like I feel for him.

That this is real.

I turn my focus back to my wardrobe, debating what to wear. I'm not planning on going anywhere, but I've got a good few hours before I have to start work. Viktor has made it clear that I don't need to work for him anymore, that I can just study, but I haven't started my course yet and I also don't like the idea of being a kept woman.

It would make me feel too much like I was taking advantage of him, and I would feel like I was dependent on him. He won't hear of me paying for anything, but at least I have the knowledge that I have my own money and the independence that gives me. After the way things turned out with my mom, I don't want to be financially dependent on anyone ever again. Not even someone as sweet as Viktor who I know would never throw it back in my face the way my mom allowed Dan to do.

I settle on wearing a pair of denim shorts and a yellow tank top. I might go and sit outside by the pool for a bit and read my book. I have to do something to occupy myself, otherwise, I'll just end up starting work earlier than I'm scheduled to do, and Viktor has caught me doing that once before. He sat me down and explained to me that if I kept doing that, he would have to let the maids go. I was horrified to think I could cost my friends their jobs. In the end, he laughed and told me he was joking, but he also reminded me that he pays the maids, so it was bad practice to buy a dog and bark yourself.

I don't see the big deal myself. I'm just here rattling around this big house waiting for him to come home and I figured I might as well make myself useful, but I'll respect his wishes. It's the least I can do when he has respected mine and not made a big fuss about me wanting to keep working. I have noticed that I'm only ever scheduled to work on his estate now though which makes me think I was right about my theory that Viktor is worried about my safety.

I'm sure he won't have to worry much longer. He'll find the bastard who torched the restaurant, and he'll deal with him. He won't talk to me about that much though. All I've managed to get out of him is he suspects it's a man called Igor. An old enemy. He showed me a photo, but I think he only did so I'll be on my guard if I happen to see him around anywhere. Not that that's likely at the minute. I'm practically on house arrest. Other than that one little snippet of information he shared with me, he just tells me it's all under control and I don't need to worry about it.

I finish getting dressed, grab my book, a historical

romance novel that I'm getting into much more than I care to admit, and go downstairs. First, I go to the kitchen and pour myself a coffee, then I head out for the balcony. I open the gate and move down towards the pool. Viktor has said he will teach me to swim, but until then I give the water a wide berth, choosing one of the loungers on the grass further away from the pool than the ones that line it. Almost drowning has given me a newfound respect for water.

I take a sip of my coffee and open my book. Lady Katherine, the heroine, is just about to kiss her prince for the first time when I hear the buzzing sound of the intercom. Great. Just as things were getting interesting.

I debate ignoring the buzzer, but it could be a delivery and I know the maids are at the back of the house, and it will take them far longer to get to the door than me. Viktor probably won't be impressed if I answer the door to a stranger, but it's not like I won't be able to see who it is on the screen before I open the door. Plus, they've already been vetted by the security staff manning the gates anyway.

I get up and hurry back towards the house. At the front door I check the screen to see who is there. My heart slams harder in my chest when I see my mom standing on the doorstep. As I stand staring at the screen, hardly believing my eyes, she reaches up and presses the buzzer again.

What the hell is she even doing here? How does she even know where I am?

For a second an evil little voice in my head tells me not to open the door. She chose Dan over me after he had tried to rape me. But my heart cries out for her. She is still my mom, and despite her faults when it comes to men, we've some good, happy times when she was between boyfriends, and she worked her ass off to keep me when I was a kid. For her to have tracked me down and turned up here, some-thing must be wrong. At the very least, I should hear her out.

I tell myself I'm just curious as to why she's here as I take a step closer to the door, but the truth is, there's a part of me, the part of me that's still the little girl my mom used to tuck into bed at night and read a story to, that wants her to have seen the error of her ways. That part of me wants her to apologize to me, to say she's seen Dan for the pervert he is and tell me she loves me more than she ever loved him.

I pull open the door and my mother smiles too brightly at me.

I don't return her smile because I already know from her false smile, she is going to disappoint me. "What are you doing here, Mom?"

"Is that any way to greet your mother, Amelia?" she answers cheerfully.

"I'm just a little surprised to see you here, that's all," I say.

"We need to talk. Can I come in?"

I nod. "What did you tell security at the gates?"

"I told them I was your mom, of course." She sighs and rolls her eyes. "I had to show them ID. This guy you're dating seems like a pretty big deal. Now can I come in or not?"

If I don't let her in now, she's only going to keep coming back if she's set her mind on us having whatever conversa-tion she plans on having with me. And this would be much more awkward and uncomfortable if Viktor was here.

I step back and pull the door open wider, letting my mom step past me. She stops in the hallway and looks around, letting out a low whistle. "You sure fell on your feet with this one. Maybe you should teach me how to pick a good one," she says with a nervous laugh.

"Do you want some coffee?" I ask, ignoring her insinuation that I'm only here for the lifestyle Viktor is offering me. That's the least attractive thing to me about Viktor. I'm not my mom, and I never will be.

She nods and I lead her through to the kitchen. I pour her some coffee and pour myself a fresh one. My coffee outside must be cold by now. I gesture to the table and we sit down.

"So, what brings you here, Mom?"

"What? I need a reason to come and see you? Can't a mom pop in to see her daughter without it being a federal case these days?"

"Well, I'm sure in normal families it can work that way, but let's be honest, we're far from normal, and after the way we left things, I wasn't exactly expecting regular coffee mornings with you."

"Fair point," Mom concedes. She sips her coffee, but she's still not telling me why she's here or what she wants.

I let the silence ride. The ball is in her court now.

"I regretted it the moment you left you know," she says suddenly.

"You did?" I'm not ready to accept her lame attempt at an apology.

"I've been trying to find you ever since you left, but it was like you disappeared into thin air. I was terrified something had happened to you. I mean, you hear these stories don't you, of young women on the streets being raped and murdered."

"Yeah, but I was one of the lucky ones apparently. I only got to deal with shit like that at home," I snap instinctively.

My mother has the grace to look down into her coffee cup, and for a moment I think she is ashamed of her behavior, but she takes another sip and goes on like I haven't spoken.

"When I saw your picture in the newspaper, I thought it was a sign from God. That he was leading me back to you," she says, still not looking at me.

"Since when did you start believing in God?"

"I don't. God is probably the wrong word for it. I guess I thought maybe it was fate or the universe trying to reunite us or whatever. Anyway, I had something to go on and I had to work hard to track down Viktor's address. He's a very hard man to find."

Somehow everything my mother has said so far makes me feel even worse than if she had never come. I'm hurt. "Yeah," I lash out bitterly. "He likes to try and keep the riff raff out."

I wait for the cutting comment. Something questioning why Viktor has shacked up with me if he has issues with riff raff. Instead, my mom surprises me. She gives me a sad looking smile.

"I deserved that one, but I didn't come here to fight with you, Amelia."

"Why did you come?"

She still hasn't really explained why she's here and I wish she would just spit it out. Get the disappointment over and done with.

"I came to say I'm sorry," she says, finally looking me in the eye.

28

AMELIA

"For what, Mom? Taking Dan's side over mine? Accusing me of trying to seduce him? Making out that my almost being raped was my own fault?"

"All of that. And mostly for being stupid enough to fall for Dan's charms and bring him into our lives in the first place," she says.

Now we're getting somewhere. It sounds like Dan has ditched her and now she's got no one else so she wants me again.

"I know what you're thinking, Amelia and it's not like that."

She likely does know what I'm thinking. We had this conversation after husband number three left. She pushed me aside in favor of him consistently throughout their relationship, but when he cheated on her and discarded her for someone else, she wanted her daughter back. I made no secret of the fact I knew the game she was playing back then.

"What is it like then?" I ask, curious as to what she would say to redeem herself.

"The day you walked out on us, I did a lot of thinking. And I saw, too late, that you were right about Dan. He's nothing but a scumbag, a piece of shit. I mean, you did wear some pretty revealing shit and you know it, but that's no excuse for what Dan did to you. And it's not an acceptable excuse for what he did to me. I mean if he can't control himself around my own daughter, what's he like when he's in a bar or something?"

"Honestly, Mom, I don't think you need to worry on that score. I can't imagine he could find another woman stupid enough to want to have sex with him," I say.

I know it's a low blow and my mom winces, but it's true. Dan is no one's catch.

"Well anyway, like I said, I realized Dan wasn't the man I thought he was. And I told him it was over between us. I packed up my things and I left him. Cynthia on the next block to us had a spare trailer and I'm renting that from her."

"So, you left Dan and still stayed in the trailer park?"

"Well yeah. It's not like I could afford anything else. We don't all have sugar daddies," she smiles to take the sting out that masterpiece of an insult.

I glare at her.

She gives a long-suffering sigh. "Look, Amelia, I'm doing my best with what I've got ok? But my trailer isn't like Dan's. It's clean and tidy and the curtains actually fit the windows."

It was a little joke we shared when we first moved into Dan's trailer, and I can't help but smile at that and my mom smiles too.

She takes a deep breath. "It's almost starting to feel like a home, but there's something missing, Amelia. You. I guess I wanted you to know how sorry I am for everything with Dan, and I hoped you would be able to forgive me and maybe come back home? I mean, I can see why you'd want to stay at this place, but you and Viktor haven't been together long, have you? And besides, family should be together. And you're the only family I've got left. You're young and you've got plenty of time to grow up and move in with your boyfriend at a later time."

She's playing the emotional blackmail card with her family should be together line. She never thought of that when she chose her husbands over me, although in her defense, I've never been asked to leave the family home. Despite knowing she's trying to emotionally blackmail me; I can't help but feel something inside of me stir at her words. I can't help but crave the mom she used to be. Maybe going back wouldn't be so bad if it was just going to be the two of us, and though I love Viktor with all my heart she's right about Viktor and me being too new to move in together. He's only letting me live here because he's afraid something bad could happen to me if I stay alone at my apartment. It could be a good thing to live with my mom until Viktor and I are truly ready to make that commitment.

Basically, she's given me everything I hoped for. Her admission that she was wrong about Dan, and she's even apologized, several times, for choosing him over me. I craved those words, but now that she's said them, I'm still wary. I've heard this kind of thing before from her, but it never lasts.

And I have to wonder if I'm really ready to blindly trust

her and go back. Am I really ready to go back to living in that trailer park and risk running into Dan every day? Basically, living a life where I'm just waiting for her to find her next boyfriend/husband before she throws me back out into the emotional cold?

I feel really confused. Right now, she seems genuine enough, but experience has taught me that the nice mom, the mom who says we can get by better with just the two of us, doesn't last long.

"Amelia? Please say something," she urges.

"I don't really know what to say," I tell her honestly. "I mean, I want to believe you've seen through Dan, and that you'll be a little bit more selective with men in the future, but let's be honest, Mom. Your track record doesn't really fill me with confidence on that score."

"I know that Amelia," she says with a heart-felt sigh. "But I promise you I've seen the error of my ways and I really would like a chance to prove that to you. Give me this one chance? Please. Even if you don't feel ready to come home, maybe you could at least drop by and see the trailer... and me."

She smiles and nudges me with her elbow.

"Come on, baby, what do you say? It'll be like the old days. We'll have movie nights, eat popcorn, and sit up all night chatting." She grins, that old grin that I haven't seen for years. "Just us two gals against the world."

She's making it sound so appealing that I'm desperate to say yes. I love my mom and I'll always love her. Maybe I should give her a chance, but I force myself to not give in so quickly. I don't want to rush into anything. I smile at her.

"That does sound good, Mom. Let me talk to Viktor

about it tonight and I'll give you a call tomorrow. How's that?"

She smiles again, a genuine truly happy smile. There is even a glimmer of tears in her eyes. "It's more than I deserve."

She stands up. "Well, I won't keep you. I just wanted you to know that I love you and I'm sorry, my darling girl. Really." Her voice breaks. "You'll call me tomorrow? Definitely?"

Definitely," I say as I walk her to the door.

THE CONVERSATION with my mom plays on my mind as I walk back to my book. I take the coffee cup back to the kitchen, so the maids don't have to. They still treat me like a friend, but there is a slight distance between us now. They are all very much aware that I'm now their boss's girlfriend. I don't want them to think for a second that I think it was ok to leave a mess lying around for them to deal with.

Part of me wants to move back in with my mom, and the other part thinks I'll miss Viktor too much. Even a few hours apart is hard for me to bear. I'm standing in the middle of the kitchen holding the coffee cup thinking and just staring into space when Justine comes in through the door.

"Amelia, what's wrong?"

"Oh nothing," I say.

She raises an eyebrow and looks at me. "That's clearly not true. Something's obviously bothering you."

"It's nothing," I insist. "It's stupid really. My mom came by earlier asking me to give her another chance and I'm a little torn. See, my mom has a history of choosing bad men to be with and then siding with them over me. Her last one led me to leave altogether. Now she says she's seen the error of her ways and it's over. Now don't get me wrong, I love my mom and I really want to have some sort of relationship with her, but I don't want to fall back into the trap of letting myself believe things will be different this time, only to get burned again."

"Oooof... that's a tough one." Justine agrees. "Families are complicated."

"Damn right," I say. "What would you do in my situation?"

"I don't know, honey. That's not my decision to make, but I will say this. Your mom, she's probably trying her best even if it doesn't seem like it right now. She's made mistakes, but maybe she's genuinely trying to make amends for them. And I'm not saying you should do this for her, because I genuinely believe that if you do decide to do it, I think you should do it for you. You know, just to stop that little voice in your head. The one that says what if."

"That's what I'm afraid of," I admit. "I'm afraid that if I give her another chance, I'll just get hurt again. But if I don't, then maybe I'll regret it."

"You have to follow your heart, Amelia. That's all you can ever do with things like this."

I nod. That makes sense. But my heart is keeping pretty damned quiet on this one. I figure I'll feel better once I talk to Viktor about this. Maybe he'll make it easy for me and push me in the right direction. Normally I wouldn't let him make a call like that for me, but on this occasion, I really think I would. It would stop this dilemma in my head if nothing else.

Our conversation is interrupted by a loud crashing

sound coming from the living room. I whirl in the direction of the sound, then turn to Justine and we just stand there, looking at each other in surprise for a second.

"What the hell was that?" I ask. "Is Lacey smashing up the house or what?"

"Lacey's upstairs," Justine answers.

It hits me then what the noise was. Breaking glass. It has to be the patio door that leads out onto the balcony. Someone must have climbed over the fence to avoid security. I don't think in that moment; I just take off in anger in the direction of the living room.

"Amelia, wait. It could be anyone. Let's call the police," she says.

I shake my head. "Whoever it is, Viktor won't want the police involved. He'll want to deal with this his way."

She runs to hit the alarm button hidden behind the fridge. "Just wait here, Amelia. The security guys will already be on their way to the house."

That's when we hear a loud bang that can only be a gunshot, followed by a scream of pain. This time, neither of us hesitate. The scream was Lacey. It sounds like someone has shot her. The only tiny bit of comfort I find in the situation is if she is screaming in pain, she isn't dead.

I'm almost at the living room door, Justine a step or two behind me. I burst into the living room ahead of Justine and freeze in my tracks.

The scene in the living room is crazy. Broken glass litters the floor. The patio door has been broken completely out of its frame. Lacey is on the ground and she's bleeding. Thank God, the blood seems to be coming from her leg. She's sitting up clutching it. Tears are running down her white face, but she's conscious and I think she'll be ok.

But none of that caused me to freeze. I froze because I see who is in the room. Igor. And his gun is now pointed at me, and not at my leg but my chest.

"Don't come any closer or I swear I'll shoot you. Where the fuck is Viktor?"

29

VIKTOR

I really didn't want to be late leaving the office and getting home tonight. In fact, I had planned on finishing work a little early and surprising Amelia by turning up early with her favorite take-out curry. I'd wrapped everything up in the office, and things were looking good for me getting away early when I got a call from Jerome.

He'd gotten word of a safe house where Igor was supposedly staying and the exact location of it. He found out it belonged to an old friend of Igor's and Igor was the only person staying in it. I abandoned my plans for an early finish and told Jerome to come pick me up and head over to Igor's.

Now I'm sitting in Jerome's car, cursing the traffic that's turning the journey into a frustrating nightmare. I'm buzzing with energy, sitting on the edge of my seat, adrenaline rushing through my body. I'm finally going to get the revenge I'm due for my restaurant, the people who lost their lives and were injured there. And most of all, I'm going to get my revenge for the fact that Amelia could have been hurt in that fire.

"How much further?" I ask.

"Not far. Another couple of blocks," he says. "If the traffic stays like this, ten minutes maximum. And it'll be quicker if it thins out a bit."

I nod impatiently. I just want to arrive there, get this whole thing over with, and go back to having a quiet life. Once I've dealt with Igor, I'll be able to relax about Amelia. I'll be able to go out to places, even places I don't own or haven't vetted, without me looking over my shoulder, paranoid that something bad will happen to her.

I can see now that's no way to live, not for either of us.

We finally catch a break in the traffic and Jerome puts his foot down. We have to hurry, not just because I'm hell bent on getting this over with tonight, but because Igor could move again. Jerome's men have obviously been asking questions, and while I know they'll have done their best to be subtle about it, there's always a chance someone will talk. If Igor knows we're coming for him, there's no way in hell he's going to just sit around waiting for us.

Jerome finally pulls the car up to the curb.

"This is it, boss," he says.

He nods out of the window to a mid-row terraced house. The house looks like it's seen better days and the garden is overgrown, but the same could be said for ninety percent of the houses on the block. A couple of young boys are kicking a ball around on the road a few yards down from where we've parked, and in one of the scruffy gardens over the road, a group of teenage girls are passing a bottle of cheap white liquor around between them. When I open the car door, the smell of weed is heavy in the air. I figure it's not just a bottle of liquor the girls are passing between themselves.

Jerome gets out of the other side of the car and waits for me to come and meet him on the pavement outside of the house.

"What's the plan?" he asks. "Are you carrying?"

"No. I came straight from the office. We're going to go in there, root out the little fucking rat, and I'm going to kill the fucker with my bare hands. That's the plan."

"Works for me," Jerome says with a wry grin. "Now?"

"Now," I confirm.

We go up to the front door and I stand back and smash my foot against it, just below the lock. It's an old, cheap looking wooden door and it splinters and crashes open on the first kick. I shake my head. Some fucking safe house.

I know kicking in the door has gotten the attention of both the group of teenage girls in the garden opposite us and the boys kicking the ball around down the road. This doesn't strike me as the sort of neighborhood where the neighbors get involved in each other's businesses, or the sort of place where people call the cops on someone else's behalf, but I don't want to risk getting caught here, so we have to move quickly. I estimate if there's a good Samaritan kicking around, we have about fifteen minutes tops.

"You do the upstairs, I'll do the downstairs," I say to Jerome.

He doesn't waste any time responding, he just runs up the stairs, taking them two at a time. I kick open the first door I see. It opens into a dingy little living room which I quickly see is empty. There's nowhere for anyone to hide. A tiny TV stands in the corner. I come back out of the room and check the kitchen. It's smaller than the living room and equally depressing. Again, there's no sign of anyone.

I hear Jerome jogging down the stairs, and I come back into the hallway.

"Anything?" I demand.

"Nothing," he says. "No clothes. No toiletries in the bathroom. We're too late, boss. He's already moved on."

"Fuck," I shout, slamming my fist into the wall and leaving a gaping hole in the plaster. White dust rains down onto the grubby once cream carpet. "Let's get out of here."

Jerome and I leave the house.

The boys have gone back to their football game, unconcerned with our business and the teenage girls, although they watch us, don't seem particularly worried about what we're doing. One of them, one of the braver ones I assume, shouts over to me.

"You looking for the big dude?"

Igor is pretty big. Chances are I'm indeed looking for the big dude. I nod.

"He left about an hour ago with a suitcase. I don't reckon he'll be back. He was driving a white, battered looking Ford," she says.

"Thanks," I shout, tipping her a wave as I get back into the car. "Take me back to the office, Jerome. I need to collect my car from there. See if you can find anything about this battered white Ford. It looks like he's heard we were coming for him and split, so there's a possibility he might end up spending a night or two living in it."

Jerome nods, then we pull away. There's still no sound of sirens, nothing to suggest anyone called the police on us.

Jerome heads back to my office. The roads are still busy, but it doesn't matter now. There's no rush to get back. After nearly forty-five minutes, Jerome pulls into my office parking lot.

"Sorry. I really thought we had him there, boss," he says.

"Yeah, me too. But he's running out of places to hide now. He'll fuck up sooner or later, hopefully sooner, and when he does, we'll be waiting," I say. "Keep looking for him. Don't let the trail go cold. And call me the second you have anything."

"Got it, boss," Jerome says.

I get out of his car and walk towards my own. I check my watch. So much for being early. Never mind. I can still get a curry delivered and try to salvage some of the night. The adrenaline is leaving me now, leaving me feeling pissed off and vaguely uneasy. I'm sure some quality time spent with Amelia can soon make me forget my troubles though.

I get into my car and head towards my estate. I put the radio on, but it instantly frazzles my nerves. I turn it straight back off again and drive in silence. I bang on the steering wheel as I quietly fume that Igor has evaded me once more. He's starting to make me look like a dick and no fucker gets away with that.

I'm near home when my phone rings. I almost ignore it, but it could be Amelia and so I pull it out of my pocket. It's not Amelia. It's Lenny, my chief of security up at the estate. He only ever calls me if there's a problem. I feel dread seize me. Something bad must have happened for him to be calling me, and Amelia is at the estate.

"Hello," I answer, then switching the call to speaker and dropping my phone onto the passenger seat.

"Viktor, it's Lenny. Where are you?"

"I'm almost home. What's going on?"

"There's been a breach. We believe there's an intruder in the main house. Please stay away until we get the situation under control."

"What the fuck?" I demand, furious and frightened beyond belief. "How did this happen, Lenny?"

"I don't know right now, Viktor, and I'm more concerned with containing the situation right now," he says.

Amelia is in that house. And I'd be willing to bet my last dollar that I know who the intruder is. The feeling of ennui is gone. My heart is hammering in my chest as I slam my foot down. I have no intention of staying away. I want to make sure Amelia is safe.

And deal with Igor once and for all.

Then I want to have a long, detailed chat with Lenny and his team and find out how the fuck someone got through their defenses. All Igor has done by breaking onto my estate and into my house essentially means, he's just delivered himself to me on a silver fucking platter.

I pull up outside of the house and jump out of my car. My blood runs cold when I hear a gunshot ringing out. *Please be Lenny's gun, please be Lenny's gun*, I pray as I fly into the house and follow the sound of a scream towards the lounge.

The door to the lounge is ajar and I slow myself down enough to take stock of the situation. If Lenny has the situation under control, knowing he told me to stay away, he won't be expecting me and if I burst in there, there's a reasonable chance he might shoot first and ask questions later. It's what he's been taught to do in these situations.

I peer through the crack in the door. There's no sign of

Lenny or any of his security team. Instead, I see Igor. On the ground is Lacey, bleeding from her leg. And opposite him is Amelia with Justine a step behind her.

Igor has his gun aimed right at Amelia's chest.

30

VIKTOR

"Where the fuck is Viktor?" Igor snarls.

Amelia's mouth opens and then it closes again, and I know it's time to end this shit. I step into the doorway, giving away my position to Amelia and Justine. Igor has his back to me. His shirt is clinging to his back, soaked in nervous sweat that I can smell even from here.

"I'm right here you fucking bastard," I say quietly.

Igor spins towards the sound of my voice as I hoped he would, the gun coming off Amelia. The second the gun is no longer pointed at her, I yell.

"Amelia. Justine. Get the fuck out of here."

Neither of them moves, but my focus is on Igor now. He's almost fully facing me, but his gun is still swiveling in my direction. With an angry roar, I launch myself at him. I collide with his body and send him sprawling backwards. I fall on top of him. The gun goes off, the sound of the shot muffled as it's shielded by our bodies. A half second after the gun goes off again, I feel a blinding white pain in my left shoulder, and half a second after that, I feel the warm rush of blood from my shoulder down my chest.

My heart pounds loudly. Each hard beat brings a rush of warm blood out of me.

Igor's body hits the floor with mine pouncing on top of him. I feel dizzy, but I hold onto consciousness, and punch down on Igor with my right hand. I catch him on the nose and feel the satisfying give of his cartilage, hear the crack that tells me I've broken his nose. He makes a grunting sound as blood explodes from his nostrils. I pull my fist back again, but Igor manages to get his gun arm free from beneath me. I feel the cold hard slam of metal against my temple and my vision swims in and out as the dizziness washes over me more violently now, threatening to carry me away on a wave of disorientating nausea.

Igor takes advantage of my pain and dizziness and shoves me hard to one side. He jumps up the second my body is clear of his and runs towards the empty space where the patio door's glass should be. In that crazy moment all my senses become alive. I can even hear the shards of glass crunching beneath his feet.

Pulling on some secret superhuman strength deep inside me, I get to my feet with a roar of anger and chase after Igor. I know even before I clear the decking outside of the patio and get through the gate that leads from the balcony to the pool area that I'm too late. Igor's body disappears around the side of the house. I know I won't catch him, not while I'm in this state. Agonizing pain is radiating from my shoulder, and I can feel hot blood running down my chest and arm. I'm bleeding from my temple too, but despite the blood and the pain and the sheer futility of my action, I give chase to Igor.

Amelia screams for me to come back, but I'm absolutely fuming, and the anger fuels the adrenaline inside of me, pushing me on.

I run to the corner he disappeared around, but he's nowhere to be seen. I stand there swaying with no idea which direction he's run to. Wherever he went, he's likely over the fence now and I know he's long gone. To confirm my suspicion, a car engine roars to life on the other side of the fence. I hear tires squealing as Igor speeds away.

"Fuck," I shout into the still evening air. "Fuck."

When I catch him now, he's not just dead, he's going to die in agony like the flea ridden fucking vermin he is. I'll make him wish he'd never even heard my name, let alone said it. I scream at the sky, letting my anger flood out of me. Then I turn and head back towards the house. I know I need to let some of the anger go for the minute. I need to make sure Amelia is ok and I need to call someone to get Lacey to hospital.

All of this is going through my mind as I step back into the living room. I'm almost knocked off my feet when Amelia throws herself at me. I open my arms and catch her, and she holds me tightly. It's agony and fresh blood flows from my wound and soaks into her clothes, but I keep holding her anyway, needing to feel her in my arms, needing to know she's ok.

"What happened?" I ask Justine.

"I don't know," she replies, with a shiver. "Amelia and I were in the kitchen. We heard a gunshot and then a scream and we ran in. Lacey was down and that man had a gun pointed at us. And then you appeared."

"Lacey?" I ask. "Do you know what happened?"

"Not really. I was on my way down the stairs when I

heard the glass breaking. I ran in here expecting to see I don't know what. I thought maybe Justine or Amelia had had some sort of accident. Instead, there was the man with the gun. I demanded to know who he was and what he was doing here, and he just shot me. Who was he, Viktor? What did he want?"

"Valuables I'm assuming," I lie. "Is everyone ok? Lacey, I know your leg needs attention, but other than that?"

"I'm fine," Lacey says.

Justine nods mutely. She looks like she's about to pass out and she practically falls onto a chair. I look at Amelia. She frowns and shakes her head.

"We're ok, but you're not," she says, her voice full of worry. "And don't be trying to pull any of this macho bullshit about being ok. You're bleeding heavily and you look like you're about ready to pass out. Sit down. I'm calling an ambulance for both you and Lacey."

My head is spinning again, and as much as I'd like to find out what exactly happened here first, I know if I don't get my shoulder fixed, Amelia will be proved right: I'm going to pass out.

"No ambulance," I say. I hold my phone out to Amelia before she can argue. "Call Doctor Singh. He's in my phone. He's my personal doctor. Tell him what's happened and get him over here now."

31

AMELIA

Some of the panic leaves me when Viktor tells me to call Doctor Singh.

I was afraid I was going to have an argument with him about getting looked at, and I really thought he was going to pass out from the loss of too much blood before I could call for help for him. I would still prefer an ambulance, but if Doctor Singh is Viktor's personal doctor, he's likely better than anyone Viktor would see at the hospital anyway. Lacey doesn't want to go to hospital either.

I find Dr. Singh's number in Viktor's contacts and hit call. He answers quickly, announcing his name in a business-like manner that helps to keep me calm.

"Doctor Singh, this is Amelia Madison, Viktor Leshchenko's girlfriend," I say. "We need your help desperately. Viktor has been shot in the shoulder and Lacey has been shot in the leg."

I realize Dr. Singh likely has no idea who Lacey is, but I just need him to know how serious this is. I'm kind of hoping he'll hang up and call an ambulance.

"Viktor told me to tell you the situation and ask you to get over here as soon as you can," I add.

"Are you at the main residence?" Dr. Singh asks.

"Yes," I say.

"I'm on my way. In the meantime, please apply pressure to any bleeding wounds," he says and ends the call.

"Sit down," I tell Viktor again when I see he's still standing.

He must be feeling pretty damned close to losing consciousness, because he doesn't argue with me. He just drops into a chair. I run to the kitchen and grab a pile of clean tea towels and then I run back to the living room. I hold one of the tea towels out to Justine. She just looks at it.

"Justine," I say. Nothing. I snap my fingers in front of her face. "Justine."

She rouses herself a little as I say her name for a third time. I push the tea towel closer to her and she takes it this time.

"The doctor will be here soon, but in the meantime I need you to press this against the wound in Lacey's leg and hold it, ok?"

She nods and gets up. She seems to be a little bit more with it as she kneels beside Lacey and tears the pant leg to expose the wound. She folds the tea towel and presses it onto Lacey's leg. Lacey winces but she doesn't complain. Justine starts to talk quietly and reassuringly to her.

I move back over to Viktor and open his shirt.

He smiles hazily at me. "I don't think we should do this with those two in the room."

His voice sounds a little weak, but his teasing tells me he's not too far gone.

"You should be so lucky." I try to grin but fail.

As gently as I can I peel the shirt off his hurt shoulder, wincing when I see all

the blood and the hole in his shoulder. Grabbing two tea towels, I make a thick pad and press it against his shoulder. He sucks in a pained breath.

"Sorry," I say, holding the tea towels firmly in place.

"It's ok," he says. "Let me hold that. I need to go and find Lenny and see what the hell is going on."

He starts to stand up, but I put my hand on his good shoulder, holding him down and shaking my head.

"No way," I say. "The doctor told me to do this and I'm doing it whether you like it or not."

"Fine," he sighs, accepting that I'm not giving in on this one. He smiles a little. "You know, you'd make quite the nurse. You really took charge of this situation."

"Yeah, well don't be getting any ideas about nurse outfits," I quip.

"Too late," he says weakly.

Viktor coughs and I feel a rush of blood seeping through the tea towel. His face is pasty white, and he slumps in his chair. Where the hell is Doctor Singh? I make a decision in that moment. If he's not here in the next five minutes, I'm calling an ambulance whether Viktor likes it or not.

Doctor Singh arrives with only a minute to spare before the deadline I gave myself. He comes in looking a little harried, carrying a black bag which he puts on the sofa. He moves towards Viktor who shakes his head.

"Her first," he says pointing to Lacey.

"I'm not bleeding anywhere near as much as you are," Lacey protests.

"Maybe not, but I'm paying the bill for the doctor so what I say goes."

"It'll be easier to just do it than to argue with him," I say to Doctor Singh.

It seems Viktor and I know each other well enough to know when our minds are made up and an argument is pointless. Dr. Singh doesn't look convinced it's a good idea, but that's ok, because I don't think it's a good idea either, I just know the quickest way to get Viktor seen to is to have the doctor deal with Lacey now instead of having an argument about it first and then still having to deal with Lacey before Viktor will let him deal with him.

The whole time the doctor tends to Lacey, I whisper to Viktor, trying my best to keep him conscious. His voice is a little weak, but he answers me, and I even get him to laugh a little, although I don't try that one again when I see him wincing and feel the warm rush of blood from his shoulder wound again.

In a few minutes Doctor Singh gets up from the ground and with Justine's help gets Lacey to her feet.

"What's the prognosis, Doc? Is an amputation in the cards?" Viktor asks with a wink at Lacey who smiles and shakes her head.

"It was really just a flesh wound," Doctor Singh says. "I've cleaned it up and put a dressing on it and prescribed a mild antibiotic just to prevent any infection from setting in. I've also prescribed a mild sedative for the shock."

Viktor nods and then looks at Lacey and Justine in turn. "I trust you ladies understand this won't be getting reported to the police. And I would very much appreciate it if you both kept this incident to yourselves," he says.

They both nod almost dismissively and I realize that while this might be the first time an armed gunman has broken into the house, it's probably not the first time they've had some variation of this conversation with Viktor.

"And obviously I don't expect to see either of you at work tomorrow," Viktor says. I open my mouth to interrupt him, and he laughs and shakes his head. "And despite what Amelia here thinks, you both understand that means you're to take some time off with full pay, not be sacked right?"

They both nod again and I relax. I've got to stop thinking the worst of Viktor. Of course, he isn't going to sack them.

"Lacey, how long will you need for your leg to recover?" Viktor asks.

"It's really not that bad. A day or two at the most," she says.

Doctor Singh nods, confirming this.

"Right. So how does a month each sound?" he asks.

"It's too much," Lacey says instantly.

"Yeah. I'll be in tomorrow. I didn't even get hurt," Justine says.

Viktor sighs and shakes his head. "I can't believe I have to make this an order, but neither of you are to come to work for the next month. You'll both receive full pay, and if I see either of you at work before that time is up, then I might have to sack you," he says.

"Thank you," Lacey says, looking sheepish.

"It's really not necessary, but it's very much appreciated," Justine adds.

"You'll both also find a large compensation payment dropping into your accounts in the next couple of days, and if either of you even think about arguing with me over that one, then I'll double it," he adds.

Both women thank him profusely. Their loyalty to Viktor is clear to see, and I know they would have argued if

Viktor had made any other threat but that one. That was the one that guaranteed to make them thank him and agree to the payment.

Working for Viktor might come with a small element of danger – I mean where else would a maid get shot on the job? – but it also comes with a ton of loyalty from him in return. He clearly cares about each and every member of his staff. I love that about him.

I love how loyalty isn't a one-way street with him.

32

AMELIA

Viktor turns to me.

"Amelia, would you call Jerome please? Have him organize cars for Justine and Lacey and come over when he's done that," Viktor says. "Dr Singh, I'm ready when you are."

I move away from Viktor and the doctor and find Jerome in Viktor's contacts list. He answers the call quickly.

"Everything ok, boss?"

"Umm it's Amelia," I say. "I'm..."

"Yes, I know who you are," he interrupts. His tone is all business, but it's not unfriendly. "Is everything ok?"

That's a big question, isn't it? How would Viktor answer it? I think for a moment.

"There's been a... er... situation at the house. It's all under control now, but he has asked me to call you. He needs two cars arranged to take two of the maids home, and he has asked for you to come over."

"Consider it done. The cars will be with you within

fifteen minutes, and I'll be there just after that," he replies crisply.

"Thank you," I say, but I'm talking to the dial tone.

Viktor laughs softly when he sees me frowning at the phone.

"It's nothing personal," he says. "Jerome isn't much of a talker, but he's a doer. What did he say?"

"He said the cars for Laccy and Justine will be here within fifteen minutes and he'll be here just after that," I relay.

"You three need to go into another room to wait," Doctor Singh says.

Lacey and Justine don't hesitate. They instantly head for the hallway, thanking Viktor again and saying goodbye to him. I don't follow them.

"Why? What's wrong?" I demand.

Doctor Singh looks at Viktor who nods his head. Blood is running freely from his shoulder now that the doctor has removed the tea towels to examine the wound and his face is whiter than ever.

"The bullet is embedded in Viktor's shoulder. I can get it out easily enough, but I don't carry any sort of anesthetic and it will hurt like hell. You don't need to see that," the doctor says.

"You know how once Viktor has made up his mind about something, it's easier just to do things his way and save time?"

Dr. Singh nods, looking a little confused.

"I'm very much the same myself. I'm not going anywhere, Dr. Singh, and I don't expect you to waste time arguing with me about it."

"Amelia..." Viktor starts.

"That goes for you as well," I say, giving him a determined look.

He sighs and nods for Doctor Singh to go on. The doctor digs in his bag and comes out with a syringe filled with clear liquid, a small pair of tweezers, and a metal bowl. He reaches down and removes his belt. I stare curiously, but I don't ask questions. I know the doctor isn't overly happy about me being here and I don't want him to remember that and ask me to leave or waste time explaining or arguing with me. He hands Viktor the belt. Viktor takes it with no confusion on his face, so the belt thing is obviously normal to him at least.

"Right, I'm going to flush the wound out with a saline solution first," Doctor Singh says.

He picks up the syringe and opens it up, and then he squirts the liquid into the wound, washing away the blood. I get a glimpse of the bullet embedded in Viktor's flesh and I feel my stomach roll. Maybe I should have just left the room, but I can't let Viktor go through this alone. I focus on Viktor's face. His head is back, the tendons in his neck straining against his skin. Beads of sweat have formed on his face and if it's possible, he's even whiter than before.

The doctor picks up the tweezers and looks at Viktor.

"Ready?" he asks.

Viktor folds the belt in two and puts it in his mouth and nods his head. I know what the belt is for now. It's to bite down on when the pain gets too much for him. I step closer to him and take his hand in both of mine.

"I'm right here," I say, before I faint.

When I come back around, I'm lying on the sofa with a couple of cushions under my feet. Viktor is sitting next to me. "Are you alright?" he asks.

"Are you?" I ask.

He nods and shows me the small bowl the Doctor had brought, and I see the bloody, mishappened bullet inside it.

"I'm sorry I fainted on you."

"It was a good thing you did," he replies. "It wasn't a pretty sight."

I lift my head up and kiss him. Doctor Singh clears his throat and I pull my mouth from Viktor's.

"Sorry," I apologize sheepishly.

"That's it. The worst is over. The bullet grazed the bone but not enough to do any real damage. I'll be prescribing you some antibiotics too," he says.

Headlights flash in front of the window.

"That'll be the cars for Justine and Lacey," Viktor says.

I sit up immediately.

"Steady," Viktor warns.

"I want to say goodbye to Justine and Lacey."

"Alright, but go easy."

I go out to the hallway where Justine and Lacey are still waiting.

"Is everything ok?" Lacey asks. "It sounded like someone was being murdered in there."

"I fainted," I confess guiltily, "but everything's ok now," I say. "The doctor had to pull the bullet out without anesthetic."

Lacey winces. "I honestly don't know if Viktor is brave as hell or bat shit crazy not going to the hospital and having it done while he was knocked out instead of this back street surgery." She glances at me. "Shit. Sorry."

"Don't apologize." I grin. "I was thinking pretty much the same thing myself."

"Will he be ok?" Justine asks.

"Yeah. The doctor said it didn't leave any lasting damage. Anyway, your cars are here, and I just came to see you both out."

We say our goodbyes and the two women leave the house. I close the front door and go back to the living room to find Dr. Singh smiling.

He hands Viktor two pills.

"An antibiotic and a painkiller. Take those now and then get this filled in the morning and take the full course," he says as he writes on a prescription pad.

"I'll go and get you some water," I say.

33

AMELIA

I hurry to the kitchen and grab a glass and fill it with water. I go back to the living room and hand Viktor the glass. He takes the pills as Doctor Singh packs his things away.

"I might be on the move for the next couple of days," Viktor says to the doctor. "So, email me a copy of your invoice so I can deal with your payment wherever I am."

I can read between the lines. Viktor will be living in another one of his properties until his men track Igor down, and while he trusts the doctor's medical skills, he's wary enough not to tell him where he'll be staying.

Dr. Singh nods his understanding and says his goodbyes. I see him out and go back to the living room.

"Shall I help you upstairs so you can rest properly in bed?" I ask.

"Not yet," he says. "There are a few things I need to deal with first. First, I need to call Lenny and find out what the fuck went wrong here and where the hell he's disappeared to."

"Can't that wait until you're feeling better?"

"No," Viktor says harshly, then sees my expression, and softens. He gets to his feet, wraps his good arm around me and kisses the top of my head. "There are some things that simply must be dealt with tonight, Amelia. I'm fine, I promise you. This meeting is likely going to be pretty dull if you want to go upstairs and get some sleep. I'll come for you later."

I shake my head. I'm not leaving Viktor's side for even a moment. He squeezes me a little tighter, but he doesn't say anything. He knows I won't be talked out of this one. Then he releases me and picks up his phone and speaks to someone in Russian. I go sit on the couch and wait for him to finish his business.

Viktor moves to the dining room and comes back with a bottle of whiskey and four glasses. He pours four decent amounts and hands one to me, taking one for himself. Lenny arrives as I take my first sip and feel the burning heat of the whiskey in my stomach.

Lenny sits down in a chair opposite us and picks up a glass. He drains it, refills it, then he sits back in his seat and sips it thoughtfully.

"My apologies for my absence in the last hour," he says.

An hour? It feels simultaneously more like five hours and only five minutes have passed.

"I called in a team," he continues, "and we've been scouring the perimeter of the estate. We found the breach. The intruder..."

"Igor Volkov," Viktor supplies.

"Igor Volkov? Ah that makes sense," Lenny says.

Does it? Seemingly it does to him. He probably knows a damned sight more about this whole Igor thing than I do.

"He made a hole in the fence, cleverly replacing the section he had cut out so there was no visible change to the fence. No one could have spotted that with the naked eye if they didn't know what they were looking for. Even knowing we had a breach, it was difficult to find, and eventually, we found it by pushing on each section of the fence until we found the loose part. The hole has been repaired."

Viktor nods his head thoughtfully.

"That's good," he says. "But my main concern right now is what went wrong. With regards to the hole, I will take your word for its sophistication and why it might have been missed. But when there was a breach, why the hell didn't you and your team come up to the house immediately?"

"Well, that's the thing," Lenny says. "This wasn't a spur of the moment attack. It was carefully orchestrated and has likely been planned for a while. I wasn't on duty, but as you know, an alarm sounds at my place if there's a breach in security. The alarm sounded and I attempted to access the CCTV, but it was down. And when I called the gate, there was no answer. I tried the mobile phones of the guards scheduled to be here but I got no answer from any of them, so I rushed down here. I was a little further away than you and when I called you to stay away, I was still a good five minutes away.

"I arrived at the gate. The guards were both uncon-scious. I believe they had been sedated with some sort of pill or powder in their coffees, although I won't know for sure until I get their bloodwork back. They're both fine, just deeply unconscious, but Frederick reckons they should wake up within twelve to fourteen hours, so hopefully, I can get some answers on what happened then."

"Fuck," Viktor says. "We've all massively underestimated

Igor and how far he's willing to go to settle whatever issues he has with me."

"Why didn't he shoot you?" I ask.

Both men seem startled as they turn to me, almost as though they forgot I was here. Viktor recovers first.

"He did shoot me," he says slowly, a frown on his forehead.

"No," I say, dismissing his statement with a wave of my hand. "After he clocked you with the gun barrel, he ran off. Why didn't he shoot you then? He could have..."

I trail off, not wanting to end the sentence. He could have killed you is what I wanted to say. Viktor and Lenny both understand my meaning.

"Because this, whatever this is, is personal to Igor. He doesn't want it to be over so quickly. He wants it to be slow, to make me suffer," Viktor says.

A shudder runs through me.

"What did you do to him?" I ask.

"I killed his father," he says coldly.

I gasp, shocked. "What? Why?"

"Because he tried to kill me, but instead murdered my fiancée and the baby that was growing in her belly."

My jaw drops. His whole world is so dangerous and alien to me and yet I feel no desire to run away.

He turns his focus back to Lenny. "Carry on."

"I heard a gunshot while I was still trying to make sense of what was going on. I didn't immediately come to the house because I had told you to stay away. I had no idea you would ignore that instruction."

"So, you thought the maids were ok to leave to die?" Viktor asked.

"Of course not," Lenny says quickly. "I didn't know they

were still here. Up until I heard the gunshot, all of the signs pointed to a simple robbery. The drugged guards, unin- jured. The timing of the incident. When I heard the gunshot, I ran towards the house. I saw someone, obviously Igor, running away, and you giving chase. I figured he was going to loop back as I ducked down, ready to cut him off, but obviously I misjudged the situation. I didn't know about the hole in the fence. I immediately called a team and orga- nized the search of the perimeter."

The door to the living room opens and a large man steps in. I recognize him from being with Viktor that night in the bar when we first met.

"Take a seat and have a drink, Jerome," Viktor says. He turns back to Lenny as Jerome sits down and picks up his glass. "Where are we now?"

"I'm waiting for the blood test results to come back and for the guards to wake up. In the meantime, a new team is in place and the fence is fixed. I have a guy on his way to sort the CCTV and tomorrow, we'll be having an urgent meeting to discuss increased security measures until Igor is found," Lenny says. "I will call some of my most trusted men and have them form a personal bodyguard team for you and Miss Madison."

"Call me Amelia," I say automatically.

Lenny gives me an unsmiling nod then his attention turns straight back to Viktor.

"A personal bodyguard won't be necessary at this point," Viktor says. "I will let you know if anything changes."

Lenny accepts this, but he doesn't look happy about it. "I'll set about replacing the glass tonight and get someone to come in and clean the mess up. Don't worry, I'll stay with them the whole time. No more nasty surprises tonight."

"What the fuck has happened?" Jerome asks.

Viktor fills him in on the events of the evening. Jerome listens in silence, drinking his drink and filling his glass several times.

"Jerome, you need to get a team together and find Igor as a top priority. This is no longer a covert mission that we can bide our time on. I don't care what you have to do to find that son of a bitch. I want him found, and I want him found now. Is that clear?"

Jerome nods, already getting to his feet, and moving towards the door as he pulls his phone out of his pocket.

"Lenny, it sounds like you have everything under control here. Keep on this and don't let anything slip through the cracks. If you need more men, hire them. And keep me in the loop with the blood results and what the guards tell you about the incident."

Lenny nods and he too gets to his feet.

"I'm so sorry, Viktor. I hate that any of this happened on my watch."

"Don't worry about it. Like I said, we all underestimated Igor and I don't think anyone could have prevented this."

Lenny nods to him, grateful to be let off the hook, and then he too leaves the room. Viktor and I are alone together for the first time since this morning.

"Are you ok, Amelia? I know this has been a lot to take in," he says.

"I'm fine," I tell him. "It's you I'm worried about, not me."

"You don't have to worry about me. This will all be over soon, I promise. And then we can go back to the quiet life, huh?"

I lean closer to him, and he holds me for a moment and then he releases me and gets up.

"Come on. We need to pack our things and get out of here," he says.

I get to my feet and follow him towards the stairs. "Isn't this the best place to be though? With the added security and stuff."

"Amelia, you had a gun pointed at you in this house only a few hours ago. Do you really feel comfortable here now?"

I consider his words. It doesn't make sense that I do feel comfortable here after what happened, but I actually do. I nod slowly.

"I feel comfortable being wherever you are," I say.

Viktor smiles at me. "You're one brave lady. Okay, go on upstairs and I'll join you in a few minutes. I think we both could use an early night. I'll just let Jerome and Lenny know we'll be staying here," he says.

34

AMELIA

I climb the stairs, feeling weary deep down in my bones. He's right about an early night. I'm covered in blood though and I decide to take a shower before bed. By the time I'm done in the shower and go to the bedroom, Viktor has washed the blood off himself and he's already in bed waiting for me. He pulls the covers back and I slip into bed beside him. He wraps me up in his good arm and holds me.

"Amelia, listen," Viktor says. "I've been thinking and there's something I need to talk to you about. And you're not going to like it."

I pull myself away from him far enough to look into his face. His expression is completely serious, and I feel dread eating away at me. I sit up and Viktor sits up beside me. We lay back on the pillows and Viktor puts his arm around my shoulders. I turn slightly, leaning into him, and then I steel myself for whatever bad news he's going to drop on me now.

"Like I said downstairs, I killed Igor's father, and he isn't going to stop coming for me until either he gets his way and destroys me, or I end him. You understand that, right?"

I nod calmly, but my heart is racing in my chest.

He sighs. "You have to understand the most obvious way for Igor to get to me is through the one I care most about. And that's you."

"You think he'll grab me or something and use me as bait to lure you in?" I ask.

"Maybe," he says. "Or maybe he'll hurt you so I suffer. Either way, I'm not taking that risk. You have to leave."

"What are you saying?" Does he want us to break up? I feel confused. Is this Igor guy seriously controlling my love life right now?

"I'm saying I have a safe house you can stay in. One that's not associated with me publicly. We won't be able to have any contact with each other, and to the outside world, it will look like we've split up. Igor isn't going to go after my ex-girlfriend and..."

Ok, it's not as bad as I imagined. He's not breaking up with me. He just wants everyone else to think he has. It's bad enough though. It still means we'll have to be apart.

"I don't want to do that, Viktor. No matter what happens, I want to be with you. I go crazy with worry for you if I'm away from you."

"I know," he says gently, moving his fingers on my arm, caressing me. "And trust me, I don't want to do this either, but if it's a choice between spending some time away from you and you being safe or having you with me and putting you in danger, I will always choose the safe option."

"You can keep me safe, Viktor," I argue. "Look at the fire. Or tonight. You kept me safe."

"We got lucky tonight, Amelia, and you know it. If I had

been two minutes later getting back, it might have been too late."

"We don't even know Igor will go after me. He didn't seem to know who I was earlier. He just demanded to know where you were."

"Well, if he didn't know who you were before, he does now. He knows I'm willing to risk my life for yours. So, I'm not willing to take the chance that he won't go for you," Viktor insists. "I once made a mistake like this before. I assumed something would be safe and it wasn't. My fiancée paid with her life, and I won't let that happen to you, Amelia. Not now, not ever."

I bite my lower lip. There's a sharp prick of jealousy to think of his ex. Even though she's dead, she was pregnant with his child. He must have loved her. There is still feeling in his eyes now. "How did she die?"

"She was shot. The bullet wasn't meant for her, but me. She got caught in the crossfire. She died in my arms," Viktor says, his voice breaking slightly.

"Oh my God, I'm so sorry," I say, snuggling more tightly against him.

"It's okay. It's all in the past now and it took a very long time, but I've made my peace with it. But like I say, I won't let it happen again. I can't lose you, Amelia. I can't."

I think for a moment. The last thing I want is for Viktor and me to be apart, but I can hear the raw pain in his voice as he talks about his fiancée's death, and I don't want to be responsible for bringing all of that back and making him feel like it could happen again.

"Ok," I say. "We'll act like we've split up. But I don't think a safe house is the answer. I'll go back to my mom's place.

That's what I would do if we really broke up and it'll make the whole thing seem more believable."

"Your mom's place?" Viktor asks surprised. "I thought you two hadn't spoken since you left."

"We hadn't until this morning. I was waiting for you to come home from work so we could talk about it, but obviously with everything that happened, I haven't had a chance to tell you. My mom saw us in the newspaper after you did that interview about the fire, and she's been trying to track me down ever since. Actually, she claims she's been trying to track me down since I left the trailer. She said she's seen the error of her ways and she's left Dan. She's staying in a separate trailer now and she asked me to move back home. Or at least to consider making her a part of my life again. I told her I would think about it."

"Do you believe her?" Viktor asks evenly, as if he doesn't want to show me his true thoughts.

"I want to. But I'm a bit afraid to. I worry things will be good for so long, and then she'll get bored of being single and find some deadbeat boyfriend and the cycle will start over again."

"I hope to have this Igor thing wrapped up quickly, so hopefully that won't happen before I do. And you're right. Going back to your mom's place is a good idea. Trailer parks are not his scene."

"All right. I'll go live with my mom for a while." I would have preferred to think about it longer and only go live with my mom when I'm good and ready, but I can't insist on staying here and leave Viktor with a choice of either forcing me out or being left walking on eggshells constantly.

"When this is over, Amelia, I want you to move back in

here immediately. I want us to be officially together... unless you don't want that."

I push myself away from him and look at him in wonder. "Are you kidding me? Of course, I want that. When I said I wanted to talk to you about what my mom said, I didn't mean I didn't want to be with you. I was just debating whether or not to let her back into my life."

Viktor smiles and I can see the relief in it. "So, the plan is you go back to your mom's trailer in the morning. As soon as you find her new trailer, I want you to text me the exact location of it, and after that, we will have no contact at all unless it's a life-or-death emergency. The second Igor is dealt with, I will come and get you."

"It's going to be hard, isn't it? Not even being able to talk to each other," I say.

"Yeah," Viktor agrees. "But you understand why it has to be that way don't you?"

I nod. In truth, I think it's all confusing and incomprehensible to me, but after Viktor has already lost one girl he loved because of something he was mixed up in, I do understand why he's going to such lengths to make our breakup look real and to keep me out of the line of fire.

"We should get some sleep," he says. "It's been a long night."

"Aren't we forgetting something?" I ask.

He looks at me and frowns.

I smile and lean closer to him. "The hot breakup sex, but don't worry I'll be super gentle," I say before I close my lips over his.

35

VIKTOR

Fucking hell what an evening it's been.

I can't believe how close I came to losing Amelia, and in almost the same way I lost Lisa. The cold, logical side of me says I should let Amelia go. Make the fake breakup I'm suggesting be real. That would guarantee her safety, but I just can't do it. I can't imagine my life without her in it. True, I'm being selfish, but this is the happiest I've ever been, and I won't walk away from that, from her.

Instead, I'm going to deal with Igor and once he's taken care of, then my hands will be clean, my businesses are clean, and being with me will be no more dangerous than being with anyone else.

Not having Amelia around distracting me with her sexy body and her sensuous kiss will certainly make it easier to focus on the mission at hand. And I intend to have this dealt with quickly. Amelia and I being forced to spend a day or two apart will only make it hotter when we come back together. At least that's what I tell myself in the hope of making being apart a little easier.

All of this goes through my mind until Amelia tells me we need to have a hot breakup sex session and leans in to kiss me. The thoughts scatter like fluff in the wind the instant her lips touch mine, and I become consumed in her kiss, in her. All I can think of now is her – how her kiss wakes my body up even though I'm mentally and physically exhausted. How her touch makes my body crave her more than ever.

And how hard I am already.

She pushes herself up onto her knees and straddles me, resting her ass right on my cock. Her wet pussy presses against me and makes me groan into her mouth as she kisses me passionately.

This kiss is different than all the others. It's about our connection. It's about what we've gone through tonight and how we barely escaped with our lives. It's about us having to be apart soon and knowing how hard that's going to be. It's about giving us something to think about when the nights are cold and lonely while we're away from each other.

Amelia moves her hips, rubbing her pussy over my cock, making me growl with need. I reach up to push my hands into her hair, but pain floods through me from my shoulder. My arm flops back to the mattress. I push my other hand into her hair, but she pulls back, frowning down at me in concern.

"I hurt you, didn't I?" she asks, sounding upset.

"No. I hurt myself by getting too enthusiastic."

She starts to lift herself off me and I move my good hand to her hip, holding her in place.

"Trust me, Amelia, you're worth a twinge in my shoulder. It'll hurt me way more not to do this than it will to do it," I assure.

"Are you sure?" she asks with a concerned expression on her face.

It's clear I'll have to persuade her I'm ok. The lust is written all over her face.

"I'm this sure," I say and push myself into a sitting position, ignoring the fire in my shoulder, and not showing it. I push my good hand back into Amelia's hair and pull her closer, finding her lips with my own once more. The fire of the pain is soon replaced with the fire of Amelia's touch. She's better than any pain killer Dr. Singh could prescribe for me.

She puts her arm around me, resting it on my good shoulder, and uses her other hand to caress my cheek as we kiss. Then she moves it down my body, scraping her nails gently over my skin. She pulls back from the kiss and smiles at me, pushing me back down onto the bed with one hand. Scooting backwards she takes my erect cock in her fist, working me until I'm almost ready to explode.

At the last moment she snatches her hand away from me and she sits across my thighs, sucking each of her fingers in turn. I moan as she sucks herself clean, making mmm sounds as her tongue laps over each finger and then it disappears into her mouth.

I'm so fucking turned on my head is spinning, but I'm not ready to penetrate Amelia yet. I want to give her something good to remember me by, even if we're only going to be apart for a few days.

I beckon to her, and she slides up my body, pausing on my cock. I shake my head and she frowns.

"Not yet," I say. "Keep coming."

She keeps moving up my body, leaving a trail of wetness as she comes. She's worked out my intention and she shimmies up my body with no more need for instruction. She lifts her ass and hovers over my face, clinging onto the headboard behind me with both hands. She lowers herself onto my waiting tongue, gasping when my tongue reaches up to her clit.

I lick her clit, flicking my tongue back and forth and side to side. Amelia moans and moves her hips in time with my licking, pressing herself down onto my tongue. I can feel her juices running down my chin. My shoulder might be out of action, but my tongue definitely isn't.

Amelia is moving her hips faster as her orgasm approaches and I press my tongue firmly against her sweet pussy, pressing up and moving it side to side, no longer licking her clit in teasing little laps.

Amelia moans again and I feel her clit tense up and then a wave of liquid floods over my face as she screams my name. I imagine her body going taut, elongating, her head coming back as pleasure courses through her. I keep licking her, pushing her deeper into her orgasm. I hear her gasping, panting and whimpering. I love that I have this effect on her, that I can turn her to jelly as easily as she does to me.

Her whole body shudders as another rush of liquid gushes from her as she screams my name again, her voice hoarse and ragged. The sound is raw with pure animal desire. Slowly her body relaxes, her muscles turn floppy as her orgasm begins to recede. For a moment, she comes down heavily on my face and I'm surrounded by the smell and feel of her open pussy. It feels so good having her this close to me. After a second, she lifts her ass up and I draw in a deep breath as she does the same.

Amelia begins to move, shimmying her way back down my body, being noticeably careful until she's past my shoulders. She pauses when she's straddling my belly and she leans down and kisses me. Her tongue snakes into my mouth and I know she's tasting her orgasm on my lips, on my tongue. I run my fingers up and down her spine as she kisses me hungrily.

She pulls her lips from mine and kisses her way down my neck. Keeping her body low, she moves backwards, trailing her hard nipples over my body with a feather light touch, teasing me and bringing my senses to blazing life. Never has a woman consumed all my wits the way she does. She's all I can see, hear, taste, and touch. I can still appreciate her sweetness on my tongue and smell her lustful scent in the air.

She sits over my cock and lowers herself until her lips cover it. Then she moves back and forth, making me groan with frustration. I need to be inside of her. Right now. She bends at the waist and flicks her tongue over one of my nipples, sending electricity rippling through my body. Softly she kisses the center of my chest, then covers one nipple with her mouth. She sucks it hard, then she bites down on it, making me gasp with pleasure and pain.

She comes back up, smiling down at me, looking pretty satisfied with herself. She rubs her lips across mine, but when I go to deepen the kiss, she pulls away, leaving me wanting more.

She lifts herself, and reaching beneath her pussy, grabs my cock. Holding it by the base she lowers herself onto it. We moan in tandem as she pushes herself slowly all the way down, taking my full length inside of herself. Her pussy is tight, warm, and wet.

And it's mine. All mine. She's mine.

She moves slowly, lifting herself until I'm almost out of her, before she comes back down, taking me back inside of her delicious, tortured inch by delicious, tortured inch. She does this slow, sensual movement until my eyes are screwed tight shut, my ass is raised away from the bed, my hands are balled into fists at my sides, and I'm moaning her name. Without warning she slams down hard, taking all of me inside of her.

Then, as suddenly as she had slammed down, she stops moving.

My eyes fly open, wondering what the hell is going on. Amelia is sitting still, running her hands over her body. She winks at me as her hands move to her breasts, kneading them and then tugging on her nipples. I swallow hard, watching the show as she trails her fingers down her stomach and pushes them into her pussy, lifting the hood, and massaging her clit.

She's a complete joy to watch, and although my cock is screaming at me to move and bring me some relief from the pressure in my stomach and my balls, I'm mesmerized by the sight of her. Her head is tilted back slightly, with her chin jutting out. Her eyes are almost closed, and her lips are pulled back in a half smile, slightly parted. Her tongue snakes out and runs over her lips leaving them moist and gleaming.

And her body is covered in a fine sheen of sweat that makes her skin glow, and as she moves, her breasts jiggle in time with her probing fingers. She's starting to moan as she brings herself close to the edge. I'm caught and utterly enthralled by the performance, when she starts to move herself up and down on my cock again. Once again pleasure assaults me.

I can't take my eyes off Amelia as she comes hard.

Her mouth drops open in a silent scream, her face twisted with ecstasy. Her back arches as she continues to move, riding me faster and faster. She pulls her fingers away from her lips and brings her head up, her eyes open now. She brings her hand to her mouth and sucks her glistening fingers.

Desire floods through me, making my cock throb, and my stomach clench. I don't want to let go yet though. I don't want this to be over. Amelia keeps moving, slowing the pace back down a little and I know she doesn't want this to end yet either. She leans forward slightly and pushes fingers through her pussy lips before running them over my lips. Immediately, I suck her fingers into my mouth. I taste her juices on them as I run my tongue up and down them and between them, lapping at every inch of her skin.

She pulls her fingers back out of my mouth and runs them over my chest, sending scurries of goosebumps running back and forth across my skin. She isn't holding back now. She ups the pace, throwing herself up and down my shaft. Her breasts are bouncing wildly, and she looks absolutely fucking amazing as she embraces her sexuality.

Her face contorts again as she comes hard, her pussy clenching tightly around me. She screams my name as she moves her hips side to side and then in a circle. She's driving me absolutely wild, and I can't hold back any longer. My orgasm blasts through me, sending waves of pleasure coursing through my entire body.

I spurt into her, filling her with my juices as my cock

goes absolutely nuts inside of her, pulsing with pleasure. Her muscles tighten around me in a tight grip, taking my breath away for a moment as fireworks explode inside of me. My cock spurts more into her and I suck in a breath that sears my throat and comes out in a secret whisper, Amelia's name over and over again.

Then I slip out of her, spent. She stays in place on my lap for a moment, her head still thrown back before she moves away and lays down beside me, panting for breath.

She moves closer to me, snuggling against my side. I want to wrap my arms around her and hold her close to me, but my body is like lead and I don't have the energy to move. Once Amelia's breathing returns to normal, she fixes that for me. She lifts my arm, draping it around her shoulders and then she snuggles closer, her head on my chest.

"I don't want to leave you," she whispers long after I thought she had fallen asleep.

"I don't want you to leave me either, but it won't be for long. And when you come back, we will never ever be apart again. I promise." I whisper back.

She tightens her hold on me, making my shoulder pulse with pain, but I don't say anything. I let her hold me as tightly as she wants to. Her hold begins to relax as she falls asleep, and I sigh. I really don't want her to leave me, but it's the only way I can guarantee her safety.

It's worth a few days apart to have her for the rest of my life.

I try to stay awake, to make the time we have left together feel a little longer, but my eyes have other ideas. The adrenaline has long since left my system and the testosterone that kept me awake during our lovemaking has pretty much faded away, leaving me feeling spent.

I kiss the top of Amelia's head, breathing in the scent of her hair, then I let myself fall asleep inside the circle of her sleeping arms.

36

VIKTOR

https://www.youtube.com/watch?v=pTOC_qoNLTk

These have been the longest two weeks of my life.
Every minute has felt like an hour, every hour like a day and every day like an eternity. Not to mention the nights. The nights are the worst. At least through the daytime I have something to think about other than Amelia, something to keep my mind occupied, but at night there is only her, the memory of her scent, her body, her taste... Sending Amelia away, even temporarily and even for her own safety, was by far the hardest thing I've ever had to do.

The morning she had to leave, we woke up early even though we were both still exhausted and we made love. Twice. I didn't want to let her go and I know she didn't want to either. We lay in each other's arms for a long time.

Neither of us speaking as if we knew that words would break the magical spell and the day would start for real.

I remember laying there, looking into Amelia's beautiful eyes and starting to tell myself we could have one more day. What difference would it make? For sure Igor wouldn't come back to the estate so soon. But even in that brief fantasy, there was a little voice in the back of my head that kept asking what would happen if he did.

I knew that no matter how much I wanted her to stay with me, I couldn't risk it. I had to let her go. The chances of anything happening that day were very slim, but the chances of Igor getting onto my estate in the first place had been super slim and he had managed that.

Besides, I knew with Amelia around for another day, even another hour, would mean I would want to spend it with her, and I couldn't afford to be distracted any longer. I had already let myself be distracted and it almost ended in disaster. I had to stop being selfish and put all my focus into finding Igor.

I finally convinced her it was time to go, and we got up and dressed, dragging out every step of the process for as long as we could. Amelia packed her things. Watching that was hard – it felt like she was leaving me for good, but the fact she kept stopping to kiss me told me another story. Her kiss reminded me it was temporary, that she would be back in my arms sooner rather than later, that I wasn't losing her.

When we kissed goodbye, it was a kiss that lingered, one that stayed with me long after she was gone. I felt like I could still taste her on my lips hours later. The kiss was more than just a kiss. It was a promise that this was only temporary and that we would be together again soon.

It was a kiss full of love and hope; it felt eternal.

Even on that first day, hell in that first hour, it killed me not to contact Amelia. She sent me a text message to tell me exactly where the trailer was as we had discussed and then that was it. Our contact was done until after Igor was dealt with.

The two weeks that have passed since she had to leave have been like hell on earth. Worse maybe. I could cope with torture, fire and brimstone, anything, as long as I have her. But I don't. Not now. It's been too long. I physically crave Amelia, she's like a drug that keeps me going back for more, always wanting more. Needing more.

And having her gone feels horribly similar to what happened with Lisa. How I pushed my grief and longing aside then and went looking for revenge, not letting myself rest for even a moment until it was done. Several times over the last two weeks, I've felt this overwhelming grief rising up in my chest and I have to take a few moments to breathe and talk myself down from it, reminding myself that Amelia isn't dead, isn't gone. But I'm handling the situation in pretty much the same way. Trying not to feel my feelings, throwing myself into looking for Igor instead. But at night, I can't help but think of Amelia, can't help but wish with all my heart that she was here beside me.

I picture myself kissing her sensuous lips, caressing her body. I see myself fucking her until she's lost in her pleasure. I hear her saying my name in that raw voice she uses when she's mid-orgasm. To my horror I dreamed of her. In bed with some other guy, saying his name instead of mine. I see him touching her, fucking her. In my nightmare she laughs at me, telling me she never loved me. I woke up bathed in sweat and had to slowly calm myself down by reminding myself she was coming back – that I know she loves me as much as I love her.

I swear I'm going crazy without Amelia.

Several times I've driven out almost to the trailer park, and each time I get as far as the turn off from the main road before I've talked myself out of it, reminding myself Amelia's safety is more important than my desire to see her.

And I've driven away again, empty, heartbroken, and crazy with longing. Before Amelia, I never really believed being lovesick was a real thing. I always thought it was something teenagers dreamed up because they didn't know how to put their feelings into words. I believe it exists now. How can I not believe in it when I'm fucking living it?

So yes, to say the last two weeks have been hard would be an understatement. And that's without even considering the fact that Igor seems once more to have vanished off the face of the earth. I'm confident he hasn't left the country though. I know he won't be going anywhere until he's finished what he started. And the fact that I'm still alive tells me he isn't finished.

The evening of the day Amelia left, I had a meeting with Lenny and Jerome again, demanding a progress report from the two of them. Lenny told me neither of the guards had seen or heard anything suspicious. They reported that one moment they were fine and the next moment they were fighting to stay awake. The next thing either of them remembered after that was waking up at Lenny's place. The toxicology report had come back showing they had both been drugged with heavy but over the counter sedatives – the kind anyone could buy from anywhere. The drugs had been in their coffee.

Lenny had followed up on both leads. Unsurprisingly,

the medication route had turned up nothing of any use. There were just too many options, and Igor wouldn't have had to say or do anything to stand out to get them. He would have just bought them from a pharmacy or supermarket, a face in a crowd, nothing memorable about the transaction. Even if Lenny stumbled across the right store, there was no guarantee anyone would remember Igor, and even if they did, it wouldn't give us anything useful. We already knew he bought the drugs, and it's not like he would've been discussing his plans for them with the cashier.

The coffee shop had turned up something a little bit more interesting. It was the one all of the guards used daily – the one on the road to my estate. One of Lenny's men had 'persuaded' the young barista to talk. He explained how a man had approached him and gave him the description of the two gate guards and he had confirmed they were regulars. The man had offered him a huge sum of money to put the drugs in their coffees. He had refused at first, but then he found out it was only a perfectly legal, over the counter sedative that wouldn't harm them, and he had agreed to do it. I'd been fuming then, demanding to know what Lenny planned on doing to him.

Lenny had shaken his head. He explained to me that the barista was only a kid – barely eighteen – and that Igor, or a man matching Igor's description at least, had offered him a sum of money big enough to get him through college. It was life changing for the kid for something that in his mind was essentially harmless.

Igor's story had been that he had messed up at work and he wanted to be able to put his mistake right without his colleagues watching over him. It was a stretch of a story, but I could see how the kid had chosen to believe it. As pissed off as I was, I had to admit I didn't really blame the kid for taking the offer. It really was an offer you just couldn't refuse in his position, and it's not like he'd drugged them with heroin or something.

As interesting as it was to learn how Igor had taken out the gate guards, none of this information helped me to find him. It did explain how he had gotten access to my estate though, and it saved the jobs of the gate guards, and stopped their heads from rolling. It was hardly their fault. They hadn't even broken from their normal routine.

Lenny also informed me about all the added security measures he had put in place. I was tempted to ask him to put some men in the trailer park, but it would ruin the impression Amelia and I had broken up. I had to make it look as though I didn't care one way or the other about what happened to her, and if I put men in the trailer park, it would make her more of a target because it would be clear that I did care about what happened to her.

Jerome told me his team was searching all of Igor's usual haunts and some new locations they had scouted out. And that was pretty much it. A lot was happening, but nothing was changing. We were just hitting dead end after dead end.

I felt so useless in that moment, because there was really nothing I could do but sit back and wait for Igor to be found. And plot my revenge, of course. I daydreamed constantly about how I'd make the bastard pay, while in reality I knew I would go in and deal with him quickly and efficiently. I didn't need to make him suffer or drag this out. I just wanted it over and Amelia back in my arms.

The daydreams were just another way of passing the hours without letting myself think about the smell of Amelia's hair or the feel of her lips brushing against mine.

That was easier said than done.

Every day, Jerome checked in with me and every day it was the same old story – sorry boss, nothing to report. It wasn't that his men weren't trying. They were tearing the city apart looking for Igor. It's just he wasn't in any of the places we would have expected him to be in and it was starting to seem like he wasn't in any of the places we wouldn't have expected him to be in either. It was like the guy was fucking supernatural, a shadow that was visible only when he chose to be.

37

VIKTOR

Jerome's men did come close to finding him once, but it was the same story as the day Jerome and I went to the safe house looking for him. They were always just a step or two behind him and always arrived to find him gone. They even found a mug with an inch of still lukewarm coffee in the bottom. They must have missed him by less than fifteen minutes.

The more I heard, the more I knew that I had definitely underestimated Igor. I had believed at first that he was just an entitled druggie, but he was more clever than that. So clever he was starting to make me, and my men look like idiots.

While I waited for news, I went through the motions of going about my day as normal. If Igor had people watching me, I wouldn't give him the satisfaction of letting him think that he had me running scared. I went into the office every day or to one of my other businesses and I did what needed to be done to keep my businesses ticking over nicely.

My secretary organized the compensation payments I'd

promised Lacey and Justine, and on a whim, I sent a similar
payment to Amelia's account. That would give her something to live on until we were together again, and it wouldn't
seem suspicious. In fact, it would seem more suspicious if
she didn't get a payment. This all added to the ruse. She had
witnessed something terrifying and discovered who I really
was, so she left me. She was paid off along with the other
maids to keep her mouth shut. It was a simple and effective
story, and it was much more believable than the version
where she left me the day after a shooting on my estate
without being paid to keep her mouth shut.

I'm sitting in the office now, dealing with emails and
reports. It feels so mundane when I know I should be out
there dealing with Igor, but if Jerome's trained men can't
track him down, then I can't see how I could. My cell phone
rings, and I feel a tingling of hope deep down inside myself
when I see Jerome's name on the screen. I try to ignore the
hope. I've fallen into this trap several times, assuming it was
going to be Jerome calling with good news, telling me he
had Igor's location confirmed, only for it to be an update on
a fresh disappointment or a question about something.

This time, it's different though. I can hear the excitement
in Jerome's voice the second he speaks. It's three simple
words, but they are words that send my whole body into an
adrenaline spike.

"We've got him."

"For real this time?" I ask, trying to remain cautious and
not let myself believe it's really this close to being over.

"For real. We know his exact location and I have men
positioned all around the place so there's no way in hell he
can escape. I'm outside your office now," Jerome says.

"Coming," I say.

I cut off the call, grab my jacket, and leave the office without a word to anyone. If anyone needs me for anything, they'll find out I'm gone pretty quickly. This is way more important than any phone call or signing some letter or something. I don't even wait for the elevator, I take the stairs, running down them two at a time, putting my jacket on as I go. I sprint through the lobby and across the parking lot to Jerome's waiting car.

"How far away is it?" I ask as I slide in.

Jerome fires up the engine and pulls out of the parking lot, the tires squealing. He's not messing about this time. He joins the steadily flowing traffic heading east.

"About a ten-minute drive," he says.

"He's been right under our fucking noses this whole time," I say, in wonder.

"Yeah," Jerome agrees. "But it's not somewhere we ever would have thought to look. I'll be honest, boss, getting the word on this place was a lucky break."

"So, what is it? Some sort of safe house?"

I don't know of any safe houses around these parts, and Jerome's words make me think it's not, but what else could it be? It's not like Igor was just going to rent a house in his own name when he knew my men were looking for him, and it's not like they wouldn't have found him if he had become that cocky.

"He's staying in a property registered to a Michael Fields. Like I said, it was a lucky break. One of the men stumbled onto this information quite by accident. Michael Fields is..."

"Someone who got caught up in the crossfire on one of my drug deals years ago. Just a kid really, didn't deserve to die that way. I remember," I say.

Michael Fields was a part of a rival drug gang. He wasn't

high enough up the chain to be a target of my men, but he was in the wrong place at the wrong time, and during a war over territory, Michael Fields took a bullet and he died.

"Yeah, he did. He was also a good friend of Igor's," Jerome says.

"Huh?" I say. "No wonder he hates my guts…"

"Yeah. Revenge. His plan was to destroy your business, your whole life, from the inside out and then kill you."

"And somehow, all he's done is destroyed himself and soon enough, he'll be the one who's dead."

"Pretty much," Jerome agrees.

He pulls onto a quiet suburb and drives down a short cul-de-sac.

"This is it," he says, nodding at a small but neat house in front of us. "You see now why we weren't looking here?"

I nod. It's the last place in the city we would have looked. I don't think we ever would have bothered coming here at all if one of Jerome's men hadn't gotten the word on the place.

"Michael bought this house years ago, before he got involved with the drugs or the gangs. He left it to Igor in his will," Jerome says.

I shake my head in surprise and get out of the car. Jerome gets out too.

"Wait here," I say. "I want to talk to him alone."

"But, boss…" Jerome says.

"But nothing," I say. "I take it your men are still in position?"

Jerome nods his head.

"Then he can't escape. Give me ten minutes, and if I'm not out, come in and take the fucker down."

Jerome nods his head again and leans on the hood of the car.

"Whatever you say, boss," he agrees.

I see him glance at his watch, noting the time so he knows exactly how long to give me. I'm confident Igor isn't going to be sitting in his living room holding a gun. He has no idea we've found him. I want to go in there and have this out with him man to man, and then I'll end the fucker with my bare hands for everything he's put me and Amelia through.

I make my way up to the house, being careful not to draw attention to myself. I'm dressed in my work clothes, a nice suit and tie, and I know anyone glancing out of their windows won't look at me and think I'm suspicious. In a neighborhood like this, an expensive suit blends in.

I reach the door and try the handle. I'm surprised to find the door unlocked. For all of Igor's trickery, he's gotten cocky. Complacent. He's so sure we won't find him here that he's let his guard down. A locked door wouldn't have saved him anyway. Then I wonder why a man as smart as him would ever be so lax.

I push the door open and step inside as quietly as I can. I close the door behind me, and I make my way across the entrance hall to what I assume is the living room. I take a deep breath and push the door wide open quickly. I expect to see Igor jumping to his feet, panic etched across his face. Instead, I see him sitting in an armchair watching the door. He smiles at me as the door opens and I feel a tingle of nerves run down my spine.

"You took your time, Viktor," he says pleasantly.

I have once more underestimated Igor. He wasn't getting

complacent. He left the door unlocked on purpose. His smile widens.

"I can almost see your brain ticking, Viktor. Yes, I left the door unlocked on purpose. I figured it would be nice if we could have a little chat before we get this over with, and we don't want any of my neighbors calling the police because some buffoon in a suit has kicked my door in, do we?" Igor says.

"No. We most definitely don't want the police showing up here anytime soon. How did you know I was coming?"

I hate giving Igor the upper hand like this, but I'm curious and now I know he was expecting me, there's every chance he does indeed have a gun in his hand, and I want to stall him long enough that Jerome comes in and blasts him away before he has a chance to use it.

"Because I instigated it so you would find out about this place and come here. I figured it was time to end this and it seems fitting that the end should come in my friend's house, don't you think?"

He phrases it like a question, but he doesn't give me a chance to answer him. Not that I really know what I would have said in response anyway. Igor is clever, but there's an air of someone slightly unhinged about him and dealing with people like that is like walking a tightrope. One wrong step and you're done.

"Innocent people are getting hurt now and I hate that," Igor goes on. "Your men think they're pretty clever right now, don't they? Finding the lucky break that led them to me. A talkative bartender. Such a stereotype. Except he was anything but a stereotype. He was paid handsomely to feed your men just enough information to put this all together and find this place, but not quite enough information to make it too easy and make them suspicious. Apparently, he nailed it. I might have to give him a bonus after this is done."

After this is done, the only thing you'll be doing is rotting away in a shallow grave somewhere I think to myself.

"Ok so you got me here. And you're not making a move on me. So why don't you cut to the chase and tell me what you want from me. Money? Is that it?" I ask.

"I don't need your fucking money," he snaps. "I have more money than I know what to do with."

"So, what is it then?" I ask, my voice calm.

"Is the maid alright?" Igor asks, throwing me off slightly. "The one who got shot?"

"The one who you shot, you mean? Yes, she's fine."

"I want an apology," Igor says, jumping back to the original topic. The jumping around is a known tactic, meant to throw a person, but I'm not thrown by it. I practically invented this trick. "For my father and friend."

I move to the couch and sit down, and I see that I've thrown Igor slightly with my casual movement, although he hides it well, the flicker of emotion only showing on his face for half a second before he paints the cocky expression back on.

"It was an accident and Michael's family received more than an apology at the time, Igor. They received a very generous settlement from me. As for your father. I didn't start that war. He wanted my territory and so he tried to assassinate me, but instead murdered my woman and our unborn child. Did you think there would be no retaliation? I did what you're doing now," I say.

He makes a strange high-pitched sound. "Stop talking. Stop making excuses. You killed them. You killed them. And

I want a real apology. I want to hear you say the fucking words. And I want you to mean it."

"Well, for what it's worth, I'm sorry about your friend. He was just a bit player, not important enough for my men to take out. He was just collateral damage, a consequence of the business we were all in. I truly am sorry you lost him, but I will never apologize for your father. I took pleasure in ending his life."

"Collateral damage?" he screams. "Your men killed him because he got in their way. That's almost worse than if he was the intended target."

"Don't sit there on your fucking high horse, Igor. You know how this shit works. Michael was a bit player, but he was still a player. He knew the risks of playing with the big boys. And you sit there judging me for it when you're worse than my men ever were. You shot a fucking maid in my home. An innocent woman."

"I didn't plan on that. She got in the way," Igor says quickly.

"Just like Michael did," I point out.

"But there's a major difference between Michael and that girl, between me and your thugs. Your men shot to kill my brother. I shot that girl in the leg to stop her from interfering."

"So, you're going to take the moral high ground because you're a bad shot?"

"I'm not a bad shot. I didn't want to kill her," Igor snaps.

"Whatever," I say. "You've gotten your apology. It's time to end this once and for all."

"Yes. I suppose it is," Igor says. "You must pay for what you did to my father. A life for a life."

Even after saying it he seems reluctant to act so I stay seated.

I smile at him coldly. "You don't want to kill me, do you? It's not that you don't want me to die – you do want that. But you know the moment I'm gone; your life becomes empty and the grief rushes in. While you're looking for revenge, you have something to focus on. Once I'm gone, there's nothing left to occupy your mind but memories and regrets."

"Don't fucking sit there thinking you know me," Igor snarls.

"But I do know you. Trust me. I've been you."

"You're nothing like me," Igor yells, now sounding completely unhinged.

He jumps to his feet, and I jump to mine half a second behind him. He runs at me with a roar, and I see a flash of silver. Igor has a knife. I sidestep his attack, narrowly avoiding being stabbed. It doesn't deter him, he spins around, more nimble on his feet than his size implies. He comes at me again, and this time, I have nowhere to go. My back is against the wall, but I'm ready for him. I know exactly how to stop him, but I don't get to use my skill.

Igor is almost upon me when the gunshot rings out. His face changes, going from anger to almost comical surprise as the top of his head explodes and he drops to the ground. I smile at Jerome over Igor's dead body.

"You timed that perfectly," I say.

"You said ten minutes, boss. Now I reckon we have about six or seven minutes to disappear before the cops get here."

"We'd better move then."

As we hurry from the house, Jerome pulls his cell phone out.

"It's done," he says to the clean-up guys. "Get in and out quickly. You have less than six minutes."

He cuts the call off without waiting for confirmation, then drops his cell phone back into his pocket.

Jerome pulls off and goes down the cul-de-sac calmly to not call attention to us, but within a few minutes, we're back in the throng of the city traffic, another anonymous car in a stream of endless cars.

I feel lighter than I have in a long time. Igor is gone. I'm free of worry, free of threats. I'm free to get my Amelia back.

"Where to, boss?" Jerome asks, although judging by the smile on his face, I think he knows the answer to that one.

My smile in return is answer enough and Jerome does a U-turn, heading for the trailer park and for the girl of my dreams.

38

AMELIA

The last two weeks have been bad.

Like, really bad.

Not only am I missing Viktor even more than I thought I would, and trust me, I thought I would miss him a lot, but being back here has taken me back to being some dumb, defenseless kid again. It's like my childhood reliving itself, and this time, it's even worse, because this time, I know how much better it can be for me, how much better it was away from this dreary trailer park... and my mother.

If it wasn't for the fact that Viktor would be beside himself if I texted him a new address in the middle of all of this, I honestly would have upped and left by now.

The first day wasn't so bad. In fact, I would go so far as to say the first day was good. My mom was right about the trailer. The one she's living in now is much nicer than the one we moved into with Dan. It's clean, tidy, airy, and bright. And yes, the curtains do fit the windows and unlike Dan's they got opened in the morning. We spent that first day chatting and giggling, catching up, and for that one day, I let myself believe that things would be different this time around. That my mom wasn't going to go out and make the same stupid mistakes all over again.

On the fourth day, my mom came to me looking shifty and I felt the familiar dread in my stomach, the familiar feeling that I was about to be let down. My mom told me she owed a couple of thousand dollars on a credit card – money she insisted she had to use to get away from Dan. She said she used it to pay the security deposit and the first month's rent in advance on this trailer.

I didn't believe that for a second.

There was no way that would have been so expensive, and besides, I'd already seen the clothes with their tags still on them hanging in the closet in the spare bedroom, the shoes still in their boxes stashed underneath the bed. She asked me if I could lend her fifty dollars to make the monthly payment, saying she was a little short this month, but she'd be ok next month, and making it clear how many charges she would have to pay if I couldn't lend her the money.

I knew if I gave it to her, I'd never see it again, but I had it to spare and I told myself it was only fifty dollars. What was fifty dollars compared to years she had fed, clothed and sheltered me? At that point, I was still hopeful she could be different, we could be different.

I gave her the money and she smiled coyly and started to tell me all about the interest on the card and how she would be paying back nearly twice what she had borrowed if she paid the card off monthly. I was disappointed, I wanted to cry, but I wouldn't show how hurt I was. I told her I would pay the interest, hoping she'd then give it up and walk away so I mourn the death of my little dream, but she didn't.

Delighted that she had manipulated me into agreeing to pick up her bill she then suggested I call Viktor and tell him I was owed money, more than what he had put into my account. I stared at her in shock. She had taken my card, checked the balance in my account, and seen the lumpsum Viktor had put into my account.

Without showing the sadness in my heart, I pointed out that Viktor had already given me far more than I was owed. She shrugged and grinned that shifty little grin again and told me to call it alimony. She basically suggested I bug Viktor twenty-four hours a day until he got so sick of hearing from me that he paid me to leave him alone.

Fortunately, I hadn't let her in on the truth of Viktor and my real situation. I didn't trust her not to talk – my mother was a gossip and there was no doubt in my mind that if she knew what was going on with Viktor and me, that everyone she worked with and half of the trailer park residents would soon know it too, and then whoever they told and whoever those people told, and so on and so on until the whole fucking city knew the situation.

But even if Viktor and I had really split up, I wouldn't be doing that. I was perfectly capable of living without a man paying for me and if my mom wasn't, then that was her problem.

I told her in no uncertain terms I wasn't planning on doing any such thing.

She pretended to understand, but the cogs where her brain should have been were still turning, and a couple of days later, she suggested maybe I should give Viktor another chance. It was clear why – she thought if I married into money, she'd be set for life.

Again, I made it clear it wouldn't be happening. I told

her Viktor and I were done and I wouldn't be calling him or texting him, and I certainly wouldn't be accepting any money from him. She got pretty huffy then, and tried to make out she was just looking out for me.

Learning that my mom didn't really want me back because she actually loved me was painful, but that she wanted me back just to access someone she had decided was a meal ticket was even harder to take. My mother was greedy to almost immoral proportions. I had missed that completely.

The worst part of being back in my old life came on day five. I had been into town and wandered the shops for a few hours to kill some time. I debated calling some of the girls I worked with to meet for lunch or something, but I didn't. It would've been nice to see them, but I didn't want to lie to them, and I would've had to.

When I returned to the trailer, I couldn't believe my eyes. Dan was there. He was so brazen, so smug, just spread out on the couch, his arm wrapped around my mom's shoulders, like he was the king of the fucking castle.

I didn't mince my words when I saw him. I demanded to know what the hell he was doing there. My mom explained that Dan had come and apologized to her, and they were going to try again.

The whole time, he sat there with a smirk on his ugly face.

I went to my room, praying that Viktor would hurry up and fix this mess so I could leave this place and go back to my life with him, the life I loved. I was desperately unhappy, I even thought about calling him. He'd said to call him in an emergency, but I wasn't sure this counted.

Sure, I hated Dan and the thought of him being

anywhere near me made my skin crawl, but was it bad enough for me to involve Viktor and put him in a place where he had to worry about me again?

I told myself I'd wait and see. Maybe Dan being back in my mom's life, and by association being back in my life, wouldn't last long. That, it turned out, was merely wishful thinking, because he did last.

Oh, he fucking lasted alright.

He moved out of his trailer and into ours, and I slowly put the pieces together. My mom and Dan had never really split up. That was all just a lie my mom fed me to get me here. Dan had been talking for a while about moving trailers, and that's what they had done. He'd kept his for a couple of extra days to work on the ruse that they had split up. Why? To try to get money out of me, or more accurately, out of Viktor.

My mom must have thought she'd won the lottery when I came to her with my bags packed and told her how I had spoken to Viktor about maybe moving back in with her for just a while, because Viktor and I were over. The sympathy wasn't real. She was just seeing the dollar signs lighting up before her eyes.

The whole time, she'd been playing me like a tune.

She really was the lowest of the low, and if one good thing comes out of this whole mess it's that I will never, ever be taken in by her act again. I've had my eyes well and truly opened to the person that she truly is.

It didn't hurt quite as much as it could have because I had Viktor in my life now. I had genuinely wanted a relationship with my mom again, but as long as I had Viktor, I could do without that relationship. I don't need toxic people around me who are there just to use me and drag me down.

39

AMELIA

A few times I started to worry if Viktor had forgotten about me, that he had just decided he didn't want me anymore and he wasn't coming back for me. I shook the thoughts away, reminding myself of the way he looked at me, the way he touched me.

He will come back.

I refused to give up hope. For a horrible moment around day eleven, I was struck with the idea that this was taking too long, and if I genuinely believed Viktor loved me, which I did, then that could mean only one thing. Things had gone wrong with Igor and Viktor was hurt, or worse, dead.

I dismissed the idea after a few nauseating, disconcerting moments that rocked me to my core. Viktor knew where I was, and that meant Jerome knew where I was too. If anything had happened to Viktor, Jerome would have told me.

I prayed that whatever the holdup was, it would be over soon. The pretense of Dan and my mom being over or trying to patch things up or whatever the story was soon went away and Dan moved into the trailer with us. It just kind of happened and no one even bothered to try to pretend anymore.

As much as I don't believe for a second, I did anything to lead Dan on the first time around when he tried to rape me, I've made sure to wear nothing but jeans and long-sleeved tops that don't show even the tiniest hint of cleavage. Unsurprisingly, that doesn't stop Dan from leering at me and it doesn't stop the comments. It seems that just having a pulse is enough to inadvertently lead Dan on.

The new trailer has fast become the old trailer. Closed curtains, overflowing ashtrays with empty bottles and cans everywhere. It seems my mom has stopped trying to pick up after Dan and that falls to me now. At first, I didn't do it, but I soon realized I was cutting my nose off to spite my face. Dan and my mom just didn't seem to see the mess, or if they did, it didn't bother them. It bothered me though and I accepted that if I wanted it gone, I'd have to be the one to get rid of it.

I've become a regular Cinderella, only I have a wicked mother and a wicked stepfather. But I'm confident that my prince will come. Soon Viktor please, before I turn into a pumpkin or something

There has been one spark of joy in the midst of my misery though. One thing that lights me up. Two days ago, I found out I'm pregnant. I snuck off to the doctor's office to confirm what the home testing kit had showed me, and he confirmed it. It's the thing that keeps me going. When things get bad, I lock myself away in my room and I lay on the bed, picturing Viktor and me with a baby.

I literally can't wait to tell him my news.

Naturally, I've kept my news a secret from my mom and

Dan. I can only imagine the way my mom would react. She will then see the baby as her meal ticket instead of me, and she will insist I call Viktor immediately and inform him about the baby and tell him exactly how much money she expects to receive. And Dan? Dan would make my life even more unbearable. I can just imagine the insults, the sneering, his thoughts on how I got pregnant and then lost the father.

Aside from the practical reasons I have kept my pregnancy a secret from my mom and Dan, there's another reason too. The thought of telling them, the thought of them knowing something so personal about me turns my stomach. Viktor should know first, but even after I tell him, I don't think I'll be telling my mom and Dan. Not for a while at least. The thought of telling them makes the whole thing seem tainted somehow, like my little baby will have their dirty little paws all over it, seeing what they can get out of the situation.

I'm in my room now, secretly buoyed once more by the image of Viktor and me starting a family. I know he'll be pleased when I finally get to tell him we're having a baby. He can't wait to be a father, and now he's not going to have to wait much longer. I keep picturing how the nursery will look, cream and yellow with lovely soft toys.

I wonder if we'll have a boy or a girl, and what we might name the baby. I'm thinking maybe Emma or Sophie for a girl, Alex or Riley for a boy. Or maybe if it's a boy he should be named Viktor after his father. I know I'm getting ahead of myself, but I'm so excited about it, I just can't help myself. Maybe Laura for a girl and Joshua for a boy. Or Harry for a boy and Amelia for a girl. I smile up at my ceiling. I'm way,

way ahead of myself for sure. Heck, at this rate, I'll be looking at schools and colleges next.

I hear the trailer door open, then slam closed. I sit up. Dan is out somewhere, most likely in a bar drinking away the money my mom claims not to have. The door was my mom going out to work. It was nice of her to say goodbye when she left.

I used to pity my mom, working so many hours to feed Dan's habit. But now, I just can't bring myself to feel sorry for her anymore, not after the stunt she's pulled. Now all I think of when I hear her going out to work to support Dan's drinking habit is what a monumental idiot she is. And then I feel angry that she somehow thought I would be willing to step into the role of supporting Dan through Viktor. They say the apple doesn't fall far from the tree, but in this case, the apple has landed in another freaking country, we're that far apart.

I'm glad she's gone out though, even if she didn't bother to say goodbye to me. It means I can do a bit of tidying up without having to make any sort of small talk with her, and then I fix myself a sandwich and eat it in the living room for a change. I refuse to go out there when Dan or my mom are around. I have nothing much to say to either of them, and I don't like being around Dan, always wondering if he'll try to rape me again.

I think he's likely learned his lesson with that one, but you never can tell with someone so dense and deluded. I'm pretty sure I'm safe this time around though - although my mom took his side the first time he tried to rape me, he'd be hard pushed to sell the idea of me trying to seduce him when I'm always wrapped up with only my hands and my face showing. Surely even my deluded mother couldn't believe I'm trying to seduce Dan dressed like this.

I go through to the living room, shaking my head at the mess. Let me clean up before I eat. I grab a trash bag and scoop up all of Dan's empty bottles and cans. I empty the ashtray and the aluminum take-out tray with congealed remains of a curry. I take all the trash down to the trash cans and then I come back and run the tap, rolling up my sleeves, ready to tackle the dishes. There aren't many.

Dan isn't civilized enough to use glasses or plates. There's just the plate and fork my mom used and a fork that she must have persuaded Dan to use. Plus, the cups from breakfast and two cereal bowls. None of them are mine, but it's nothing new that I end up doing the dishes too. If I don't, they'll just pile up until they're moldy and the whole trailer stinks of partially rotten food. The stale beer and cigarette smell is bad enough.

I fill the little sink with hot water and add some dish soap. I've barely gotten started when the trailer door opens. My heart sinks when a drunken, swaying Dan steps in. He pushes past me although there is plenty of room to get around me without touching me. I don't know for sure if it's intentional or if he's just so drunk that navigating around me was too hard for him.

He goes to the living room, throws himself onto the trailer's answer to a couch and turns the TV on. I keep washing the dishes, telling myself I'll be done shortly and then I'll go straight back to my room. I might even go out and stay out until my mother will be back. As much as I have nothing to say to her, at least I'm confident Dan will keep his dirty hands and his inane thoughts to himself while she's home.

40

VIKTOR

I 'm physically sitting in the car, but mentally, I feel like I'm floating on air. In minutes, I'll be with my Amelia again. I'm going to pull her into my arms and kiss her like I've never kissed her before. Then I'm going to take her home and make love to her all night long, and we'll never, ever look back.

I'm never letting her go again.

I really hope the two weeks we've been apart have gone well for Amelia and she wasn't as miserable as I've been for every second of them. I know she was hoping her mom had really changed this time, and while I don't think her mother is a useless human being, I really want Amelia to have a relationship with her again if that's what she still wants.

Jerome turns off the main road and drives down a thin, winding road with no traffic. It's the road I've driven up to so many times over the last two weeks, but I've always forced myself to turn away from. And now here I am again, only this time, finally I don't have to turn away.

I feel my heart skip a beat when I see a sign saying

Sunny Vale Trailer Park is coming up. I can feel butterflies swirling in my stomach and while I laugh at myself inside for acting like a lovesick teenager, I don't want the feeling to go away. I love being in love with Amelia and I want to feel every part of it, every little emotion that goes along with it.

We drive beneath the Welcome to Sunny Vale sign, and for the first time, I see the trailer park Amelia was living in before we met. I have nothing in particular against trailer parks, but this one is ancient looking, really run down. It looks like it might have been a nice enough place to live in back in the eighties or nineties. Amelia deserves better than this.

I give Jerome directions as we make our way through dilapidated trailers.

"Fucking hell. If I'd have known it was this bad, I never would have let her come back here."

"It's better to live a bit rough for a couple of weeks than it is to be at risk," Jerome says.

"Yeah, I guess," I agree.

But she's never going back to living this life ever again, I vow to myself. She's never going to live like anything but the queen she is from now on.

We pull up outside of the right trailer. It doesn't look as old and decrepit as some of the other trailers, but it's hardly welcoming. All the curtains are pulled tightly closed as if Amelia's mom is afraid someone might see in. It's not because she's ashamed of where she has to live since the trailers around hers are all in a worse state than this one so there's nothing she'd have to be ashamed about there.

"I won't be long," I say to Jerome as I get out of the car.

I have no intention of dragging this out. I just want my Amelia back home. If things have gone well though and

Amelia and her mom are getting along, I'll obviously have to make the effort to get to know her, so maybe I'll stay for a cup of coffee or whatever and spend some time getting to know the woman. It'll be hard to be nice to the woman knowing the way she made Amelia's childhood so miserable, but if Amelia can forgive her, then I'll have to find a way to accept her, or at least put on a damned good show that I have.

Jerome nods, opens the glove compartment, and pulls out a newspaper. I walk quickly along a short concrete path that's cracked and full of weeds growing through it.

Despite this depressing place, I am deliriously happy at the thought of being reunited with Amelia in just seconds. It's hard to believe she's behind that door, and I have to pinch myself to convince myself this is real and not a new form of torture my nightmares have conjured up.

41

AMELIA

I finish washing the dishes and grab a grubby looking tea towel. It's not dirty, it's just stained. I start drying the dishes with it. Dan looks over at me, but I ignore him, forcing myself to keep drying the bowl in my hand and pretend I haven't noticed his eyes on me. He mutes the TV.

"Get me a beer."

No 'will you' no 'please', just the demand. I debate telling him to get his own beer, or better yet, to go fuck himself and die, but I don't. It'll be easier just to give him the beer. It will keep him distracted while he has a drink in his hand. I bite my tongue, and as painful as it is to respond to Dan's commands, I put the now dry bowl down and go to the fridge and grab a can of beer. I dutifully take it to Dan and put it on the table. He looks at me with a sly smile and he reaches out towards the can of beer, but instead of taking the can, he changes direction and clamps his hand around my wrist.

"What are you doing?" I ask angrily.

"We can't possibly be back to you pretending you don't want me," he slurs. "You came back, didn't you?"

"Yes, I came back. Because my mother lied to me and told me you were gone," I reply furiously.

I try to pull my wrist from his hand, but his grip is strong for a drunk guy. I can't get it free.

"Bullshit," Dan says. "You came back to finish what we started. Well, your mom won't be home for hours so you can have it."

He gestures to his crotch with his other hand and it's all I can do not to retch in disgust.

"Let go of me, Dan," I order.

He jumps to his feet and suddenly I see he's not as drunk as he was making himself out to be. The brushing up against me was intentional. He's still holding my wrist as he steps closer to me. I back up with each step he takes towards me, but that doesn't put him off. He grins at me, knowing what I know. A few more steps and I'll be up against the wall with nowhere else to go.

I'm not letting this happen again. I won't let this man touch me. There's one way I will be able to get free. I stop backing away from Dan.

"You know what? You're right. I don't know why I keep denying it. I think I just feel guilty because of my mom."

He strokes my cheek and I have to stop the shudder from running through me. I even manage to nuzzle against his palm slightly. I hate myself for doing it, but it's the only way I can think of to get away from him.

"You don't have to feel guilty, Amelia. You've tried to fight it, but when two people have a connection like we do, fighting it just prolongs it. It was always going to happen, and I think deep down, even your mom knows that."

I nod, pretending like he's convincing me. I can't help but wonder if he really believes this bullshit he's talking about or if he just thinks it makes him sound intelligent and less like a sexual predator.

"She can't be mad, can she? I mean, we can't help being attracted to each other," I say, playing along, telling him what I think he wants to hear.

"Exactly," Dan agrees.

I smile at him shyly.

"Kiss me, Dan. Before I change my mind," I say.

My plan works. Dan releases my wrist and cups my face in his hands. I don't hesitate. I bring my released hand up and slam the beer can against his temple. Dan roars in anger and steps back from me, glaring at me in pain, shock, and pure fury. I feel fear gripping me. I really thought that would knock him out, or at least leave him dazed enough that I could run from the trailer.

Instead, all I've done is infuriate him. He pulls his fist back and slams it forward, punching me in the stomach.

"You little bitch," he roars.

The breath leaves me in a rush as Dan's fist hits my stomach. I fall to the ground, wheezing and gasping. I cross my arms over my stomach, trying to protect the precious bundle inside of me. If I lose this baby because of Dan, I swear I will kill him. I'll wait until he's asleep and I'll cut the fucker's throat.

He pulls his foot back, aiming a kick at my face. I fight the instinct in me that wants me to move my arms to protect my face. My baby is more important than me. He can do what he likes to my face, but I won't let him near my stomach again. I tense up, waiting for the agony of his foot connecting with my face, but it doesn't come.

Before his foot can make contact with my face, he's dragged backwards, pulled away from me and thrown to the floor and I see Viktor towering over him, his face the picture of anger.

My prince came back for me. Just in time to defeat my evil stepfather and save the day.

42

VIKTOR

I reach the trailer door, and raise my fist to knock on it, but before my fist connects with the door, I hear a man yelling from inside, his voice ugly and angry.

"You little bitch," he shouts.

I don't bother to knock after that. That angry voice has to be Dan's, and if it's not Amelia he's having a go at, then it's her mom. I throw open the trailer door and step inside expecting to see Dan and either Amelia or her mom arguing. I sure as hell don't expect what I see. Amelia is lying on the ground, her knees pulled up into the fetal position and she's holding her stomach and wheezing. And some scruffy looking fat bastard who smells like a brewery is standing over her, his foot pulled back like he's about to kick her in the face.

I lose it. I see red. Dan is damned lucky I don't have a gun on me or he'd be dead right now. In a flash I cover the distance between us and grab Dan by the shoulders, pulling him away from Amelia. His weight and his surprise work against him, as does the fact he's drunk.

He stumbles and I let him fall and then I do to him what he was about to do to Amelia. I pull my foot back and kick him hard, square in the face. Blood bursts from his nose and his mouth. I give him a few more hard kicks on his ribs and he writhes and screams like a stuck pig. I'm pretty sure I've broken a few ribs. At any other time I could have gone to town on him, keep kicking him until there's no life left in him, but I don't want Amelia to see that side of me.

I force myself to turn away from him and go to Amelia who has pushed herself up into a sitting position.

"Are you alright?" I ask, reaching down and helping her to her feet.

"I am now," she says with a broken smile.

I want to pull her into my arms and kiss her, but I can hear Dan getting back to his feet behind me. I turn so I can see him if he tries anything, although he is in so much pain he can barely stand. He looks angry but cowed. I return my focus to Amelia.

"What happened?" I ask her.

"That bitch smacked me in the head with that," Dan answers for her, pointing at a beer can I hadn't noticed on the ground. "I'm not proud of what I did next, but it was just an instinctive reaction. I hit her back."

Amelia laughs and I frown.

"Sorry," she says. "It really isn't funny. But I'm just laughing at Dan's fantasy story. I did hit him with the beer can. But only because he was trying to rape me."

"You asked for it," Dan says. "You told me you wanted me."

"I said that so you'd let go of my wrist and I could get away from you," Amelia snaps.

"Bullshit," Dan says. "You just don't want him to know how you can't control yourself around a real man."

He's still talking when my fist slams into his mouth. He goes reeling, falling onto the drab grey couch that runs around the edge of the living room area of the trailer. His eye is already swelling shut and my fist stops his words. I stalk over to him.

"Get up," I say.

Dan doesn't move. I reach out and grab his shirt, pulling him to his feet.

"Get up you fucking coward," I shout. "How dare you lay a hand on my girlfriend?"

I look at Dan's dumb face and I want to do something that will remind him of this day every time he looks in the mirror. I release his shirt once he's on his feet and slam my fist into his mouth. He goes back down and spits out blood and teeth. I start to reach for him again, wanting to pull him back to his feet once more when a shrill voice rings out behind me.

"What the hell is going on here?"

"Dan tried to rape me again. And sorry but this time, you can't try to blame what I was wearing. It's just because he's a worthless piece of shit. Luckily this time, I don't have to rely on my mom to protect me, the one person who is meant to be there for me through thick and thin. Instead, I have Viktor."

"Violet, call the police," Dan says.

"Yes, please do," I smile. "I'd be very interested to hear their thoughts on who is responsible when someone tries to rape a woman."

Violet looks from me to Dan to Amelia and back to me again. She shakes her head slowly.

"I'm not calling the police," she says. "I know Amelia's a troublemaker, but I don't want to make trouble like that for her."

"For me? Are you seriously this dumb, Mom?" Amelia says, shaking her head.

"I'm going to pretend you didn't just say that. Now if you don't mind, I have to go to work. I only came back because I forgot my name badge and it seems like it's a good thing I did. Amelia, I want you out and take your brute of a boyfriend with you."

She smiles nastily and turns to me.

"And by the way, she doesn't think that much of you. She chose me over you once before. Always remember that," Amelia's mom says.

I throw my head back and laugh, surprising myself, but I just can't help it. It's like these two live in some alternate universe where they live believing their own bullshit and refusing to see the real truth.

"Not only are you a terrible mother, you are also a stupid, unthinking woman," I say. "Do you really think she would choose you over me after everything you've put her through?"

Violet looks from me to Amelia in shock. "Are you going to let this man speak to me like that?"

43

VIKTOR

I don't know how this will go, whether I've overstepped the mark, but I just couldn't stand to see the glee on Violet's face as she lorded over her daughter and me.

"Why not? That's what you've always done," Amelia says.

Violet shakes her head. "You think you're better than me. Let me tell you now you'll never be able to keep a man like him. He'll be cheating on you in no time and then you'll be making excuses for him too. Just like me."

I take a step closer to her and she instinctively shrinks back from me.

"You should take notice of what I'm saying here. You and your rapist boyfriend," I say, my voice low and threatening. "Because if either of you so much as come near Amelia ever again, you might find that you disappear."

"You won't see either of us around her again. She's nothing but trouble. You'll see it for yourself." She turns to her daughter. "Just give it time. And Amelia? When he does, don't even think about coming back here."

"You know what, Mom? I'd sooner live in a fucking box under a bridge before I came back here," Amelia cries.

"Let's go, Amelia," I say.

"Just give me a minute. I need to pack my stuff."

"Leave it," I say. "We'll buy you some new stuff. We don't want anything that's tainted with the stink of this fucking place."

Amelia smiles at me and puts her hand in mine and we walk out of the trailer without looking back. I lead Amelia down the steps and start to make my way back down the short path to the waiting car. Amelia stops abruptly and when I turn back, I see she's crying.

"Hey come on, it's ok. You're safe now," I say, wrapping her in my arms, instantly conscious of her body pressed against mine. "God, Amelia, I'm so sorry. If I had any idea what I was sending you back to in there I would've found another way."

"It's ok," she sobs. "I was the one who was stupid enough to believe my mom had changed."

She pulls back from me and looks up at me, tears running down her face.

"Viktor, there's something I have to tell you," she says. "It wasn't meant to be like this. It was meant to be happy. I've been so excited about it, but now, Dan has ruined everything."

"It's ok, Amelia, just tell me," I whisper.

My heart is breaking for her as she sobs and shakes in my arms.

"I... I'm pregnant," she says. Before I can react, she hurries on. "But Dan. He punched me in the stomach. What if he hurt the baby?"

Anger floods me and I want to go back into the trailer

and finish what I started with Dan, but Amelia is looking up at me again, pleading with me with her eyes to be there for her. I swallow the anger down and hold her closer for a moment, knowing that if I go back in there, I will end him, and the fact is being here for her now is more important than taking revenge on a pathetic excuse for a human being like Dan. He's the sort of guy who will get dealt with one day anyway. He'll overstep the mark with the wrong person one day and get his comeuppance.

"Let's get you to the hospital and get you checked out," I say, my voice strange even to my own ears.

She nods sadly and I squeeze her again.

"It's going to be ok," I say, hoping it's not a promise that I can't keep.

It has to be ok. She has to be ok. Our baby has to be ok. Despite the anger, I can feel a flood of happiness waiting to erupt over me, but I hold it back, not wanting to be so happy only to come crashing back down if I find out that the baby is gone.

"Are you angry at me?" Amelia asks quietly as we start to walk again. "Because I couldn't protect the baby?"

"Never," I say, meaning it. "I'm angry at Dan. I'm just trying to reign it in so I can be the man you need me to be, that's all."

"If he's hurt the baby, Viktor, you won't need to do anything because I swear, I'll kill him myself," Amelia mutters fiercely.

I squeeze her hand and lead her to the car. I open the back door and she gets in. I quickly walk over to the other side, and I climb in next to her.

"Can you take us to the hospital please Jerome?"

"Sure thing, boss," he says, knowing better than to ask questions.

He reverses out of the road and turns around. Amelia looks out of the window.

"I'm never coming back here again," she says.

"You'll never have to," I tell her. "Because no matter what the future holds for us, I'm never letting you out of my sight again."

She shuffles closer to me, and I wrap my arm around her shoulders. She rests her head on my shoulder for a moment and then she lifts it up.

"I didn't ask you. Is everything with Igor sorted?"

"Yes," I say.

She accepts this without question. I know she knows what I mean by him being sorted, but I don't need to rub her face in it.

"And your shoulder? How is it?"

"Better," I say.

This she doesn't accept so easily.

"Better better or trying to be macho even though it's still bad better?" she asks.

"Better better, really," I say. "Look."

I shuffle my shoulder out of my jacket and shirt and show her the small scar left behind.

"Dr. Singh is good," she smiles.

"Yeah, he's the best," I agree.

"Shouldn't we go to him now then instead of going to the hospital?"

I shake my head.

"He's the best surgeon I know, but he's not the sort of doctor you need."

She lays her head back on my shoulder and puts her

hands protectively on her stomach. I reach over and put my hand on top of hers and she smiles up at me.

"It's going to be ok," I say again.

We make the next part of the drive in contemplative silence and I let myself think for a moment. I'm overjoyed that she's pregnant and terrified that she may have lost the baby. As much as I tell myself not to get too excited until we know for sure that everything is ok, I can't help but be excited. I can't help but picture myself with a baby. It tells me I did the right thing with my business too. If I'm going to be a father, I want to be a good one, one who shows his child the right example.

"Have you ever cheated on your girlfriends?" she blurts out suddenly.

I know it's the poison her mother has poured into her ear that makes her ask me that. I look into her eyes. "Never. I have never cheated on any woman in my life. I always make it perfectly clear that I am not on the market for serious relationships."

She chews her bottom lip. "But won't you miss the thrills and excitement of having many different women?"

"Oh, don't worry about that. I have all the thrills, all of the excitement, I'll ever need right here in my arms. I haven't even looked at another woman since I found you in that dive bar."

"Really?"

"Really."

Jerome pulls into the hospital grounds and takes us right up to the entrance to the emergency room. Some of the easy jovialness between Amelia and me falls away as the looming hospital building reminds us of the reason we're here.

"Do you want me to wait for you?" Jerome asks.

"No, it's ok. I don't know how long we'll be here. I'll just call one of my drivers when we're done. Just get back with your team and make sure they haven't left any loose ends behind."

He nods and we get out of the car. It pulls away and I take Amelia's hand. She puts her other hand on her stomach.

"It'll be ok, won't it?" she asks, her eyes begging me to reassure her.

"Of course it will," I smile. "Us Leshchenkos are made of strong stuff. And something tells me you are too."

44

AMELIA

Viktor ushers me into the emergency room and immediately the smell of antiseptic hits my nostrils.

I keep my hands on my stomach, shielding the fragile life that is hopefully still growing inside of me as Viktor leads me to the front desk, his arm wrapped protectively around my shoulders.

"My girlfriend is pregnant and she's been hit in the stomach," Viktor says. "We need to see a doctor right away please."

The receptionist asks me for my details, and I give her everything she asks for. My name, my address. I give her Viktor's address and I feel a warmth inside of me as I say it. Then I tell my medical history and my insurance details.

"Thank you," she smiles. "Please take a seat in the waiting area."

"I don't think you understand," Viktor says, his voice level but with anger simmering just beneath the surface. "She needs to be seen by a doctor right now."

"I appreciate that, Sir, but as you can see, there are a lot of people waiting to be seen and..."

"I'm going to say this one more time," Viktor interrupts her. "She needs to be seen by a doctor right now."

I cringe slightly, sure he's going to threaten the woman, but once again, he surprises me with what he actually does, and once again, I tell myself to stop thinking the worst of him.

"I can forgive you for not knowing this," he tells the receptionist calmly, "but I've donated more money to this hospital than anyone else in the city. You have a whole wing named after me. I didn't do that to be recognized or worshiped or any of that shit, but when my girlfriend and my baby are in danger, I expect to be seen in a timely fashion," Viktor says.

Her jaw drops open. "Oh, you're Viktor Leshchenko?"

"Yes," Viktor admits.

"I'm sorry, Sir, I had no idea," she stutters.

Viktor smiles his most charming smile. "It's fine. I didn't come wearing my name badge, so you're forgiven. I trust we can go through?"

"Yes. Yes of course, Mr. Leshchenko," the receptionist says. "I'll page Doctor Patrick right away."

"Thank you," Viktor says.

He leads me down a wide corridor towards the back of the emergency room. Curtained cubicles line the walls and harried looking doctors and nurses swarm in and out of the engaged ones.

"You paid for the hospital?"

"Not all of it, but a lot of it. This is one of the few hospitals in the state with the resources to see people without insurance. Growing up, we were one of those families without insurance and it's nice to be able to give something back now that I'm in a position to be able to do it. And for the record, that's the first time I've ever played that card."

A man in a white coat appears from a door to our left. "Mr. Leshchenko? Miss Madison? I'm Doctor Patrick. Come this way please."

He leads us to one of the cubicles and pulls the curtain around us.

"What happened Miss Madison?"

"Umm..." I start hesitantly.

"I gather you are pregnant, and you took a blow to your stomach?" Doctor Patrick says.

I nod and he goes on, his voice gentle. "I'm not here to judge you and I'm not here to make trouble for you. I just want to establish what happened, so I know how best to treat you."

Viktor nods to me and I tell Doctor Patrick what happened. He shakes his head solemnly.

"Some men aren't fit to be around other people. Miss Madison, I'm so sorry that happened to you."

"Thank you, Doctor. Have I lost the baby?"

"It's possible I'm afraid, but let's not jump to any conclusions. Have you experienced any blood loss or spotting?"

"I don't know," I admit. "We came straight here, and I haven't had a chance to check."

"Please do so," the doctor says, turning his back subtly.

I quickly open my jeans and push them down, relieved to see my panties are clean, dry and not dotted with red. I pull my jeans back up and re-button them.

"No," I say. "No blood."

"Any pain or discomfort in the area?" he asks.

"No more than I would expect after being punched," I

say. "I'm a little tender, but there's no sharp pains or anything."

"That all sounds promising. Why don't you hop up onto the bed for me with your jeans open and top lifted past your stomach while I go and fetch the ultrasound machine?"

I do as he says as he leaves the cubicle, the curtain swirling around where he parts it to leave.

"That sounds good, right?" I say to Viktor.

He nods and smiles at me, taking my hand in his.

"It does," he confirms. "I don't think he would have been so quick to do an ultrasound in front of you like this if he thought there was a chance you lost the baby."

I lay on the bed, taking comfort from Viktor's words. The doctor returns quickly, with a nurse pushing a cart with a machine on it. She stands the machine beside me and switches it on. The doctor picks up the scanner and turns to me.

My heart is starting to race as nerves overcome me. This is it. The moment I will know if my baby is ok or not. The doctor apologizes in advance for the cold and then he rubs some icy cold jelly over my tummy. He smiles reassuringly and then he begins to move the scanner around my stomach. I hold my breath, watching Dr. Patrick look at the screen.

His expression doesn't give a lot away, but I can see a slight frown on his face as he peers at the screen. I feel my heart sink. I've lost my baby. I turn to Viktor with tears in my eyes, biting them back, not letting them come. He squeezes my hand tightly and reaches out and brushes the hair back from my face. He doesn't say anything. There's nothing to say. Our baby is gone.

Suddenly, a thump, thump sound fills the room and Doctor Patrick's face changes. He beams widely at me.

"That sound is your baby's heartbeat, Miss Madison. The little mite gave me quite a scare there, but it turns out you just have a shy one," Dr. Patrick says.

Relief floods me and the tears I was holding back come now, tears of pure joy as I laugh at the same time.

"The heartbeat is nice and strong, and you can rest easy. Your baby's fine," the doctor says. He turns the screen around so that Viktor and I can see it. "Look here."

He points at what looks like a tiny peanut on the screen.

"That's your baby," he says.

"Hi Ava or Jack," I whisper.

"Oh, so we've chosen the names already, have we?" Viktor says, laughing with the same relief that makes me cry.

I grin happily. "Well, they're not definite or anything."

He leans down and kisses my forehead.

"We can call the baby anything you want Amelia," he says. "All I care about is that you're both happy and healthy."

Doctor Patrick moves the scanner away from me and hands me a wad of tissue which I use to wipe the jelly off my stomach. I want to beg him to let me listen to the baby's heartbeat for a little bit longer, to see him or her on the screen for a bit longer, but I don't. My baby's fine and that's all that matters, and I'm suddenly very much aware that not everyone waiting to see a doctor will be getting such good news. I don't want to hold the doctor up from seeing people who still need treatment.

"Thank you so much, Dr. Patrick," I say as he shuts the scanner down.

"Yes, thank you Doctor," Viktor echoes.

The doctor waits until I have my jeans fastened, my top pulled down and I'm sitting up again.

"Amelia," he says gently. "Excuse my language, but if you want to prosecute the bastard who did this to you, I can call the police and have them here in minutes."

"No," I say quickly. "I don't want to go through all that stress. I just want to forget any of this happened and look to the future. Thank you, though."

"Well, if you're sure."

"I'm sure."

He shakes my hand then Viktor's.

"Your baby is well and you're now free to go."

We stand up and thank him again then we head back outside. First, Viktor calls his driver to come and get us, then he turns to me. "Well, I guess I'll be making another sizable donation to this hospital."

"I guess you will," I echo.

He pulls me into his arms then and I melt into him. He leans down and his lips touch mine and fire and longing flood my body. It feels so good to be back here in Viktor's arms, where I belong.

He kisses me like we've been apart for years rather than weeks, and I feel the kiss in every part of my body. My pussy responds to Viktor's kiss, getting wet and clenching hungrily, wanting him to take me home and fill me up. I hold him tightly against me, needing to feel the solidity of him, to know this is really happening. I've dreamed of this moment every day for the last two weeks, but not even in my wildest dreams did it feel this good.

Finally, Viktor pulls his lips from mine. We stand in each other's arms, looking into each other's eyes. Viktor smiles and his eyes twinkle.

"I didn't want to stop kissing you, but I had to. I don't think I could have stopped myself from going any further if I hadn't, and a hospital parking lot doesn't feel like the right place for me to show you how much I've missed you," he says.

"I've missed you too," I say. "So much. More than I could ever begin to explain."

"You can show me when I get you home." Viktor winks.

I laugh and nod eagerly.

He laughs too and he squeezes me a little tighter and then he releases me from his hold and takes my hands in his, still looking me in the eye. "I can't wait to be a father."

"You're going to be the best dad in the world." I beam. "I only hope I can be a good mom."

"You're already a good mom," he smiles. "Dan was about to kick you in the face when I came into the trailer, and still, it wasn't your face you were protecting. It was our baby."

He releases one of my hands long enough to rub his palm gently over my stomach. He takes my hand again. "I love you, Amelia. More than anything in this world, and when our baby comes along, I'll love him or her so much too."

"I love you too, more than words," I tell him.

He kisses me again, his worry about not being able to control himself forgotten. We finally break apart when we hear an awkward cough beside us. Viktor's driver stands at the curb, the back door to the car open. I laugh and Viktor laughs with me. We didn't even hear the car pull up. We get into the car and Viktor asks the driver to take us to his estate.

"We need to go shopping tomorrow," he says. "Get you some new things."

"Oh, never mind me," I say excitedly. "We need to get a crib and a stroller and a changing table. And paint samples and a fluffy white rug, and teeny tiny clothes and diapers and toys. Pacifiers and teething rings too."

Viktor laughs beside me.

He grins wolfishly. "Maybe I should clear my schedule for a week or two rather than a day."

"Make it a month." I smile. "Someone has to paint the nursery you know."

He laughs as he pulls me into his arms again. I sit with my head on his shoulder, my hands on my stomach, and I realize that I've never been happier than I am in this moment.

EPILOGUE
AMELIA

https://www.youtube.com/watch?v=LjhCEhWiKXk

-just the way you are-

One Month Later

There's a quiet tap on my bedroom door and I tear my eyes away from the mirror long enough to turn towards the sound.

"Come in," I say, expecting to see Lacey or Justine.

Instead, Viktor steps into the room. He smiles when he sees me.

"God, Amelia, you look absolutely stunning," he says quietly as he looks me up and down.

I adore my wedding dress. Its floor length and pure white. A straight, elegant, timeless dress because I've always hated poofy wedding dresses. My hair is curled and I'm wearing a silver tiara and a matching choker with diamond earrings that sparkle in the light. I feel stunning today.

"Viktor, what are you doing here?" I screech, waving my hands to shoo him back out of the room. "You know it's unlucky for the groom to see the bride before the wedding."

"Amelia, I'm marrying the most amazing woman in the world. How can that be unlucky?"

I feel myself melt at his smile, at his words. He's right. I am the luckiest girl in the world, marrying my prince. Some old wives' tale can't spoil this day.

Viktor comes towards me and wraps his arms around me. He leans down and kisses me. I kiss him back. Yeah, there's nothing unlucky about this. It feels right. And it's not like we've done anything the traditional way. The way we met, the way we fell in love, none of it followed the rules. And that's what I love about us. We found each other when neither of us was even looking for love. We saved each other when neither of us even knew we needed saving. And our love grows stronger every day.

Viktor pulls his lips from mine and smiles at me.

"We don't have long before the ceremony and you might want to fix your lip gloss."

I look at myself again in the mirror and laugh. Most of my lip gloss is gone. I pick up a tissue and wipe it from Viktor's mouth and then I pick up the lip gloss and reapply it.

"I just came by to give you this."

He pulls an envelope from his pocket and holds it out to me. I smile and take it, ripping it open. My jaw drops and I squeal with excitement when I see what's inside.

"You told me you couldn't take time off work right now

and we couldn't have a honeymoon," I laugh, swatting his arm playfully.

"Yeah, I lied," he admits. "I wanted it to be a surprise. I did promise to take you to Rome though, didn't I?"

I squeal again at the thought of two weeks in the most romantic city in the world with the man I adore more than anything. Viktor laughs at my excitement as I wrap him up in a tight hug.

"No kissing," I warn him quickly. "I don't have time to fix my lips again."

He laughs, shaking his head and then he releases me.

"Do you still think me coming here now was unlucky?" he asks with a gleam in his eye.

"No. I know I'm the luckiest girl in the whole world," I tell him. "Now go or we're going to be late for our own wedding."

He nods and heads for the door.

"Viktor?" I say as he pulls it open. He glances back at me, and I smile at him. "I love you."

"Not half as much as I love you," he replies.

He leaves the room and I spin in a circle, laughing with delight. I can't believe that Amelia Madison, trailer trash, is about to become Amelia Leshchenko, the luckiest woman in the world.

The End

SAMPLE CHAPTERS - HEAT OF THE MOMENT

Prologue
Willow

I opened my front door surprised to find, Tiffany, my step sister standing outside. A bit of a surprise since I hadn't seen her in more than three months. Her pouty lips seemed more bee-stung than ever, and her hair was an even whiter shade of platinum. She was wearing pearls and a pretty blue dress that made her eyes look almost turquoise.

Right off the bat I should say, we don't get on so I was very surprised to see her.

"Hello. Aren't you going to let me in?" she purred.

Wordlessly, I opened the door wider and stood back. She walked through in a cloud of exotic perfume and made her way to my old couch, where she perched at the edge of it as if she was afraid to soil her clearly expensive dress.

"Where's your dog?" she asked, looking around her warily.

"Pogo is the dog groomers," I informed.

She visibly relaxed. So she should. Pogo hated her with a passion. He snarled, growled, and snaped whenever she was around him.

"Do you want something to drink?" I asked.

"Perrier with a slice of lemon, please."

My lips twisted. Tiffany never failed to amaze me. She really thought the whole world existed only to serve her. "I don't have Perrier. You can have a glass of tap water if you want," I offered, even though I had bottled water in the fridge.

Her nose wrinkled. "I'll pass." She flashed a fake smile and patted the space on the sofa to her. "Come sit with me."

I suppressed a shudder at the thought of being that close to her. Now it was my turn to be wary. "What's going on Tiffany?"

"Nothing. I just wanted to talk to you... to tell you something."

I moved to the sofa, but sat away from her. "Tell me what?"

She took a deep breath. "Okay. It'll be best if I just came out and just said it."

"Go on then."

"Steven and I are in love."

For a second I thought I'd heard wrong, because the words she said didn't make sense. Unless... unless by some weird coincidence it was a different Steven. "Steven?" I echoed.

"Your Steven," she confirmed artlessly.

The shock was incredible. Never in my life had I felt so utterly shocked. Steven and her! Even the idea made me sick to my stomach. "What?" I blurted out.

Tears pooled in her big blue eyes, then spilled down her beautiful face in rivulets. She always could turn on the tears as if they were on tap. She opened her purse and pulled out a tissue.

"We didn't mean it to happen," she sobbed, as she dabbed her cheeks. "It just did. You have to believe me."

"What a little bitch you are. You stole my boyfriend and you didn't mean it to happen?" I think I was still in shock or disbelief because my voice sounded strangely calm compared to her hysterical crying and sniffing.

She blinked with surprise. It was very rare I was ever confrontational or horrible to her. From the time we were children, I learned, it was better to let Tiffany have her way. That way my stepmom would not complain to my dad, and my poor dad wouldn't have to stand up for me and be trapped into fierce arguments about how he spoiled me. Arguments that lasted for days on end and made my stepmother resent me even more.

Tiffany, for her part, very quickly understood she could walk all over me with no consequences. And walk all over me she did until the day my dad died, then I took a step back from my whole family, and reduced my interaction with her to a strictly necessary level.

Until now.

Unbelievable. She was unbelievable. First, she helped herself to my boyfriend, then she invited herself to my home to give me the news.

A malicious, almost cunning look came into Tiffany's suddenly dry eyes. She tossed her head and her long white-blonde curls bounced on her shoulders. "I don't know why you're being so mean about it. Steven and I tried hard to resist the pull, but we simply couldn't. We fell madly in love with each other. It's not like what you had with Steven. Steven told me the two of you were just fucking around."

My eyes widened. Wow! Just fucking around!

I swallowed the sharp stab of pain. Bastard. *That* was what he thought we were doing for the last two years. The coward did not even come to tell himself. He'd left Tiffany to do his dirty work. Typical. The betrayal was like a knife in my chest, the pain sharp, but I took a deep breath. No matter how much it hurt I would not give Tiffany the satisfaction of knowing just how much she had hurt me.

She was staring at me curiously, intensely, as if she was actually drinking in my pain. Keeping my face expressionless I looked back at her. And without warning something clicked in my head, and suddenly, I was nine years old again and we were both standing in my bedroom. She was laughing cruelly and holding out my favorite blue blouse with the colorful dogs on it. It was ripped. She had ripped it right in the middle.

And now here she was, in all her blonde glory, at it again. She simply couldn't bear for me to have anything she didn't, not even the cheap blouse my mom had given to me before she died. And here she was again, holding out my ripped relationship... just because she couldn't bear for me to have anything she didn't.

But things were very different now. My beloved dad was gone forever. I didn't need to protect him anymore. I forced the most confident smile I could muster on to my lips.

"The only person Steven Harriman loves is Steven Harriman, and you're either stupid or deluded for imagining you'll be anything more to him than I was." Then I threw my head back and laughed. It sounded a bit crazy, but it was a real laugh, because it was true. He was as narcissistic as she was. She had finally met her match. They deserved each other.

"I'll prove how wrong you are. You'll see," Tiffany promised heatedly.

I stopped laughing and stared at her. Her eyes were glittering with a strange light and her fingers were clawed as if she wanted to scratch my eyes out. And I finally understood what I had never understood. She was jealous of me. She had always been jealous of me. Why, when she was the beautiful, loved one, I would never know.

Shocked by the intense hatred and insane rage I'd glimpsed in her eyes, I jumped to my feet. I couldn't wait for her to get out of my sight. I never wanted to see her again.

"Get out," I snarled.

"With pleasure," she cooed. The mask was back on her face. There was a satisfied smile on her face as she stood, then looked around my small apartment dismissively. "You should invest in some air freshener. The whole place of stinks of dog. Ugh. How can anyone live like this?"

"Get out," I screamed.

Satisfied she had inflicted maximum pain on her victim, she sailed out of my home, her head held high.

Chapter One
Willow
Three Months Later

"I'm so sorry to have to tell you this, Willow, but Tiff and Steven are getting married," Olivia, my half-sister informed gently. Her voice was full of pity.

I clamped my free hand over my mouth to stop any sounds. Thank god, we were on the phone and she could not see my reaction. My knees felt like jelly, so I quickly sat down. The taste of failure filled my mouth. All kinds of thoughts filtered into my mind unchecked. Crazy, angry, negative thoughts.

I was wrong when I predicted their relationship would not work out. They seemed so different. He was commit-ment shy. She was hopelessly flighty. Based on her past behavior, I assumed she would break it off once the novelty of taking what was not hers wore off. She didn't want my blue blouse, she just didn't want me to have it.

It was just a matter of time.

But even in my worst nightmares, I'd never thought it would get this far. Tiffany had won again. She had proved me wrong and showed me that she could get and keep my man. They were actually getting married!

I frowned. I suppose, if I was fair, why wouldn't she keep him. He was a good catch. Great career prospects, hand-some in a boyish way, and there was something else that was very important to her. He came from a good family. A rich family.

It hit me then that he must really want her too.

Steven and I were together for two years and marriage had never come into the conversation. He never even hinted of wanting it. His career came first. Everything was always about him.

With hindsight, I guess, I should have seen this coming when he left his high-powered job and moved to our small town in South Dakota. I'd laughed when I heard that, thinking he would not last. Steven loved the city. There was no way he was going to last more than six months there.

I'd even imagined the scenario where he came knocking on my door and begged me to take him back. Telling me he did not realize how selfish she was. How she wouldn't lift a finger to do any housework, how she always wanted to be waited on. In my head, I saw myself tell him to go fly a kite. Not only did I have my pride to consider, I could also never trust him again. The joke was on me. Instead of begging me to take him back, he was getting married to Tiffany.

So, there they were, the two most selfish people I knew, out there happily making plans for their wedding while I sat here in my little flat alone.

My shoulders slumped.

My personal life was in shambles. After what Steven and Tiffany did, I left everything that was familiar to me and moved into the city where I was still finding it hard to make friends. My neighbors preferred a nod and a polite smile to anything real, and I was still too raw to actually go out and make new friends. Hearing that Tiffany was getting married made my nonexistent social life seem even more pathetic.

"Willow? Are you still there?" Olivia asked. A note of worry had crept into her voice.

"When is the wedding?" I croaked.

"Er... in eight weeks." In my mind's eye I could see her wincing as she said it.

"January? Tiffany is getting married in the dead of winter?" I noted, surprised. For as long as I could remember she had always planned a spring wedding for herself.

They must be in a hurry to get hitched. I really read them both completely wrong. Tears filled my eyes and I quickly wiped them off with the back of my hand. I hated that even now they could still hurt me.

"Willow darling, are you okay?" Olivia asked.

"Yes, of course," I replied immediately, even though I was clearly not okay. Not by a long shot. I felt mortally wounded. As if I was a small animal in the woods and someone had thrown a spear at me, and now it was stuck in my side.

I gripped the phone tighter and gritted my teeth. I was not a loser and I was not going to let my family see my pain. My whole family had all taken Tiffany's side. Had my father been alive, he would not have tolerated that kind of behavior in his family. Dad had been the fairest man I'd ever known.

Tiffany would have been the outcast, not I. After I left, the family had embraced them both, even though they all knew she had stolen him from me. Suddenly, a wave of grief came over me, almost knocking me over, as a deep longing for my father swept over me.

"Um... one more thing..." Olivia trailed.

"What?" I asked, dreading her answer.

Olivia hesitated for a couple of seconds. "Tiff is pregnant."

I thought of petite, glamorously skinny, snake-hipped Tiffany and for a few seconds, I couldn't even imagine her pregnant, but it sure explained the January wedding.

"Poor thing suffers from terrible morning sickness," Olivia mumbled into the bruised silence.

I was the oldest, my father's child, Tiffany was my step-mother's child from another marriage, the spoiled one who got her way all the time, but Olivia was the youngest, the child who belonged to both parents. Consequently, she took her their love as a given as she never had to win favors from either parent. That made her confident of her place in the world and she became the one who tried to make everyone happy. And she was doing it now too.

"Of course, Tiffany suffers terribly," I said bitterly." Tiffany can't get a cough without thinking it's lung cancer."

"Yes, she can be a bit of a drama queen," Olivia agreed with a small awkward laugh. There was another uncomfortable silence before she rushed into it with what was obviously a prepared pitch. "Um… are you going to come for the wedding? Obviously, we'd all love you to come, but you don't have to. I mean, no one would blame you if you didn't. It would be awkward for Tiffany and really difficult for you. Why should you put yourself through the pain of watching Tiffany marry your ex-boyfriend—"

"I'll be there," I cut in firmly.

"Willow—"

"It's fine, Olivia," I interrupted in a weirdly crisp voice. "It won't be difficult for me at all. To tell the truth Steven is a narcissist. We would eventually have broken up, anyway and I'm actually quite happy he's found someone who suits him better."

"Really?" Olivia asks doubtfully.

"Yes, really. To be perfectly honest, I've moved on and even met a nice guy. While it's early days, things are looking promising," I babbled on while a part of me stood aside and watched incredulously at the brazen lies that were coming out of my mouth.

"Oh! You already met someone?"

"Yes," I squawked. My whole body felt hot with guilt.

"Well, that's really great news, Willow. I'm so happy for you. I tell everyone at home. They will be so relieved. We were all worried you might still be broken-hearted. Family gatherings have not been the same without you." She paused for a second, then said the words that made my head spin. "I know... why don't you bring him along to the wedding?"

"Okay, I will," I heard myself say calmly, but my eyes were squeezed shut with horror at the mess I'd dug myself into.

"Fantastic. Can't wait to meet him. What's his name?"

"Look, I've got to go. Got a pile of work I've to get on with. I'll talk to you soon, okay?" I said and quickly cut the connection.

Chapter 2
Willow

WITH POGO hot on my heels I hurried to the kitchen. I stood at the window and stared out of it. My cheeks were burning. Did Olivia really believe me? She could be a bit naïve, but Tiffany or my stepmother would never believe it.

The view from the kitchen had been the selling point of this tiny apartment. If you crane your neck out of the window on a good day you get a partial view of San Francisco Bay Bridge.

A scream filled the air.

At first, it sounded as if it was coming from the apartment above. Pogo gave a frightened yelp and ran off to cower in a corner. I sank down on the cold, tiled floor and began to sob. Pogo came out of his hiding spot and tried to get into my lap. He made strange growly noises of confusion and distress. It was not his fault. Poor baby. I stroked his silky head.

"It's okay, it's okay," I soothed, again and again, like a monotonous mantra. I didn't know if I was saying it to calm him or myself. But it helped us both.

Pogo started to relax. He draped his small fat body over my thigh and let out a sigh of contentment. If I knew Tiffany at all, for sure the wedding would be a lavish affair at the country club where all the crème de la crème of society weddings were held. The easiest thing would be to make up an excuse for being ill and not attend the damn thing, but I was not going to give her and Steven the satisfaction of hiding away.

I could see Tiffany crowing to Steven, "See, I told you she was lying. She hasn't found a man at all, and now she's too embarrassed to show her face."

And they would both imagine I was still hurting over their betrayal.

No, I had to show everyone I'd moved on. I was happy. I didn't need Steven. Which was the God honest truth. I was well over Steven. In fact, I was eternally glad I didn't waste another second with him. Two years was enough. The thought of them getting married didn't really hurt that much. I could go to that wedding no problem. The thing that hurt the most was my family's treachery. The way they had all taken Tiffany's side and turned their backs on me, abandoned me as if I was the one who had done the unspeakable thing, not her.

I sighed heavily. If only I had not told Olivia I had found someone new.

But I had, which meant I now had to bring a date.

Where the hell was I going to get a date from? There was Emma's brother. He was pretty dishy, and a nice guy to boot.

I chewed my bottom lip. No, that wouldn't work. I told Olivia I'd found someone new in the city.

No, I needed a brand-new suitor, someone who would make Tiffany rethink the idea that she'd gotten the better of me. It came to me like a lightbulb. I could hire an out of work actor to be my date for the wedding.

But paying someone was risky. My family were inquisitive and one little mistake on his part and they would know it was all a sham. My stepmother is like a ferret for gossip and rumors. And the humiliation that would bring would be intolerable. I could already imagine the delight in Tiffany's eyes. It would be the best present I could ever give her.

No, I would just get on one of those online dating sites. If that didn't work, maybe, I could hang out in some of the trendier bars in town.

How hard could it be to find someone respectable in such a big city?

I decided there and then I was going to attend that wedding with my head held high, and my wonderful new boyfriend on my arm, and afterwards, I was never going back to my sleepy hometown ever again. Once this was over I wanted to stay as far away from my family as I could.

Feeling greatly cheered, I scooped Pogo into my arms and went to pour myself a glass of wine.

I buried my nose in his soft neck and breathed deeply. I loved him so, so, so much. Pogo turned his head and licked my cheek. "You were right about her all along, my darling. She's a manipulative grade A bitch. And all that strong perfume she wears day and night has killed off her sense of smell. You don't stink. If fact, you smell heavenly," I told him as cold wine splashed into my glass.

Pogo made an almost cat-like purring sound at the back of the throat. He was happy, and I had my drink and my brilliant plan.

The crisis, I was certain, had been averted.

Chapter Three
Willow
Seven Weeks Later

Except it hadn't.

Turned out the meme going round was true: good boyfriends were not so easy to find. Hanging out in the trending bars had yielded nothing. Not that I hadn't been hit on. I had, but they were mostly assholes looking for a quick hook-up.

And after my latest conversation with Olivia where I got the distinct impression that both my stepmother and Tiffany didn't believe I'd actually found a man, I decided that my date for the wedding had to be above reproach. Handsome. Sexy. Successful. A man who would make Steven look like a wet-behind-the-ears boy.

But time was running out and I was starting to despair. I was not going to find such a legend especially since there was hardly a week left before the wedding. Not that I was ready to give up the search, but I was starting to get more than a little despondent.

As I got ready for the company's yearly Christmas party, the temptation to skip it and spend the time curled up on my couch was huge, but I squared my shoulders with determination. No, I needed to go out. Maybe what I really needed to do was get talking with some of my colleagues. Maybe they knew someone who could help.

I tried on several outfits, not quite achieving the look I wanted. The bed was a mess of discarded outfits.

"We need a new strategy Pogo," I told my beloved cat who was lazing on the bed, staring at me as I slipped into a red dress. "Clearly I'm not going to get a date through the conventional ways, so I must think outside the box."

Pogo yawned.

I adjusted the long sleeves of the dress. They were the only respectable thing about the dress. For a second, I wondered if it was too sexy for an office party. There was a lot of leg on show.

I took a couple of steps towards the mirror. It was not too sexy, not really. Yes, the dress was short and it clung to me like a second skin, but in a classy way. And anyway, I was in the big city now. Some of the girls at work came to work dressed as if they were going directly to a party afterwards.

If my stepmother could see me, she would definitely have said I looked like a whore. We were brought up to clutch pearls and show as little skin as possible. but I wasn't living in South Dakota anymore. I was in San Francisco, home of the daring and brave.

My stepmother had no control over me anymore. I would never again let her shame me into behaving in a way that she approved of.

I applied a layer of cherry lip gloss, kissed Pogo, and left.

****

The party was a disastrous waste of time.

I knew very few people so I stood in a corner, clutching my fifth glass of bubbly, and pretended to admire the Christmas tree as everyone else talked, laughed, danced, and generally had a good time.

A familiar song blasted from the speakers, pulling me from my introspection. And draining my glass, I popped onto a ledge and began swaying to the beat. That was when I realized just how sloshed I had become. I decided to go to the restrooms and splash some cool water over my face.

I left the big hall and walked into the corridor when I turned the corner and slammed into a brick wall, well it felt like one, but it had warm, strong hands that curled around my forearms and kept me upright.

Shaken, I lifted my head all the way up, and stared into the face of a hot, like magazine-cover hot man. He was easily the most beautiful man I'd ever seen in my entire life and that's even counting magazines and movies. God! His eyes, they were piercing blue. And they robbed me of all thoughts except one.

This here, was exactly the kind of man I was looking to take to the wedding and fate had delivered me right into his hands.

"Whoa! What's the hurry?" the utterly gorgeous beast drawled, his voice dripping with amusement.

Chapter Four
Rex

"ARE YOU SINGLE?" she asked breathlessly, as she stared at me with a dazed expression.

"Guilty," I admitted, stepping away from her warm curves, and watching her closely. I didn't know what to make of her.

She had the obligatory long blonde hair that I usually went for in a woman, but she was not exactly my type. There was too much intelligence and warmth lurking in those honey-brown eyes. I preferred my women, blonde and dumb... Still, something about her intrigued and fascinated me. Probably those fantastically long silky legs. I could already see myself opening them and tasting her. That was surprising since I couldn't remember the last time I had reacted so viscerally to a woman.

"Oh good," she said, a slight slur to her voice, "because I have a proposition for you."

My eyebrows rose. Well, well... She didn't look like that type of a girl, but these days, you never knew.

"Oh no! No, nothing like that. This does not involve sex. Not at all," she gasped quickly.

Pity.

"Come with me and I'll explain," she said, and started to walk away.

For an instant, I thought about walking in the opposite direction. She was clearly tipsy, and I wasn't exactly in the mood for a tanked-up woman, but then thought was gone in an instant, when the sway of her hips mesmerized me. I was staring at her firm round bottom and her long, long legs when she looked over her shoulder, and asked in an almost melancholic voice, "Aren't you coming?"

That must have been what the song of the siren was like for those unfortunate sailors.

I followed her and she led me to a deserted canteen and gestured for me to take a seat at the closest table. I leaned a hip at the edge of it and regarded her. The bright, white led lighting made her appear almost unreal.

"Would you like a bottle of water of something?" she offered, jerking her head in the direction of some fridges at the other end of the room.

I shook my head.

"I supposed I could snag us a glass of champagne from the party, but I think I might have had too much already," she mused aloud.

"I'm alright for drink," I said quietly.

She smiled sunnily and it lit up her whole face. Yes, there definitely was too much intelligence and warmth in those eyes.

"I haven't seen you around before. Which department do you work in?"

"I'm... er... visiting from a different branch of the organization," I replied evasively.

"Oh, which branch?"

"You had a proposition for me..." I reminded pointedly.

She licked her lips, a suddenly nervous gesture, and to my astonishment, I felt my cock jerk to life.

"How do you feel about a weekend trip to South Dakota all expenses paid?" she blurted out with what was obviously false bravado.

I kept my face straight. "All expenses paid, huh?"

"All expenses paid," she agreed solemnly while nodding eagerly. "In fact, I will even pay you for your time."

Curiouser and curiouser. I rubbed my chin thoughtfully. "Pay me for my time? Just how much are we talking about?"

She had obviously not thought about it until now,

because she frowned, then pulled a figure out of the air and let it hang in the air as if waiting to see my reaction to it. "A thousand dollars?"

A thousand dollars? What a laugh, but how cute of her. I nodded and pretended to be impressed with her figure.

The relief in her posture was unmistakable. "And if it all goes well, I'm even prepared to double the figure."

Somewhere between the time she said 'all expenses paid' to 'I'm even prepared to double the figure', I started to enjoy myself. Nothing like this ever happened in my life. All I ever did was crunch numbers so that I could then use the information to wrestle chunks of bloody meat out of the mouths of emotionless sharks. Could I really take a whole weekend off?

Of course, I could.

I just never did.

Until now.

"And what would I have to do in return?" I asked softly.

One thing for sure. She was a terrible actress. She slapped her forehead in a dramatic, over the top gesture. "What am I like? I didn't tell you, did I? Well, you'll be very pleased to hear you won't have to do anything much in return."

I raise my eyebrows.

She stopped to swallow audibly, then flash another big, bright smile at me. "You'll just have to pretend to be my new boyfriend."

Now *that*, I did not expect. I stared at her curiously. "You want to pay me to pretend to be your boyfriend?"

"Well, I know it sounds a bit weird, but it's not. Really, it's not. You see, my step-sister stole my boyfriend and now she marrying him... and I just need someone to go with me to the wedding, you know, to show them all that I'm not broken-hearted or anything like that, and then I saw you, and I thought you'd be absolutely perfect, so I stupidly thought you wou¾"

Midway, her voice broke, and tears began to roll quickly down her cheeks.

"I mean, you look like a straight-up, hardworking guy so you can just consider it a weekend away. A free, no strings attached, treat that you probably deserve. You really should take the deal. It's a good one. You'll be staying at a really lovely hotel. It overlooks a lake, and even though it will be frozen this time of the year, you could go for long walks around it. It's so beautiful around Green Bison Lake Club it's almost like walking into a postcard."

More tears ran down her cheeks as she continued babbling, so fast her words tripped over each other.

"And they make the best margaritas at the main bar. I promise you, you won't regret going with me. We'll have to share a suite, of course, but I'll be busy all day and you'll hardly know I'm there, or have to spend much time with me. Except during the wedding, of course. And that'll only last for a couple of hours. We don't even have to attend the reception."

The words were still tumbling incoherently out of her, when I pushed myself off the table and walked towards her. Casually, I curled a lock of her blonde hair between my fingers.

She was so startled she stopped talking and went as still as a statue.

The air between us hung heavy as her eyes widened and her lips parted. Unexpectedly, something happened deep in my gut. The place where the first warning of danger usually came from. It was different this time. It was a craving. A craving so deep that it actually throbbed inside me.

Pretty insane!

My finger grazed her wet cheek and a spark of electricity shot through me. Hell, I hadn't had such a reaction to a woman in a very, very fucking long time. Perhaps because I had designed my life in such a way that all my sexual interactions with women were meaningless, casual, and deliberately impermanent.

I released the lock of hair and stepped back. "The best Margaritas, huh?"

"The absolute best," she whispered hoarsely.

"So... a frozen lake and walking trails are on offer?"

"Totally. I'll even throw in a couple of dark chocolate muffins from the local bakery. I swear they are to die for. You could never get enough of them."

"Hmmm... I am rather partial to dark chocolate, but... will I have to be nice to the bitch, though?"

A startled expression crossed her eyes before a tremulous smile trembled onto her lips. A little giggle she couldn't contain slipped out. "Nope, being nice to Tiffany is not included in the deal. However, you will get bonus points if you don't fall for her manipulative machinations."

I smiled lazily. A female shark. I knew well how to handle them. "Ah, one of those."

A bitter expression crossed her face. "Yes, one of those. She uses her beauty to blind people to her real intentions."

"I'll consider myself warned."

"Good," she said heartily.

The smell of her shampoo was still in my nostrils. Lemon with a twist of something sweet, apricots perhaps. I had an insane desire to bury my face in her hair. "What weekend are we talking about?"

She bit her bottom lip. "This weekend coming."

I stared at her plump mouth. An image of me plunging my cock into it popped into my head. "A bit short notice, isn't it?"

"I know, but I couldn't find anyone suitable, until tonight when I ran into you."

"Who else besides the bitch will I have to convince?"

"My father died three years ago, so there'll just be my stepmother, Nicole; my half-sister, Olivia; Tiffany, the bride; and of course, her bridegroom or my unfaithful ex, Steven."

"Whom you're still madly in love with, I suppose?"

Her head jerked back and her voice was hard with disgust. "God, no! He's a selfish, narcissistic, untrustworthy jerk. They deserve each other."

I hid a smile at her outburst. "So why the elaborate charade?"

She seemed suddenly agitated. "Because I did a stupid thing. I told Olivia I'd found someone and things were going well. I only told her that because I didn't want her or anyone else to pity me and think I was still nursing a broken heart, but it backfired when Olivia asked me to bring the new guy along, and now I'm committed to bring someone. Either that, or I'll look like a liar, or even more humiliating, like someone who can't keep a man."

"I see."

"I know it must be impossible for you to understand, but I just want to attend this wedding with my head held high, and once and for all stop the rest of my family from thinking I'm a total loser, or that I'm hurting because I want him back. Also, if I'm honest, I don't want to give Tiffany the satisfaction of thinking she has something I want."

"So the job description is for me to leave no doubt among your family and friends that I'm head over heels in love with you?"

She clasped her hands and nodded enthusiastically. "Yes."

By now I should already be in a plane flying back to head office, but being a part of this little adventure was surprisingly entertaining and intriguing.

"Okay. I'm Rex. What's your name?" I asked.

"Willow, Willow Garrett," she replied, and staggered a little. She was more drunk than I originally thought. "So you *will* do it?"

"Yes. Yes, I think I will," I murmured.

Chapter Five
Willow

"YOU REALLY MEAN IT? You'll go with me?" I squealed excitedly, part of me, still not quite believing he had said yes.

"Sure, why not. I have nothing better to do this weekend, anyway."

"Oh my God! Thank you," I cried breathlessly.

Rex grinned suddenly, and the butterflies in my stomach went crazy. There was no two ways about it. Rex was smoking hot. He had everything I found insanely attractive in a man. Beautiful eyes, a body that clearly saw the gym a lot, and a slow smile that made my insides swoon.

When his finger grazed my skin something weird

happened to me. My breath quickened and my heart started racing like mad. The kind of juvenile reactions I used to have as a teenager when a super cute boy looked at me.

Rex glanced at his watch. "I have to be somewhere else now, but how about dinner tomorrow? We can hammer out our strategy then."

Wow, he was really serious. "Dinner tomorrow sounds great. Thank you so much. I'll pick up the tab."

He frowned slightly, but only said, "Okay. You pick the restaurant then."

"We could go to the Italian at the end of this street. They do an amazing Ossobuco."

"Sure. Seven-thirty good for you?"

"Seven-thirty is perfect," I agreed happily.

"Put my number into your phone and call me if any problems arise."

I fumbled around in my purse, located my phone, and pulled it out. When I had it open, he called out his number, and I put it into my phone.

"Now give me a missed call," he instructed. The way he issued the command gave me the impression he was used to giving orders, and it made me curious about him.

I heard his phone ring from inside his jacket and killed the call.

"See you tomorrow," he said.

Then he was gone.

I stood in the deserted canteen alone, not quite sure if it had all been a dream. Then I looked down at my phone. His number was still there.

I felt as if I had just won the lottery. A lottery called Rex Hunter.

And all that pent up frustration and anxiety came out of

me in a rush and I laughed hysterically like a demented hyena. No one would feel pity for me with him at the end of my elbow. With a whoop of pure joy, I did a happy dance all around the tables.

Yesssss! I did it. I actually did it! I found a date for the wedding, and what a date I found. I couldn't wait to see the expression on Tiffany's face. This was no blue blouse she could rip into two. She would go green with envy. Rex made Steven look like a boy still in schoolboy shorts.

My best impression of an evil laugh reverberated all around the empty room as I practically skipped and danced my way out there.

Yesssss, Willow. You did it, girl. You did it.

Please pre-order the book here:
Heat of the Moment

ABOUT THE AUTHOR

If you wish to leave a review for this book
please do so here:
Mine To Possess

Please click on this link to receive news of my latest releases
and great giveaways.
http://bit.ly/1oe9WdE

and remember
I **LOVE** hearing from readers so by all means come and say
hello here:

ALSO BY GEORGIA LE CARRE

Owned

42 Days

Besotted

Seduce Me

Love's Sacrifice

Masquerade

Pretty Wicked (novella)

Disfigured Love

Hypnotized

Crystal Jake 1,2&3

Sexy Beast

Wounded Beast

Beautiful Beast

Dirty Aristocrat

You Don't Own Me 1 & 2

You Don't Know Me

Blind Reader Wanted

Redemption

The Heir

Blackmailed By The Beast

Submitting To The Billionaire

The Bad Boy Wants Me

Nanny & The Beast

His Frozen Heart

The Man In The Mirror

A Kiss Stolen

Can't Let Her Go

Highest Bidder

Saving Della Ray

Nice Day For A White Wedding

With This Ring

With This Secret

Saint & Sinner

Bodyguard Beast

Beauty & The Beast

The Other Side of Midnight

The Russian Billionaire

CEO's Revenge

Printed in Great Britain
by Amazon